ABOUT THE AUTHOR

David Tolfree is a retired chartered physicist with fifty years' experience in nuclear research and business consultancy in technology exploitation. He has over 160 publications including articles in journals, books, newspapers and conference proceedings, and has co-authored the books *Commercialising Micro-Nanotechnology Products*, *Roadmapping Emergent Technologies* and is the author of *The Millennium Conspiracy*, his first novel, published in 2012.

ACTS OF RETRIBUTION

David Tolfree

Matador
Troubador Publishing Ltd
9 Priory Business Park
Kibworth Beauchamp
Leicester LE8 0RX, UK
Tel: (+44) 116 279 2299
Email: books@troubador.co.uk
Web: www.troubador.co.uk/matador

ISBN 978-1783063-093

A CIP catalogue record for this book is available from the British Library

Matador is an imprint of Troubador Publishing Ltd

To

Carolyn e Steve

Best wishes

David Isyfree

21.12.13.

ACKNOWLEDGEMENTS

I want to thank all those readers who enjoyed the story in my first novel *The Millennium Conspiracy*. I am fortunate to have many good friends who still read books. It was their positive comments and those of other readers that gave me the incentive to write this sequel, without which my late journey into novel writing would have come to an abrupt end.

I owe a debt of gratitude to many people whose knowledge I used in the writing of this story but for reasons of security and confidentiality their names cannot be mentioned. My special thanks go to my wife Valerie and to Clive Davenport for painstakingly reading the manuscript and making corrections to the text. In matters of aviation, I am grateful to Derek Fielding and Lynn Jenkins for their advice on aircraft design and operations, and also for their constructive feedback on the story. I wish to thank my sister Pamela Rogers in New Zealand for her encouraging comments on my last novel and the draft of this one. Final thanks go to the helpful staff at Troubador Publishing for the production of the book.

AUTHOR'S NOTE

This book is a work of fiction and, except in the case of historical fact, any resemblance to actual persons, living or dead, is purely coincidental. Characters, organisations, situations and philosophies are either the product of the author's imagination or, if real, have been used fictitiously without any intent to describe or portray their actual conduct.

Acts of Retribution is a sequel to *The Millennium Conspiracy*. The story is in two parts and involves of some of the main characters from the first book.

Part one is mainly set in London and New York in 2001 and is about the hunt by special agents of MI6 and the US Counter Terrorist Unit for foreign terrorists who were responsible for blowing up a plane over the Thames Estuary in London that killed 349 people. The hunt reveals new sinister al-Qaeda plots to attack US cities and installations. It also uncovers a political conspiracy to assassinate a Russian oligarch resident in London.

Part two takes the reader back to the UK and a terrorist plan to attack a cruise ship and then to the US on 11 September 2001 where al-Qaeda terrorists hijack planes and fly them into the twin towers of the World Trade Centre in New York and the Pentagon in Washington.

It is an historical fact that Osama bin Laden and many of his followers who were responsible for the attack on the World Trade Centre have now been killed or captured, but terrorism and fundamentalism in their many manifestations still threaten democratic countries. The war on terror, in its various forms, is far from being over. Terrorism is a crime against humanity and must never be justified for political ideology or religious conviction.

Many official reports, books and films have been written and produced about the events of the last decade. But only a limited number of people know the real facts. This gives fiction writers opportunities to create stories around what they believe really happened in the period before and after the attack on the World Trade Centre. This is one such story.

CONTENT

CAST OF CHARACTERS

MAIN CHARACTERS

Paul Cane	Journalist
Valerie Cane	Cane's Wife
Robert Carville	Cane's Friend and Agent
John Nicholas	Commander of UK Counter Terrorist Unit
Rupert Arnold	Head of UK CTU
Henry Barrington-Smith (BS)	DG MI6
Lord Clifton Davenport	Property Tycoon and Advisor
Jayne Clayton-Browne (Angel)	MI6 Agent
Bob Bradley (Alex Newman)	Jayne's Assistant at MI6
Bill Simpson (Spear)	SAS Marksman (retired)
Alan Leeke (AL)	MI6 Firearms Expert
Christopher Rogers	Captain of Cruise Ship *Prince Charles*
Matthew Jones	First Officer on *Prince Charles*
Tracey and Maria O'Brien	Singers and Curly's sisters
Alicia Garcia	Head of US CTU
Sean O'Brien (Curly)	Alicia's Private Agent
Guy Hadrian	New York Publisher
Jack Linderman	President's Chief Political Advisor
Sheikh bin Abdullah	UN Delegate

Brad Walker	Senior CTU Analyst
Pat King	Senior CTU Analyst
Rob Burger	Security Advisor to the Vice President
Mark Brooks	Head of FBI Counter Terrorism
Gregori Seperkov	Russian Assassin
Oleg Detroski	Russian Oligarch
Boris Surak (Voss)	Detroski's Bodyguard
Katrina Vasalov	Russian Diplomat
Mohammad bin al-Zarak	Arab Informer
Khalid Sheikh Mohammed (KSM)	Head of al-Qaeda Operations in US
Abdel Malik	al-Qaeda Courier
Kasim Hadjab	al-Qaeda Southampton Cell
Ali Baba (AB)	al-Qaeda Chief in New York

ACRONYMS AND ABBREVIATIONS

CIA	Central Intelligence Agency
FBI	Federal Bureau of Investigation
NSA	National Security Agency
SAS	Special Air Service
SIS (MI6)	Secret Intelligence Service
COBRA	Cabinet Office Briefing Room
CTU	Counter Terrorist Unit
KGB	Soviet Union State Security
SVR	Sluzhba Vneshney Razvyedki (Russian Foreign Intelligence Service)
FSB	Federal Security Service of the Russian Federation
NCTC	National Counter-Terrorist Committee
GCHQ	British Government Communications Headquarters
SUV	Sport Utility Vehicle
PM	Prime Minister
DG	Director General
BA	British Airways
IRA	Irish Republican Army
BMW	Bavarian Motor Works
GPS	Global Positioning System
PDA	Personal Digital Assistant

PART ONE

CHAPTER 1

The Thames Estuary
May 2001

Paul Cane tried to open his eyes, but his eyelids were heavy. The misty dawn light limited his vision. It was like looking through a dirty window. He could just make out dark shapes rising up in front of him, silhouetted in the hazy light. His ears were ringing, but he could just hear the sound of lapping water and a faint commotion in the distance – muffled sounds of voices, of sirens and engines.

Cane couldn't move his legs; they were trapped by something heavy. Except for his head, his hands and the rest of his body were numb with the cold. Slowly he started to regain some of his senses and realised that most of his body was immersed in muddy water.

Was he experiencing some kind of bad dream? He took some comfort knowing that he would soon wake up in a warm bed. But as his consciousness returned, the full horror struck him: it was icy-cold, flowing seawater. Why was he in seawater? How did he get there? Where was he? Fear and despair consumed him. He could feel his heart thumping in his chest; that meant he was alive.

After some effort, Cane managed to raise his arms, which had been plunged vertically into the mud. That movement caused his face to fall forward and his nostrils to fill with water. Its smell and taste made him feel nauseous; it was like rotten eggs. But he was now able to move his head high enough to see he was near some kind of small bank, not a nice sandy bank, but a smelly, muddy one.

He had to get free, but couldn't see what was pinning him down. Groping in the mud under his body he felt the seat. Why was he strapped to a seat? He ran his numb fingers over it to find a belt across his chest. Eventually he located a buckle and after some exhaustive tugging, it snapped open, relieving the tightness around his body and the pain in his chest. His legs were still trapped, but he was now able to raise enough of his body out of the water to see what looked like a metal bar across his legs.

The mud was soft so, after some effort, Cane wriggled his legs free from under the heavy weight of the bar. First one leg, then the other. He felt no pain in his legs since they were numb from the cold. He rolled over and tried to stand up, but the mud was sucking him back. There was no ground firm enough to stand on. The effort drained his energy. He found breathing difficult. At each small breath he inhaled the stench of decay. It made him feel sick. Vomiting into the mud was difficult and painful. He felt sicker as each cough emptied whatever was left in his stomach. Each movement released more stench.

Finally, after feeling a little relieved, he forced himself to swim through the watery mud to a bank, which appeared to have some blades of grass growing on it. He thought it might be firm enough to support his weight. Although the effort had exhausted him, Cane managed to haul himself up onto the bank to get a better view across the water.

He wanted to sleep, but an inner voice said, '*Don't go to sleep, stay awake and keep moving.*' The cold, the increasing pain in his chest and the confusion added to his misery. He could only breathe in short puffs. He tried to call out, but no sound emanated from his mouth. He felt like dying, but not here on a muddy bank.

Nobody wants their life to end unseen, ignored in a desolate spot where their body might never be found. Many wounded soldiers in mud-filled holes on battlefields must have felt that sense of desperation. In the First World War, thousands lost their lives, unseen, in such places.

Cane's despair diminished when he saw faint lights moving in the distance. But when he realised they were from fires burning on the water it returned. What he saw looked like a battlefield littered with debris from the aftermath of a massive bomb explosion. It was a scene out of hell. The water was on fire and water doesn't burn. A strong, sickly smell of burning fuel oil pervaded the air.

Dark clouds of black smoke were hanging over the river like malevolent monsters poised to devour their prey. Bits of flotsam were visible everywhere. Some were sticking out of the water displaying gruesome twisted shapes. Some were burning, some just floating and moving with the current. It was a scene of carnage. He could see that he was on a bank of a river estuary with the water flowing out to sea.

Cane then saw a half-submerged object moving slowly towards him. The mud on his face covered his eyes as he tried to wipe them with his hand. But he was able to focus on the object since it was partially illuminated by the light from the distant fires; it looked like a charred body floating face-down. He felt sick again. At first he kicked it away; but then for a brief moment caught a flash of light reflected from the metal of what looked like a wristwatch on the blackened flesh of the arm. He reached out and pulled the body back towards him. Surprisingly, it was an undamaged watch. He recognised it as a Casio, one of the latest digital models. Movement of the body caused it to turn over, revealing a ghastly sight. The face had been completely burnt away leaving just a row of white teeth and parts of a hollowed-out, blackened skull. It smelt of burning kerosene.

After considerable difficulty and still feeling sick, Cane removed the watch from the charred wrist. Why was he doing that? There was something deep in his memory that urged him. He went to place it in the pocket of his jacket only to find it had been torn away along with most of his coat. The metal watchstrap was undamaged. After fumbling with fingers still numbed by cold, he managed to place the watch on his own wrist. Then he saw that his own one was missing. He always wore a watch so perhaps instinctively he wanted one. The figures on the dial showed a time of 6.40. It would be many days later when the significance of the find would be realised.

Then reality hit him. What had happened? How did he get here? Fragmented parts of his memory were slowly returning.

The air attendant was collecting the breakfast trays. An announcement was made asking all passengers to secure their seat belts for landing. Cane vaguely remembered his wife, Valerie, moving in the seat next to him to look out of the window as the plane banked over the estuary of the River Thames on its glide path to Heathrow.

The man on the seat opposite was looking at his watch. Was it the Casio watch he had just found? Were the charred remains that man? It would explain why the body was so close to him in the water. He had a vague recollection of a blinding light and hearing a thud – like the wheels of the plane coming down, then nothing – a blank. He tried to fill in the blank, but couldn't. The horror of what might have happened then overtook him. The plane must have blown up and crashed. It was the only rational explanation for how he came to be in the mud. Was the sight out on the river parts of the plane wreckage burning? It would explain the fire on the water since it would be burning fuel.

Cane's mind couldn't comprehend the situation. He was confused. Where was Valerie? Where were the other passengers? *God, are they all dead? That can't be.* Maybe he was in a twilight world between life and death, if such a place existed.

He was beginning to feel dizzy. His sight was deteriorating. The pains in his head, his chest and legs were taking hold as his body warmed up. Was this the end of his life? Surely not now after surviving a plane crash.

He tried to be rational and stay conscious, but slowly the cold and the pains in his body were driving him into oblivion. He was in shock, made worse by the thought that the new Boeing 777 on which he was travelling to London had crashed into the River Thames on its descent into Heathrow. But these planes, the most reliable and accident-free planes in the world, don't crash.

There had to be another explanation. He had to think, but his mind was oscillating between fact and fantasy. By now, if the plane had crashed, the area would be teaming with rescuers since it was close to one of the largest capitals in the world, but no one was nearby. Cane was slowly drifting into unconsciousness when he was aroused by a bright light and the heavy thud of propeller blades.

Minutes later he could just make out dark figures moving around him and hearing someone shouting.

'Quick, over here, there's a man lying in the mud.'

He felt himself being lifted onto a soft, warm surface. People were scurrying around, some crying out commands, some splashing about in the water. He was being carried to the source of the sound. The deep thudding noise was getting louder. Then he felt the sharp pain of a needle being inserted into his left arm. He heard a door slam shut and a deafening roar as the rescue machine quickly took off and sped towards the city of London. He drifted into a deep sleep.

During the flight Cane was oblivious to the surreal scene of carnage below. Arriving boats and helicopters contributed to a cacophony of sound that now pervaded the area. Powerful searchlights lit up the surface of the water, which rippled as the wreckage made its journey down the river. The light was amplified when it hit small fires burning fiercely on the surface. These extended beyond the river to the banks on either side.

The heavy parts of the aircraft – the engines and undercarriage had disappeared and were probably buried in the river's muddy bottom. No large parts were visible. Boats searched in vain for survivors. They only found bodies and body parts. Most were unrecognisable. Identification was going to be a major task.

Cane regained consciousness. The first thing he saw was a young woman's smiling face peering down at him. She had deep blue eyes and in a soft voice asked, 'What is your name?'

Too dazed to answer, he just muttered some incomprehensible sound. He then felt what was left of his clothes being removed and a blanket being wrapped around his body. The warmth was wonderful. He drifted back into blissful sleep.

The emergency room in the hospital was made ready for expected casualties, but none came. The staff hadn't been briefed on the reality of the event. At this time Cane was alone. He was their only patient.

The early morning radio newsreader interrupted programmes to announce a news flash.

> *'At 6.30 this morning a British Airways Boeing 777 en route to Heathrow from New York exploded in the air above the Thames Estuary. Emergency services have been mobilised to the scene where debris has been spotted. So far no survivors have been picked up, but an intensive search is in progress. It is believed, but not confirmed, that this may be the work of terrorists. The Prime Minister has called an emergency meeting of the National Counter-Terrorist Committee. Further bulletins will be made when more information is available.'*

At 7 am there was a further announcement on television and pictures of the scene were shown. The presenter said:

> *'London woke up this morning to the shock of a possible terrorist atrocity in the blowing up of a civilian aircraft over the River Thames Estuary. It is believed the bomb was meant to explode when the plane was directly over the city or at the airport. Its premature detonation over the estuary had minimised damage to property and loss of life on the ground. This did not, however, diminish the horror of the act, the consequences of which will be far-reaching. All emergency services are at the scene. Further bulletins will be broadcast throughout the day.'*

Further broadcasts did continue as the world's media became aware of what had happened. A later announcement claimed that some bodies had been found and a vigorous search was being made for the black box flight recorder.

Air Traffic Control at Heathrow had given permission for the aircraft to land and a recording of the conversation with the pilot indicated that everything was normal and the aircraft was set to make a perfect landing. At exactly 6.30 the aircraft's transponder and all its wireless communications stopped working. This was followed by a loud explosion, which was heard in the city. Distant clouds of black smoke were seen from the Heathrow Control Tower.

Coming a year after the planting of terrorist bombs in London and New York on the eve of the millennium, this latest act shocked the government and the security services. Only a few top level members of the security services and the Prime Minister knew about the failed atomic bomb that was planted on a barge tethered to the millennium wheel. Further attacks by al-Qaeda were feared. Unfortunately, it looked like these fears had now been realised.

Was the destruction of this aircraft an act of vengeance? No intelligence of a planned terrorist act had been received by anyone on both sides of the Atlantic even though surveillance on the movement of suspected terrorists had been greatly increased. This time there would be no hiding from the inevitable public outrage. Questions would be asked by people around the world and answers would be required on how a powerful explosive device capable of totally destroying a large aircraft could have been placed on it undetected.

As soon as it was established that the explosion was not accidental, the Prime Minister telephoned the US President, who had already been informed. They agreed on the text of public statements that would be made about the bombing and that top priority would be given to finding those responsible. An urgent investigation was already in progress on both sides of the Atlantic. They vowed that their respective security services would work closely together to defeat the common enemy, assumed to be al-Qaeda.

Realising what had happened under the former US president, the new one was determined to take a hard line on terrorism. But this latest terrorist act was a devastating blow to the intelligence services who were again found wanting.

There was surprise and alarm when the passenger manifest and the flight plan were revealed to members of the National Counter-

Terrorist Committee (NCTC). They discovered that flight BA66 had been diverted to Schiphol Airport in Amsterdam owing to the closure of Heathrow because of a bomb scare.

The captain had been told by BA to pick up some passengers stranded after a flight from Dubai had to make an emergency landing at the airport due to a failure of one of the aircraft's engines. The decision to divert was made by British Airways because the New York flight was only fifty per cent full and an hour ahead of schedule. Unknown to the airline, Amsterdam had been the city where the London millennium bombs had been loaded onto a ship. Was this proof of a connection to al-Qaeda? Members of the NCTC didn't know that two US agents were on the aircraft to keep an al-Qaeda suspect under surveillance. The information was kept secret from the airline.

The NCTC was a joint operational committee comprising of the heads of MI5, MI6, GCHQ, the Metropolitan Police Counter-Terrorist Section and the Home Office Minister. It had been established by the Prime Minister, who also chaired it, after the millennium bomb incident. The committee was set up to ensure that every relevant agency and authority received all intelligence information at the same time so decisions on any actions could be coordinated. In the past a lack of coordination between the services had resulted in delays and poor management in dealing with terrorist acts, often resulting in the perpetrators escaping capture. Many useful lessons had been learned during the IRA bombing campaign, but very few put into practice. The millennium bomb incident had been a wake-up call.

Rupert Arnold saw the names of Paul and Valerie Cane on the passenger list. He knew they were on the plane as he had authorised protection for them on arrival at Heathrow after the call had been made to John Nicholas by Robert Carville from New York who was concerned about Cane's meeting with the Saudi.

In view of Cane's close involvement with the millennium bomb incident, was it, he wondered, a coincidence that he was on this particular flight? Cane was not on any mission or, to his knowledge, involved in any clandestine activity. When he later discovered that Cane and three others had survived the explosion, he immediately arranged for them all to be taken to a secure ward in a private London hospital.

Cane's injuries were not life-threatening, but the other survivors were in a critical condition. It looked like everyone else on the flight had been killed. So far, less than half of the bodies had been recovered amongst the wreckage that was scattered over a wide area of the Thames Estuary. Many were disfigured beyond recognition. Others had been washed out to sea by the fast-flowing tide, making recovery very difficult. Matching the body remains to the names on the passenger list was going to be a long and heart-breaking task for relatives and officials.

Divers had recovered the flight recorder embedded in the soft mud on the river bank. Fortunately, it had been ejected when the plane broke up and wasn't badly damaged. Being lightweight and stored in the lower part of the plane, many items of luggage were also expelled by the force of the explosion.

A security zone was set up around the crash site, but the river couldn't be stopped from flowing out to sea, so divers had to work quickly to recover as much as they could, including any evidence of the source and materials used in the explosives. Experts were being flown in from the US to help since at first it was believed the bomb could have been placed on the aircraft at Kennedy Airport. All people involved with the flight at Kennedy Airport were being held in detention while investigations were carried out.

Paul Cane was taken to a secure room in the hospital for treatment. Rupert Arnold asked John Nicholas to go to the hospital to talk to him as soon as it was possible.

Nicholas had been promoted to the rank of commander for his outstanding work in catching the millennium bomb terrorists and was placed in charge of the investigation. He had no doubt about the formidable task that confronted him.

John Nicholas called the senior medical consultant at the hospital, who told him that Cane had three broken ribs, a fractured leg and was suffering from concussion. He was also traumatised by shock and couldn't be interviewed for some days. Nicholas asked to be kept informed when it would be possible.

Three days later the consultant agreed to allow a short visit. The commander was asked to limit his questioning since the patient would be confused and shouldn't be stressed. He told Nicholas that Paul Cane's survival and relatively light injuries were a miracle. It was probably due to the front part of the plane, where he had been seated in first-class, being blasted away from the main fuselage. The seat in which he was strapped broke away from the structure and fell into the soft mud on the river bank, which had absorbed the energy of the fall. This was possible because the aircraft was only about a thousand feet above the ground and travelling at low speed on its approach to Heathrow.

He added quietly, 'Mr Cane has repeatedly asked about his wife, but we haven't told him yet that she is missing, presumed dead, since her body hasn't been recovered. Telling him now might worsen or delay his recovery.'

Nicholas knew the couple had recently married and returned from their honeymoon in Switzerland. After what they had endured together during the millennium bomb crisis in 1999, he was surprised they had gone to New York. It was, however, important to talk to Cane as soon as possible since he was likely to be the only survivor and might have valuable information.

The consultant also told him that two of the other survivors, the co-pilot and a flight attendant, were also in the front section of the plane. The third survivor, a male passenger who was in the tail section, had also fallen into the mud strapped to his seat, but he was not so lucky as Cane and unlikely to survive. That section had also broken away from the main body during the explosion. The other two had serious head injuries and were in intensive care. He didn't think they would live. No other survivors had so far been brought in, but the search for bodies was still in progress.

Nicholas entered the room to see Cane, who was connected to a bank of monitors and sitting in a semi-upright position on a bed. His face was swollen making him almost unrecognisable, his leg was set in plaster and the rest of his body partially covered in bandages. He looked up at the visitor with a wry smile indicating some recognition.

Feeling uncomfortable, John Nicholas said, 'The Prime Minister and my colleagues are devastated about what has happened and are glad you have survived. They convey their best wishes for a speedy recovery. If you don't wish to talk now I will come back and see you at a later time, but there are some urgent questions I would like to ask you if you feel up to them.'

It was a poor statement to make to a man who was distraught with pain and distress. Cane looked up at him with his swollen eyes and tried to compose himself. He muttered, 'My memory is hazy, but I will do my best and try to answer your questions.'

Nicholas asked, 'Do you remember what took place just before the explosion and if any passenger on the plane was acting suspiciously?'

'Vaguely, there was a well-dressed man of Arab appearance in the seat on the opposite side of our cabin who appeared to be agitated after the *Fasten Safety Belts* sign was switched on. It was also announced by the pilot as we approached the river estuary. I had my suspicions of the man during the flight. Just before everything went blank I remember he was making some adjustments to a digital Casio watch. I particularly noticed the watch because it was large and didn't fit well on his wrist. The watch may be significant because when I was in the water a charred body floated past me.' Cane paused. The memory of that horrific sight unsettled him and a tear ran down his face.

Seeing his anguish, Nicholas said, 'Take your time.'

After a few minutes, he continued.

'On the wrist was a watch. I instinctively removed it from the arm and placed it on my own wrist. I don't know why I did it. Only then did I notice that my own watch was missing. I didn't realise until later it was the Casio watch I had seen on the plane. I think it's in my locker beside the bed.'

Nicholas had never forgotten his police training and always carried with him a pair of plastic gloves. He stretched them over his hands and went to the locker and took out the Casio watch.

'What's significant about the watch?' Cane asked.

'I'm not sure, but we need to have forensics examine it. The time shown is when it stopped working, which is ten minutes later than the time when signals from the aircraft's transponder ceased and the plane exploded. That's the time when the plane would have been directly over the centre of London, near the Houses of Parliament. The watch seems unusually large and, not surprising owing to its tumultuous journey into the river, the case is badly damaged. The brief immersion in cold sea water probably saved it. Taking it apart will require special tools. Fortunately, the body you saw, Paul, was, with others, removed from the water and is now in a special mortuary awaiting a post-mortem. DNA results will assist in determining the person's identity if we can match it to any found on the watch. Then we can find out if it's the person you saw on the plane and, from the seat number, identify him. This could be crucial evidence so I need to take it away.'

Cane looked disturbed at giving up the watch. It had become an important artefact that related to his survival.

Seeing this Nicholas said, 'Don't worry, when it's been examined you will get it back, Paul.'

Nicholas put the watch in a polythene bag and placed it in his pocket. He told Cane that for security reasons his name as a survivor would not be released to the press and a police officer would be on guard outside the room around the clock. Seeing Cane was tired and becoming upset, Nicholas thanked him and said he would see him again soon. A nurse came into the room to check readings on the various monitors connected to his body. Before leaving the hospital, Nicholas asked the consultant about his patient's medical prognosis.

'He should fully recover from the physical injuries in about a month, but the trauma of the explosion and the death of his wife may last for a long time. It could affect his mental stability and is likely to change his outlook and attitude to people and events. We want to limit the number of visitors he receives; having a secure room will help. My staff will deal with any enquiries from friends

and relatives. It would be useful for us to have their names.'
Nicholas agreed to provide that information.

John Nicholas returned to Scotland Yard and was briefing his team
when he received a call from a very distressed Robert Carville in
New York. He had heard about the explosion and anxiously
wanted to know what had happened to his friends, the Canes.
Nicholas told him that Paul Cane had survived and was in hospital,
but Valerie was missing, presumed dead. It came as a devastating
shock to Robert; particularly since he had booked them on the
flight. He felt blame for what had happened. Robert told Nicholas
he would take the next flight to London. Nicholas warned him
about the strict security now in place at airports. He told him to
report to his office when he arrived so arrangements could be made
for him to visit Cane in hospital since a high security cordon had
been placed around it.

Extensive searches were being carried out for evidence at Kennedy
and Schiphol airports and around the crash area. Divers and land
teams had recovered aircraft parts from the river and the
surrounding banks. The recordings from the aircraft's black box
were being analysed. The backgrounds of all passengers on the
flight were being scrutinised by the FBI and British police. All
security services were on high alert. It was believed the terrorists
intended to bring down the plane over central London, but
something had gone wrong with the timing and the bomb had
detonated prematurely. There was a lot of work to do. Many
questions needed to be answered.
   A total of 346 people had been instantly killed on flight BA66,
which made it the worst terrorist attack on a civilian target. It had
a similar pattern to the destruction of the Pan Am flight 103 over
Lockerbie in Scotland in December 1988 by a terrorist bomb. On
that occasion 243 people onboard died. There were no survivors.
One crew member, a flight attendant who was in the front section
of the plane that was blown clear of the fuselage, was thought to
have been alive when it hit the ground but died shortly after.

Unlike BA66 there was no soft mud to absorb the impact, so it was miraculous that anybody had survived such a descent and impact on the ground. It was thought, but couldn't be proved, that on that flight, the crew found strapped to their seats on the flight deck may have been alive until they actually hit the ground.

During the days that followed, Paul Cane had been told more about the explosion and that his wife was lost, presumed dead, along with all other passengers. None of the other three people who had survived the explosion was still alive. The death toll had now risen to 349. Cane was devastated and found it difficult to come to terms with the news. He was living a nightmare and had to be given sedatives to sleep. His physical injuries were healing well, but he would require extensive trauma counselling. The medical staff protected him from the press and media, who had heard about the plane survivors and were using a range of clever means to get into the hospital.

Two uniformed policemen were assigned to his room. The only non-official visitors were Valerie's parents, Sir George and Margaret Day and her aunt Flo. Naturally they were extremely distressed and in a state of shock and disbelief at what had happened. They were surprised he and Valerie went to New York following their honeymoon, particularly after what had happened previously in that city. He knew they blamed him for her death. He wished he hadn't survived. Added to his grief, he felt a deep sense of guilt for taking her to New York. But it was Valerie's wish to see the city that persuaded him to accept Robert Carville's invitation. He personally didn't want to go. Except for his friend Robert Carville, his New York publisher, John Nicholas and the airline, nobody else knew they were on the aircraft. It was an unfortunate coincidence – an act of fate that had placed them on the doomed plane. Their first meeting in Washington and short time together had been fated by a series of coincidences.

During the time that Cane had known Valerie she had been disturbed by bad dreams and premonitions that something bad was going to happen to her. It had always disturbed him, but he could do little to dispel them. Now those worst fears had materialised. He had lost the woman he loved before they had really started their life together. Coming so soon after the attempt on their lives in the previous year left him emotionally drained and deeply depressed. He saw little purpose in living. He had reached a pit of despair. Seeing his condition, the medical team placed him on suicide watch.

Cane's memories of the events of the last month were stirring his investigative instincts. They hardened his resolve to find those responsible and take retribution for the death of his wife and all those people on the plane. He knew that finding those responsible was also the objective of the security agencies, but he was now personally involved. He was convinced in his mind it was the same group who had been behind the millennium bombs, even if the individuals were different. Thinking about what he would do after he left hospital helped to relieve his anguish. In a strange way, it helped to speed his recovery.

Robert Carville's journey to London had been delayed because, having knowledge of his involvement with the millennium bombs, he was questioned rigorously by the FBI. But after a call to Alicia Garcia, who was now the director of a new Counter Terrorist Unit (CTU), established to provide intelligence directly to the President and his security advisors, he was allowed to take a flight to London.

Alicia Garcia had been a member of the last president's Task Force set up in 1999 to find the terrorists who threatened to blow up New York with an atomic bomb. After surviving the Senate enquiry and spending a short time as Head of the White House Security, she was praised for her part in bomb investigations and given the new post. One outcome of the Senate enquiry on the millennium bomb incident showed the lack of information sharing between the White House, the CIA and the FBI.

The infiltration of the agencies by terrorist moles contributed to the new president's decision to set up a Counter Terrorist Unit independent of the CIA and the FBI and directly reporting to the President's national security advisor. It was to the FBI's annoyance that it was located at a secure site near Langley, the CIA headquarters. They saw it as a lack of presidential confidence and a bias towards the CIA; it also went against the recommendations of the enquiry.

Alicia Garcia had impressed the new president's advisors and was given the job of its first director with the freedom to recruit her own staff. The unit was unpopular with her former colleagues because she could bypass their organisations and report directly to the White House if the security issue was considered serious enough. This resentment would later prove to be a barrier to the very purpose for which the unit was established.

Having placed two of her top agents on flight BA66, Alicia was now in a difficult situation. She knew nothing at the time about the Canes being on the flight, but felt an intense sense of guilt because she believed the man who was being tracked by her agents could have had some involvement with the bombing. It had all the hallmarks of an al-Qaeda bomb outrage.

The Canes had become her friends over the years after helping to save New York from an atomic bomb. That incident raised serious breaches of security and proved the enemy still had extensive assets in the US.

A week after the tragedy, Robert arrived at the hospital. He was shocked when he saw the state of his friend. Although recovering well from his physical injuries, Robert could see a marked change in the man who, only a week before, had been the happiest man in the world, having married the one woman he truly loved. Robert felt depressed with a deep feeling of guilt, having been the person who had asked his friends to come to New York to meet with the publisher of Cane's book. He had actually booked and paid for their flights on BA66. But, of course, he knew nothing about the existence on the plane of the agents and a suspected terrorist or that it would be diverted to Amsterdam. It reminded him of the set of coincidences that led them to become involved with the millennium bomb threats. History seemed to be repeating itself.

The strange behaviour of Valerie at the World Trade Centre in New York had also worried him. She did show some reluctance to board the fated plane.

The exchanges between the two men didn't last too long since Cane was tired and too depressed to say much. Robert told him he was staying over in London and would come back to see him in a few days.

Robert returned to his hotel and immediately called Alicia Garcia using the private secure cell phone number that she had given him during his time in Washington. She answered immediately. He told her about Paul Cane's situation. She said her team was working around the clock to find those responsible.

Al-Qaeda had denied any responsibility for the destruction of the plane. But nobody believed them. All intelligence agencies across the world were now working together and sharing intelligence. All-out war was finally declared on al-Qaeda by Western nations and their allies. The whole world shared in the horror of the event. There were mixed feelings in some Arab countries, who, although not openly supporting the terrorists, believed it was a consequence of the continued US support of Israel against Palestine.

It was to everyone's surprise that the British Prime Minister was developing a good relationship with the new Republican President. They publicly declared a common intention to share intelligence and strengthen their alliance in the war on terrorism. In the years to come, this would become controversial. Politicians have their own agendas, not always obvious to their voters.

The destruction of BA66 was clearly in retaliation to the failure of the millennium bombs. It was a direct attack on the West, less serious than the atomic bomb explosion would have been if it had been successful, but showed there was now a determined enemy who threatened world peace. It had to be eliminated as soon as possible. The big question that faced the governments and their security services was how to do it within international law. The enemy didn't recognise such a law, so new ways would have to be found to deal with them. But the US President and his advisors had already worked out their own strategy for dealing with the terrorists.

Not being aware of the threat to a civilian aircraft was a public relations disaster for the intelligence services. The FBI, the CIA and their British equivalents were furious about not being informed of the suspected al-Qaeda terrorist on the plane until after the event. Once again the cultural divide between the services was shown to still exist. This was the last thing anyone wanted at a time when both governments had pledged full cooperation in the war against the terrorists.

Alicia locked her office door and dialled a number.

The receiver of the call was told, 'We need to meet at ten o'clock tonight at the usual place.' A reassuring Irish voice simply said, 'OK.'

She left her office unseen and drove out of Washington into the darkness of the night.

CHAPTER 2

England
One Month Earlier – April 2001

Paul Cane had finished writing his book in early 2000 and sent it to an American publisher. It was when his then fiancée, Valerie, was in hospital recovering from the horrendous car crash. The police were still investigating the incident, which was almost certainly an attempt on their lives by Christine Hunter.

In writing the book, Cane relived the tumultuous few months of the previous year that he had spent in Washington, New York and London when the world was taken to the brink of nuclear Armageddon by al-Qaeda. He still found it difficult to come to terms with how, through a series of unexplainable coincidences, he had become intimately involved in one of the most dangerous terrorist events of the century.

In agreement with his agent, Robert Carville, and the American publisher, a decision was taken to delay publication of the book until after the completion of the US Senate hearings and the UK government's enquiry into the millennium conspiracy. Since he was still a terrorist target Cane decided to use a pseudonym in preference to his real name as author.

A shake-up in the security services in the US and the UK had already taken place. Many senior people on both sides of the Atlantic had lost their jobs or been demoted. New people had been recruited and internal communication systems improved. The hunt for the terrorists responsible was on-going, but most of the leaders of The New Order had been quietly eliminated. Little progress, however, had been made in capturing leading members of al-Qaeda. Bin Laden had narrowly escaped being caught on a number of occasions and was hiding somewhere in Afghanistan. He was now the CIA's prime target.

Paul and Valerie had postponed their marriage from the previous year because Valerie's father, Sir George Day had a second stroke, which left him partially paralysed. It also took Valerie much longer than expected to recover from her injuries, so the year had been difficult for the couple. Finally, after Christmas, Valerie and her father had recovered enough for the wedding plans to be made. The wedding took place on 30 April at the parish church in the village of Farncombe, near Godalming.

It was a sunny spring morning when the bride walked down the aisle with her proud father. Sir George was a little unsteady walking, but with some help he made it to the altar. Robert Carville was Paul's best man. Their US friends were invited, but couldn't attend. John Nicholas, representing the police, did come to the reception and wished the couple every happiness, knowing the traumas they had been through during the previous year.

Paul and Valerie flew to Montreux in Switzerland for their honeymoon and stayed at the world-renowned Chateau de Chillon overlooking Lake Geneva. Paul had informed the hotel they were on their honeymoon so a bottle of Moet et Chandon champagne in a bucket of ice was waiting for them on arrival.

It was during dinner on their last night at the hotel when Paul noticed a well-dressed man and a woman sitting at a nearby table. The woman was much younger than her male companion, who was of Spanish appearance, while she was more English-looking. After Valerie left to explore the desserts laid out on a far table, Paul saw the woman staring at him. Her dark, penetrating eyes and severe facial expression made him feel uncomfortable. He sensed she was trying to send him a message – a warning. Did he know her? She seemed to know him. The man, who had his back to Paul, was talking to the woman, but it was clear she wasn't listening to what he was saying. Shortly after, they left the table and walked out. Paul noticed how much older the man was to the woman. There was a noticeable similarity in their physical appearance; he could easily be her father. Valerie returned with a plate of food and observing her husband's worried expression, said, 'What's wrong, darling, you look like you've seen a ghost?'

'Nothing, I just feel a little sick; it must be all this rich food. Let's go for a walk alongside the lake and get some fresh air, I don't feel like eating much more.'

On the walk, Cane kept thinking about the woman at the table. Then, like a cold shower, it hit him; it was the eyes. Last time he had seen them was in the rear mirror of his Mercedes before the vehicle the woman was driving forced his car off the road and into a tree. Was she Christine Hunter? The daughter of Diana Hunter, the deceased British Cabal member of The New Order. He decided not to tell Valerie since it might spoil their honeymoon. He could be wrong, but no woman had ever looked at him in such a disdainful way. She would see him as being responsible for her mother's downfall and death. The police had supposedly tracked her to Spain and then lost the trail. Nobody really knew what she looked like, but her father's face was well known. If the man proved to be her father then it would be a positive identification. He was tempted to call John Nicholas, but he didn't want to be pulled back into the millennium saga. Now the book was written, all that was behind him. He just wanted a quiet life with his new wife and family.

When they arrived back in Knightsbridge the next day there was an urgent telephone message from Robert to call him. Paul dialled the number and put the speaker on so Valerie could hear. Robert answered immediately.

'I apologise for contacting you so soon after your honeymoon, but the book publisher has been in contact and wants to meet with you urgently about some important legal issues that need sorting out before they can proceed with publication. Can you and Valerie possibly come to New York for a meeting with the publisher?'

Paul didn't want to go back to that city. He knew that Valerie would share his reluctance. Detecting a concern by Paul's hesitation in replying, Robert added, 'I will pay for first-class flight tickets.

The publisher is still willing to pay you a hundred thousand dollars and agree on generous royalty terms. If you both can come I will reserve you a suite at the Millennium Plaza Hotel in Manhattan. You will not need to be in New York for more than a day.'

Robert's expectations annoyed Paul. It reminded him of what had happened previously when Robert made arrangements for a meeting in Washington before consulting him.

'I will call you back after I have spoken to Valerie,' he said and put the phone down. It was the last thing Paul wanted to be bothered about after his honeymoon. Valerie had overheard the telephone conversation. Unlike her husband, she hadn't been to the Manhattan part of New York, having spent most of her time in the US working in Washington.

'We could do some sightseeing while in the city. Let's go, Paul, that is, if it doesn't bring back too many bad memories for you. Sorry, that was insensitive of me,' she said.

Reflecting on Robert's offer, Paul said, 'If you're sure you want to go, then I guess I do need to have the meeting. The publication of the book is important. It's my way of recording the truth about the millennium conspiracy. I owe that to David Simons and all the other people who died.'

Now that Valerie wanted to go to New York, Paul called Robert back and agreed he would go to the meeting. He asked Robert to book them on the first available flight and make the necessary arrangements. It was to be a fateful decision.

CHAPTER 3

Manhattan, New York

The Canes were met by Robert Carville at Kennedy Airport. He drove them to Manhattan passing over the Queensborough Bridge and along First Avenue to the Millennium Plaza Hotel, located opposite the United Nations Building.

Their suite, on the forty-second floor, gave a commanding view of the Manhattan skyline. To the right could be seen the Chrysler and Empire State buildings. To the southwest, the twin towers of the World Trade Centre were clearly visible. On the left side was the rounded dome of the United Nations Building; not a particularly impressive one considering it housed what could be described as the embryonic world government. Unknown to most New Yorkers, a vigorous debate was in progress about Iraq's expulsion of the weapons inspectors and the prospects of new UN sanctions.

Robert, who was staying at another hotel, agreed to return in the evening to take them out to dinner with the publisher, Guy Hadrian, the director and owner of Hadrian Books.

The Millennium Plaza Hotel was normally used by delegates and officials attending UN meetings and sessions. Unknown to Paul, Robert had also arranged for him to meet what he described as an important man, who was staying at the hotel. The man, whose name he didn't disclose, was attending a meeting of the UN Security Council. The mystery deepened when Paul learned that the man couldn't leave the hotel for security reasons so the meeting had been arranged in his suite on the top floor. Paul was annoyed that Robert had made such an arrangement without asking him first. It made him suspicious that Robert was up to his old tricks again. Last time it resulted in them being sucked into working for the CIA.

Paul looked out across the New York skyline from the bedroom window and thought back on how close the city had come to extinction in late December 1999 when the army team shot the al-Qaeda terrorist only seconds before he was going to detonate a nuclear bomb on the barge on the Hudson River. A city like New York with its closely packed, high-rise buildings was so vulnerable to terrorist attacks. It had nearly happened twice and failed; would they dare try again?

Sheikh bin Abdullah was a member of the Saudi Royal Family and leader of the Saudi delegation to the UN. A crucial meeting of the Security Council was in session to discuss sanctions against Iraq for their treatment of the weapons inspectors. Paul had just finished dressing when the phone rang.

'Hello, Paul, can you come on your own to suite one on the top floor for the meeting?'

Robert sounded nervous as he put the phone down. Paul told Valerie that Robert wanted him at the meeting with the so-called important person. She wanted to bath, wash her hair and get dressed so told him to call her when the meeting was finished.

Two smartly dressed Arab men in Western-style business suits, obviously armed guards, stood outside the door. They frisked Paul for any concealed weapons and recording devices before he was allowed into the room. Robert opened the door and gave a guarded smile. He led Paul into a suite of luxury furnished rooms. A formally dressed Arab was seated on a padded chair. Paul thought he recognised the man as one he had interviewed in Kuwait. Sitting on the other side of the room was a younger man, also dressed in a traditional Arab dishdash.

'Paul, may I introduce Sheikh bin Abdullah and his son Faisal.'

The Sheikh's outstretched hand displayed a wrist fitted with gold jewellery and a very expensive Gucci watch. Paul shook their hands, but decided to not show any recognition of the Sheikh. His name was different so Paul wasn't completely sure it was the same man he had interviewed. He looked similar, but had a longer beard. Saudi families are very large, comprising of many sons, brothers and sisters so similarities are quite common. This one looked like a prince and was probably a member of the royal family.

Tea was brought in by a servant and the three men sat down to talk. Paul's curiosity was soon put to rest when the Sheikh said, 'Mr Cane, you interviewed my cousin, Prince bin Ahmed, in Kuwait in 1999. It is with great sadness that I have to tell you he was killed in a car accident a month after you interviewed him. I believe he was murdered. It was not long after your friend Abdel Salam met a similar fate.'

The Sheikh seemed to know about the Kuwait operation.

'We don't have much time, Mr Cane, so I will come quickly to my reason for meeting with you. I know about the traumatic experiences you endured during the millennium bomb crisis. I have to tell you that I believe a major terrorist attack on Britain and the US is imminent. There are powerful people in my country who support al-Qaeda and are secretly aiding them. I don't know yet what form it will take or the identities of the leading figures involved. Our king and members of the royal family are also targets, so we have tightened up our security. Those people we suspect are being watched and at the right time we will arrest and deal with them. Meanwhile we would like your help.

'I would like you to warn the US President and the Prime Minister through people you can trust, not the CIA, FBI or MI6 because al-Qaeda still has sympathisers working for those agencies.'

Looking puzzled, Paul said, 'Why have you sought me out? I am now married and don't want to be involved anymore in politics or terrorist threats. Anyway I'm sure the CIA and FBI are following up such threats. Both governments are expecting further attacks so any additional warning from me wouldn't add much.'

'Mr Cane, I understand that after the millennium bomb you don't want to become involved, but unfortunately you are high on al-Qaeda's hit list. Because you're not officially a government agent you are the only one we can trust. You will know that intelligence often comes from unknown sources. After the failings of the CIA and FBI and the British equivalents to find and stop those responsible for the millennium bombs, we have little confidence in them preventing further attacks. We know the President has set up a new Counter Terrorist Unit under the direct control of the National Security Agency and the White House. We know the identity of its director, Alicia Garcia, someone you know well. My people don't want to contact her directly so would like you to act as our intermediary. If you agree, you will be handsomely paid. If required, you will also be provided with protection.'

Paul didn't like the implication. He didn't want to be a paid agent for the Saudis and involved in any of their clandestine activities. Once again he felt like a trapped man. Forces beyond his control were moving him into a situation he didn't want to be in. He wanted to walk away, but knew that wouldn't be easy. Why did Robert agree to set up the meeting with the Sheikh? Was it for money? Knowing Robert, that would have been the main reason, but there might be others. Once agreements are made and money is accepted these people never let you go. The Sheikh shook hands with both men showing an expectation that his requests would be granted. Most men obeyed his requests; it was the nature of the culture in which he lived. Paul was extremely angry about being placed once again in the invidious position where he might have intelligence that could be useful to the governments.

The Saudi Royal Family seemed to be able to do whatever they wanted working outside official channels. They possessed this ability because of their vast wealth and extensive commercial interests with Western countries. Being key players in the Middle East also gave them a strategic position and influence over politicians. But many Saudis supported Wahhabism in its purest extremist form, which is fundamental to the al-Qaeda doctrine. Most of the leaders of al-Qaeda are Saudi Arabs. Wahhabism is a sect that is intolerant to Islam, Judaism, Christianity and Hinduism. It seeks to challenge and destroy these faiths and considers their followers as non-believers. They claim to be the champions of Islam, but are, in reality, the enemies of that faith.

The US government had needed Saudi support in 1991 for the invasion of Iraq in Operation Desert Storm. The setting up of US military bases in Saudi Arabia was essential but unpopular with many Saudis. This arrangement together with the need for continuing oil supplies made the agreement with the US necessary. Paul was angry with Robert.

'Why have you involved me in this?' he said angrily.

'The Sheikh specifically wanted to speak to you as he knew you were in New York.'

'How did he know that?'

'I don't know. A letter was handed to me when I arrived at my hotel. They obviously knew where I was staying. It looks like they have been spying on us.'

That really worried Paul.

'Robert, don't tell Valerie about the content of this meeting. She thinks it's related to the publishers.'

'OK, but we do have that meeting with Guy Hadrian over dinner later.'

Paul called Valerie to say he was coming back to the room. Valerie came out of the bedroom and seeing Paul staring out of the window said, 'You're very quiet, darling. Is there anything wrong?'

'No,' he said.

She looked at her husband and by his tone knew that he was lying, but said nothing.

Inside the Yellow Cab taxi on the way to the restaurant at the Waldorf Astoria Hotel on Park Avenue, Robert explained to the Canes why Guy Hadrian had concerns about the book's content. He was worried that too much information was given about the activities of the CIA and FBI. They would certainly want to stop publication on grounds of national security. Therefore, in its present form they would need to see and approve it.

The Waldorf Astoria was world-famous for its culinary creations and used by the rich and famous who wanted to impress their guests. Their host had booked a private room in the Peacock Ally Restaurant so they could talk in private. Guy Hadrian was a multi-millionaire and the owner of Hadrian Books, a company his father had founded after he arrived from Greece many decades ago. It specialised in high value, high quality publications and, although fictional novels were not normally published, owing to its content, they made an exception for Paul's book. They had published many bestsellers written by celebrities and business leaders so had a reputation to uphold. Paul had met Guy previously at one of Robert's functions in London and knew he had shares in *The Global Economist*, the journal that commissioned him to write articles on the Middle East. The publisher clearly saw the commercial potential in the book by offering a one hundred thousand dollar fee for its exclusive copyright to publish. If Paul had been a well-known fiction author then he could have commanded an even greater payment.

The taxi arrived at the hotel and Robert immediately made a call on his cell phone. A well-dressed woman, who introduced herself as Emma, Guy's PA, came to meet and escort them to a private room. A table displayed ice buckets with bottles of champagne and wine. She was followed soon after by a portly man in his late fifties who introduced himself as Guy Hadrian, shaking hands first with Valerie, then Paul and Robert. A waiter came in and poured out the champagne. Paul noticed that Guy's eyes were transfixed on Valerie, who was dressed in a figure-hugging low-cut black evening dress. He congratulated Paul for having such a beautiful wife. After the usual small talk, the group sat down and dinner was served.

Guy Hadrian was an astute businessman so didn't waste time in talking about the issues of publishing Paul's book. He wanted the book edited to remove many references to the CIA who had the power to stop it being published. The alternative would be to submit it to them first for approval.

The fact that the story had fictional characters but was based on actual events made their identity obvious. Paul was unhappy about submitting it to the CIA because he knew it would never emerge, but agreed to edit the book himself. Guy told him the book would be a blockbuster because many people didn't believe the Senate Commissions Report on what had happened in 1999. He was willing to publish it under Paul Cane's pseudonym after the edits had been carried out. Robert wanted a contract drawn up and agreed. Guy had no problem with providing an up-front fifty per cent payment prior to receiving the final manuscript. He shook hands with his guests and took the opportunity to kiss Valerie and whispered to Cane, 'You have a very beautiful wife. I wish you all the very best and happiness for the future.'

A taxi was waiting to take them back to their respective hotels.

The next day Robert took the Canes on a sightseeing tour of Manhattan. He drove along Sixth Avenue to Central Park, then to Broadway and Times Square. The Square was, as usual, bustling with sightseeing crowds and billboards advertising shows. It was a kaleidoscope of colour and noise, a mix of nationalities and all types of people weaving around each other. They were drawn to this famous area of the performing arts like insects attracted by light. But Broadway was special. Everybody knew it and loved to go there and experience the magic. Americans have an uncanny marketing ability for their films and shows.

After passing slowly through the crowded streets of Broadway, Robert drove to the financial district of lower Manhattan then turned into Church Street and stopped briefly outside the World Trade Centre's twin towers. Robert had some client companies with offices on the 83rd floor of the North Tower. He had visited them on a number of occasions and told his passengers what a fantastic view of Manhattan and beyond there was from the top. Each tower had one hundred and ten floors and rose to a height of a fifth of a mile above Manhattan. They were the pride of New York and America and symbolised what America represented; the centre of capitalism and world trade.

'Would you like to go up there?' he said, pointing upward at one of the towers.

Paul saw Valerie shudder at the suggestion. Valerie's face was white as though she had seen a ghost.

'What's wrong?' Paul asked.

'Can we drive on? I don't want to be here,' she replied with tears in her eyes and gripped Paul's hand so tight that it hurt. She was visibly shaken. Something associated with the towers had affected her. But she wouldn't say what it was.

Paul knew that people had been killed in the underground car park when al-Qaeda exploded a bomb there in 1993. Had Valerie sensed that? Had she picked up something from the buildings? The two men were not affected by any such vibes.

Robert started up the car and drove on towards the boat terminal at Battery Park. As they passed the Trinity Church at the junction of Wall Street and Broadway, Valerie called out, 'Please stop.'

Robert pulled over into a small car park at the rear. She got out and walked swiftly into the church, followed by the two men who were becoming increasingly worried about her strange behaviour. Valerie walked slowly down the aisle, stopped and, without moving, just looked at the altar. Paul and Robert stayed back watching in silence. After ten minutes, Paul walked to her as other people were coming into the church. Noticing him at her side, she smiled. Paul took her hand and noticed that her face now showed an expression of serene calmness. Colour had returned to her cheeks. Gone were the worried look and sadness he had seen earlier.

She smiled and whispered, 'I'm fine; now let's go out.'

He took her hand and gave it a reassuring squeeze. Robert took her other hand and without saying anything the three walked back to the car. Paul decided he wouldn't ask any questions for now. Once again he realised that his wife had sensory powers beyond anything he understood. Whatever had happened or was going to happen in this place had affected her.

One of New York's historical landmarks, the church was a classic example of Gothic architecture and on the tourist route.

Later in the year the historical significance of the church would be greatly enhanced.*

Robert parked the car on the road at Pier A, near Battery Park. They walked to the water's edge to get a view across the Hudson River of the Statue of Liberty standing tall on Liberty Island. It was America's icon, a symbol of freedom and democracy to immigrants arriving from abroad; a suitable target for its enemies.

They looked out across the river to the south bank where over a year ago the al-Qaeda terrorists had planted the millennium bomb on a barge. It brought back sad memories of their friend David Simons. Paul still felt guilty about his death. If he and Alicia hadn't tracked him down he would still be living in retirement in Tucson. His life was an essential part of the story in Paul's book, which was why it had to be published. He was not named, but those who took part in the calamitous events of 1999 would know him.

Now being more composed, Valerie said, 'Let's take a boat trip around the harbour and get that famous view of Manhattan.'

'OK, I'll get some tickets,' replied Paul and went off to the ticket office.

Robert saw Valerie looking at him, expecting him to say something now that Paul wasn't present.

'Robert, who was the meeting at the hotel with last night? Paul didn't tell me so I assumed he didn't want me to know.'

Feeling embarrassed not knowing that Paul hadn't told her, he was left with little choice but to tell her about the Sheikh's proposition to Paul. She became visibly distressed, saying, 'Paul promised never to become involved with terrorist threats again.'

Robert said, 'I didn't know what the Sheikh wanted when he asked me to arrange the meeting. Paul told the Sheikh that he didn't want to become involved. Afterwards, I told him to walk away.'

Paul returned with the tickets and said, 'The next boat will be here in ten minutes.'

---

* On 11 September 2001, debris from the World Trade Centre rained on Trinity Church, at Broadway and Wall Street where people fleeing from the falling towers took refuge. The church survived the devastation.

He saw that Valerie was looking unhappy again. He glanced at Robert, who was looking away, clearly uncomfortable.

Noting his predicament, Valerie said, 'I asked Robert about the meeting at the hotel last night that you didn't tell me about. He told me about the Sheikh's request.'

Paul immediately went on the defensive, saying, 'I didn't tell you because I have no intention of getting involved and didn't want to spoil our visit by worrying you again about terrorists. I am, however, concerned about how the Sheikh's people knew so much about our movements. When we get back to London I will go and see John Nicholas and ask for police protection.'

'What time does your flight leave tonight?' Robert asked.

'About 7 pm.'

'I will pick you up at the hotel at 4 pm and take you to Kennedy. You have first-class reserved seats so your baggage can be checked through as priority passengers. I will call John Nicholas and ask him to arrange for you to be pushed through the VIP channel and taken to your apartment in Knightsbridge after arrival at Heathrow. Last year he agreed to provide you protection if it was needed. It seems it might now be needed.'

The sightseeing harbour boat arrived at the jetty. The fine weather and calm water had brought out a number of tourists. They were in front of what was now a long queue. Paul hadn't brought his camera, but had one on his cell phone. He went ahead and took a photo of Robert and Valerie walking onto the boat along with other people. It was then he noticed an Arab man and woman just behind who seemed to be observing them more closely than normal. Paul wondered if he was now getting paranoiac about Arabs after last night. They were probably just tourists like them. But he captured them on a photo.

The boat pulled away from the jetty and headed for Liberty Island to give visitors a close-up of the Statue, but not to land. It swept around the back of the statue to give them a panoramic view of Manhattan with it in the foreground. Paul took the iconic photo. Once dominated by the Empire State Building, the skyline was now dominated by the twin towers of the World Trade Centre.

They rose up to the heavens proclaiming the land on which they stood, demanding to be noticed. Al-Qaeda's failed attacks on New York unfortunately didn't mean that they wouldn't try again. He wondered if the CIA and FBI had learned any lessons from these past attempts.

The boat went close to Ellis Island where all early immigrants had passed through on their way to becoming US citizens. It was the gateway to a new life. Robert had visited the island before and was impressed by the efficient system that had been in place between 1892 and 1954 for processing people. Unfortunately, time didn't allow the visitors to land on this occasion. It was now approaching midday and the high sun was warming the air with only a little cooling breeze. The cloudless sky made even the Hudson River look blue. It was a perfect setting.

Kennedy Airport was, as usual, busy when they arrived. Robert wished them well and told Paul security had been arranged in London on their arrival. He had called John Nicholas and told him about the meeting with Sheikh bin Abdullah and his warning about renewed terrorist threats on London and New York, breaking the confidentiality the Sheikh had wanted. Nicholas dismissed it as nonsense saying that it was just an example of inter-rivalry between different factions of the Saudi Royal Family. He told Robert to tell Paul not to become involved. Both governments now had reliable intelligence sources in the Arab world and were in a much better position than they were two years ago. The Canes shook hands with Robert as they departed to the VIP lounge. Paul noticed that Valerie was very quiet and seemed reluctant to leave New York.

CHAPTER 4

Flight BA66

After checking in, the Canes were escorted to the VIP lounge at Kennedy International Airport by a BA staff member. Someone in London had pulled some strings. Robert had done a good job. Six other people, presumably all first-class passengers, were already sitting on plush leather seats being waited upon by men in tuxedos. In the centre of the room was a table on which a variety of food delicacies were displayed, around which ice buckets with champagne and wines were conveniently placed. The escort took them to a table in the corner of the room. He gave them a phone to use if they needed to call any member of staff.

Valerie would have preferred to be treated like any other passenger as they were now attracting attention. The lounge was usually occupied by business people, celebrities from show business and the media, and bankers from Wall Street. VIPs were usually well known unless they had special reasons to be kept out of the sight of other passengers. Paul Cane knew they were in the VIP category for security reasons. Would there be someone assigned to protect them? Last time they travelled back from the US, the FBI did have an agent on the plane although he never revealed himself. Unknown to them, two CTU agents would be on the plane, but for a different purpose.

Valerie thought she noticed at least three film or TV stars in the room, but couldn't recall the names. The others were dressed in business suits. Paul asked the waiter for some champagne and a plate of seafood. The king prawns were too good to miss, but Valerie didn't want any food. Something was still bothering her.

An air attendant escorted the Canes to their seats, which were located in the middle of the first-class cabin in the front section of the plane. They were the first passengers to board. During the next ten minutes the remaining fourteen seats in the cabin were filled. Paul looked around at the other passengers and saw that Valerie was one of only three women in the section. People travel first-class for the comfort and privacy it provides, so the seats were arranged to make it difficult to observe other passengers. But the man in the nearest window seat was just visible. Dressed in a dark business suit, he was of Middle Eastern appearance and reading a book, making no attempt to make himself known to other passengers. The film people, who knew each other, were grouped together in seats behind them and talking amongst themselves about the latest films or celebrities. One was obviously a producer or well-known script writer from the nature of the conversations that took place.

Valerie was looking at the dinner menu and reading the flight entertainment programme when the flight attendant who had shown them to their seats brought glasses of champagne and introduced herself as Anne. She was actually the Cabin Services Director who was in charge of all the flight attendants and cabin services. Anne handed Paul a sealed envelope with the compliments of the captain. The letter gave details of the special security arrangements for them on arrival at Heathrow. Now the air crew would know the Canes were not just ordinary passengers. Thinking back to the meeting with the Sheikh, Paul wondered who else on the plane knew their status. The man in the window seat opposite looked up from his book as the envelope was passed to Paul. For the few seconds it took, Valerie saw the man looking at her. He then went back to reading his book.

The first-class cabin was isolated from the rest of the plane, but Paul could hear the noise of the other passengers coming aboard. The Boeing 777 could accommodate up to 350 passengers across its four classes. It was the most advanced aircraft in the British Airways fleet and was fast becoming the airline's favourite for long haul flights owing to its lower fuel costs and advanced instrument technology. It was the first plane that had been totally designed using a computer. The innovation was the automatic flight control system for take-off and landing in times of poor visibility or in bad weather.

Being able to travel in the stratosphere at over 600 mph in an aluminium tube a few millimetres thick, the only separation between life and instant death, is truly a marvel of twentieth-century technology. It wasn't comforting to dwell upon such marvels for too long since humans were still in control and humans are fallible. Air accidents had been reduced over the years to make flying the safest form of travel, but sometimes things go wrong due to human error. It's a sad fact, but it usually takes a disaster to make airlines improve the safety of their operating systems.

With a good tail wind the flight time to London Heathrow would be about eight hours. Paul liked his flight to Washington on Concorde, but enjoyed the extra comfort and facilities offered by the present aircraft. It was the first time he had travelled on a 777; all his previous flights had been on 747s except for the one flight on Concorde in 1999.

The plane was over the Atlantic and most passengers were asleep when the pilot announced that the flight was changing course to divert to Schiphol Airport in Amsterdam because there was a bomb alert at Heathrow and the airport had been temporarily closed. All incoming flights had been diverted to other airports in the UK and in Northern Europe. The only slot left was Amsterdam. The captain was asked by London control to refuel at Schiphol and pick up some passengers who had been stranded after their flight from Dubai had to make an emergency landing owing to engine problems. He didn't give many details, but told passengers that since the flight was only half-full and owing to following tail winds, it was an hour ahead of schedule so the diversion would only place a short delay in the eventual arrival time at Heathrow, assuming it was open later. He added that any passengers inconvenienced would be compensated and expressed apologies on behalf of British Airways.

Valerie was also asleep when the announcement was made. The only other passenger in the cabin who was awake and writing notes was the Arab-looking man in the window seat. During the flight, Paul couldn't resist observing him. He had refused food and only drank water during the flight, making it obvious to the flight attendant that he didn't want to be disturbed. He hadn't slept so kept his jacket on, spending all the time reading a book. Paul wasn't sure, but he thought the book was a copy of the Koran.

Something wasn't quite right. He couldn't figure out what it was, but the man's dress and physical appearance didn't seem to match. He looked like an actor dressed for a part. He was clean shaven, although it was clear from the marks on his face that he had only recently removed a beard. His hair was cut short and, although black, didn't look like it was always short. He also displayed a number of rings and other jewellery, including an extra large Casio digital wrist watch that also didn't look right. If he was a Muslim then why had he taken steps to disguise the fact?

Cane thought about the meeting with the Sheikh. Was the man in the seat connected to him in some way? Would every Arab he saw make him believe he was being followed or observed? Again, was it paranoia making him suspicious? The odds of being on the same plane as a potential enemy made such a possibility extremely unlikely. The events of 1999 still lingered in his mind. He was still angry with Robert Carville for setting up the meeting with the Sheikh. Robert's explanation wasn't convincing. He had tried to redeem himself by alerting John Nicholas at Scotland Yard to the Sheikh's warning. It did result in the Canes being granted VIP status and receiving protection in London. The downside was it meant they were back on the watch list when all they really wanted was to be left alone.

The plane landed at Schiphol Airport. Most passengers were unhappy about the interruption to their sleep since airline regulations made it necessary for them to be awake before the plane actually landed. During the time it was on the ground Paul heard a lot of noise associated with new passengers coming onto the plane and the extra luggage being loaded into the hold. Since all the seats in first-class were occupied new arrivals had to take seats in one of the other sections on the plane. But the flight time to London was short so any inconvenience would be more than off-set by the compensation they would receive. The first-class cabin was guarded by two attendants to ensure no one entered.

Paul looked out of the window to see a trailer loaded with luggage being brought to the plane, presumably transferred from the grounded flight from Dubai. To save time it was expedient for it to bypass the usual security checks since they would have already been carried out at Dubai Airport. Unknown to the crew, some new extra luggage had been surreptitiously added.

Looking around the cabin, Paul noticed that the Arab was not in his seat. The light was on indicating the toilet was occupied. He had been in there for a long time. After he came out and returned to his seat, driven by need and curiosity, Paul went to the cubicle. He searched the small toilet compartment, but found nothing. He didn't notice that the door lock on the inside had been replaced. The new one had been hollowed out to accommodate a screwed insert. Afterwards he went forward to the area occupied by Anne, who was busy preparing trays with drinks, located between the passenger cabin and the pilot's cockpit, the latter being always locked. Only she knew the code to unlock the door. She was surprised to see Paul standing behind her. In a commanding voice that inferred he shouldn't be in the space, she said, 'Mr Cane, is there anything I can get you?'

'No, thanks, but I would like some information on the man sitting in the window seat near me.'

'Information about passengers cannot be revealed,' she answered.

Paul noticed the passenger list on her table. The name of the man by the window was Abdel Malik.

'I understand, but I'm just curious about the Arab sitting by the window. He seems a little strange.' Noticing that Paul had seen the passenger list, Anne asked, 'You mean Mr Malik?' Paul nodded.

'Since he doesn't speak English and due to a dietary condition he does not eat our food and takes only the medication he has with him; he has requested not to be disturbed during the flight.'

'Is he a US citizen?' asked Paul.

'No, he is a Saudi businessman, but has US and UK visas. I'm sorry, but I can't give you any more details.'

Alarm bells began to ring in Paul's head. It explained the man's behaviour but not his dress. He thought it strange for a businessman not to be able to speak English when he had visas for both English-speaking countries. He wondered if he was concealing his real identity.

Paul thanked Anne for the information and could see by her expression that she too had concerns. He was about to walk away when she said quietly, 'I shouldn't be telling you, but there is something else. I think he may have a colleague or associate who came aboard from the Dubai flight since he was asking at the transfer desk if Mr Malik was on the flight. According to the man's passport, he is an Emirati businessman going to London. The desk did acknowledge Malik was seated in first-class, but told him that access to passengers in first-class was not permitted unless there were exceptional reasons. The man seemed satisfied with that.'

Paul thanked Anne and returned to his seat. She then continued to prepare food and drinks for her passengers.

He noticed that Valerie had been very quiet during the stop-over at Schiphol. She had slept a lot and looked unwell.

Gripping her hand, Paul asked if anything was wrong.

'I had a terrible dream,' she said.

With some hesitation, Paul asked, 'What kind of dream?'

'I was on my own in a dark forest. I don't know how I came to be there, but I heard you calling out, but couldn't see you. I tried to shout, but no sound came out. Then your voice became fainter and fainter and I was lost. I cried out for my mother to help. But this time my mother didn't come. I ran and ran, then tripped and fell. I could see a tree walking towards me. Its outstretched branches were trying to grab my legs as I crawled away. I could see you running in the distance and called out, but you didn't hear me. I was in despair. I was alone. Then I saw a light in the distance. It came nearer and got brighter and I woke up. It was just after the plane had landed at Schiphol and the cabin lights went on.'

Paul saw that she was shaking and looking very pale. He remembered the incident at the site of the World Trade Centre in Manhattan where she had acted strangely. Was she again sensing something? She didn't explain what had happened in Manhattan and at the time he had decided not to quiz her, but it left him worried.

He put his arm around her saying, 'Everything is OK. You're safe now. Have a drink.'

Anne had placed a pot of coffee and some sandwiches on their table. Valerie composed herself and started to read the in-flight magazine.

Within thirty minutes the captain came over the intercom to welcome the new passengers aboard and told them that the plane would be taking off in ten minutes, and assured them of a speedy and comfortable flight to London.

The plane sped along the runway, making what seemed like an extra loud roar as its engines throttled up to maximum power. It then rose effortlessly like a bird in flight as the programmed guidance system was activated to take it directly to London Heathrow. Dawn was just starting to break as a glimmer of light separated the North Sea from the dark sky. It illuminated the tops of some grey-white clouds rapidly being left behind as the aircraft ascended to 30,000 feet. There was little to see at that altitude, but the knowledge that the English Channel below was the last step to England and London was a comforting thought.

Anne came to all the passengers in the section and stated that owing to the short time before arrival, a full breakfast would be available in the Concorde lounge at Heathrow. She distributed drinks and light snacks to those that wanted them. Cane noticed that Malik was wide awake, but not interested in drinking or eating. He looked worried as if he was expecting something to happen, constantly looking at his large Casio wrist watch. Perhaps someone was meeting him at Heathrow. When planes were diverted or late, one was always concerned that people waiting at arrivals may not know the new arrival times. But the flight was almost on schedule.

Paul Cane's thoughts went back to the day in 1999 when he last flew across the Channel from Kuwait after an ordeal that set him on a life-changing path. One's destiny was rarely predictable. Any unexpected event, large or small, could shape it.

It was only a short time before they would be over the Thames. The dawn light was shining through the cabin windows. Valerie had woken up and was looking better with some colour in her face. The plane descended and banked giving its passengers a view of the Thames estuary and the mud flats below. Valerie pointed at the window when a blinding flash of light and deafening sound filled the air. It was momentarily experienced by everyone – then, for most of the passengers it was a deadly silence and oblivion. It was like a giant hammer had crushed the plane – the end came quick for most. The plane exploded and broke up. The force of the explosion tore the front and rear sections away from the main body and they spun away to earth, disappearing in the river below.

Cane felt a sensation of falling down a mineshaft. Alternately, he sensed light and dark. He heard muffled sounds and felt hot and cold. But nothing was discernible, nothing made sense. Numbness and darkness then took over.

CHAPTER 5

The Rendezvous

Alicia Garcia pulled up outside the building. In the past she went to the multi-storey car park at the rear, but now the relationship with her employee had changed. She rang the number on her cell phone. After four rings she switched off the phone and waited. When the blinds on the window of the top floor became slightly raised she knew the occupant was in. It was their agreed sign. The electronic lock on the front door of the building sprung open and she went inside. It automatically closed behind her. After climbing four flights of stairs she reached the door to the apartment that had been left open. She stepped warily into the darkned room, not quite sure what she would find.

Sean 'Curly' O'Brien was standing in front of the window, looking directly at her. His six-foot-two, well-built body was partially illuminated by a single table light in the corner of the room. As she drew closer to him she saw his penetrating eyes staring at her like a hunter confronting its prey before the kill. She became excited. A slight widening of his lips displayed the beginnings of a smile. Without uttering a word she fell into his arms and felt the warmth of his stiff body pressed against her; she knew what he wanted. It was always what he wanted.

Pulling away slightly, she said, 'You will know about the plane that was blown up over London. We have a serious problem. There is urgent work to do and—'

Curly pulled her back, put his hand over her mouth and, looking down into her dark brown eyes, said in a soft, low voice, 'I know, but let's talk later.'

He removed her jacket and the holster containing the Glock 22 strapped around her body, unbuttoned her blouse and placed his large hands on her firm round breasts, caressing them with one hand while undoing her bra with the other. He had learned the importance of continuity in sex. Seeing and feeling her breasts always aroused him. Her nipples started to harden. She responded by pulling down the zip on his trousers and felt his hardness.

They slowly took off their clothes, becoming more and more aroused as each item dropped from their bodies. She laid down on the floor with her head propped up on a cushion that had been thoughtfully positioned for the purpose. Curly had thought about it before she arrived. He planned everything down to the finest detail. She liked the hardness of the floor as it produced a solid, almost painful reaction to his movement. He always had a new position to offer – something she looked forward to with eager anticipation each time they met. He rolled her over so she was lying face down and came up from behind. Without hesitation he entered her and continued with swift almost uncontrolled movements. He could feel her yielding beneath him. She sighed with delight. He liked it when she sighed. He was in control of a woman who always liked to be in control, which for him enhanced the experience.

He had long abandoned the missionary position at the start, it was boring, but they often ended up doing it that way when exhaustion took over. For the next twenty minutes they indulged in passionate sex involving different positions. That's all it was, just pure physical sex. For them it provided the best physical and mental therapy for removing the stress and tension of their daily jobs.

It had taken many assignments before Alicia had succumbed to Curly's desires. Before him she had never had a serious relationship with any man. In fact she despised men after her father had abused her as a child. Unlike most women, she didn't need men, but Curly was different. With him she enjoyed sex to the point where it had almost become an addiction, but one she could control. There was no love, no commitment, no illusions, but just pure physical enjoyment. At a physical level it was an ideal situation that many would envy. Both were ruthless, driven by their work, but they learned to respect and satisfy each other's needs.

Alicia was married to her job and wanted it to stay that way. She had been brought up by her mother after her Italian father left the family when it was discovered he had been sexually abusing his young daughter.

Her mother's family, originally from Kenya, went through difficult times in the 1960s during the time of racial segregation in the South. They didn't report the abuse because in those days black people rarely received justice from white juries. Her grandfather, Silas, eventually took the family to Washington where he obtained a job as a car cleaner and the family slowly prospered. They lived in a tough neighbourhood so Alicia became streetwise at an early age and became capable of looking after herself. Being an extremely able and intelligent girl, she became the top pupil in her school. She obtained a scholarship to the University of Georgetown to study law. After graduation she went to work for a local law firm, but after witnessing too many guilty criminals being acquitted because they had clever lawyers or were rich enough to pay off prosecution witnesses, she eventually became disillusioned with the law. She preferred to be on the other side, catching the bad guys rather than defending them.

One day, after the trial of a corrupt politician, whom she reluctantly defended but lost the case, she was approached by a man who asked to speak to her privately. She had seen him in the court, but, as far as she knew, he had no connection to the case. They went to a café near the court. The man ordered coffee and introduced himself as Simon, but it was obviously not his real name. He told her she had the skills wanted by the CIA at Langley. He refused to give his name or any other details, but did give her a card on which was a telephone number. He told her that if she was interested, to ring the number. It was a strange and puzzling brief encounter. Clearly she had been under observation by the CIA for some time, which worried her.

Out of curiosity she made the call to Langley. After answering some basic questions, she was told she might be asked to attend a preliminary interview. Three months later, she was invited to the interview at Langley. She was asked many personal questions about her childhood, her upbringing, education and career ambitions. She believed the interviewers knew the answers and were just testing her truthfulness.

A month passed before she was asked to attend a second interview, but this time it was followed by a series of intelligence and aptitude tests. Her background had been thoroughly investigated. A week later she was offered a job in their legal department. But it soon became obvious to her new employers that she was better suited to investigative work. She was transferred to the analysis department. It was just one step to fulfilling her ambition to become a field agent.

The CIA and FBI had been criticised after the bombing of the World Trade Centre in 1993 for not analysing and sharing intelligence information that could have caught the suspects before the act. The two agencies started to recruit new people and set up protocols for sharing and integrating intelligence information. Alicia was one of those new recruits. She was given field training and sent to the FBI headquarters in Washington to act as a CIA liaison officer but with field responsibilities. It was to be the start of an exciting but dangerous career.

Sean 'Curly' O'Brien was one of a small number of independent agents unofficially contracted by the CIA. He went under the codename C5. His identity was known only to Alicia Garcia and her boss, the Agency's Director. Contractors like him worked alone and often outside the law of the countries in which they operated. If caught, injured or killed, they were on their own, not protected by the Agency, who would always deny their existence. They were *persona non grata*; the unknown foot soldiers who dispatched enemy assassins and undercover agents, using any means at their disposal. There were no rules, no questions were asked, no explanations required. The financial rewards for success were high. Success was all that mattered. Failure was not an option. Their names never appeared on records or in files. Their actions were listed as 'unexplainable' in case histories. Only their employers knew about their deaths. They had no known graves.

Born in Belfast of an American mother and Irish father, Curly had served as an army SAS officer before being recruited as an undercover agent for MI5 in Northern Ireland during the IRA troubles. He resigned after the Northern Ireland Peace Agreement was signed because he could no longer abide by the agreement that required the release of many of the terrorists whom he had put behind bars. The justice system gave criminals and terrorists human rights denied to soldiers. Except in time of war, soldiers were not allowed to shoot such people unless they were shot at first and had to defend themselves. This often resulted in the death and injury of soldiers by terrorists before they could retaliate. After the Agreement, revenge killings on both sides followed.

Curly was involved in tracking down the IRA people who were responsible for the Warrenpoint massacre near Newry in Northern Ireland in 1979, where eighteen British soldiers were killed in an ambush; it made him many enemies. He was about to retire and live a quiet life in obscurity when the murder of his parents by the IRA forced him to return to his former life but as a free independent agent.

MI5 agents were never really free. A number of transatlantic phone calls were made. It wasn't long before Curly was recruited by the CIA as a freelance agent. He was contracted to their Russian station in Moscow to seek out ex-KGB agents who would make useful contacts. After the fall of communism and break-up of the Soviet Union, many such agents became highly paid gunmen for private Mafia-type organisations that controlled much of the business in the cities.

Curly was intelligent, self-centred, ruthless, hated rules and liked to work alone, so had the right qualities for the CIA job. He only accepted assignments if they involved removing his country's enemies. Coming from a family with a military background, he had a strong sense of patriotism. He actually didn't enjoy killing for the sake of killing and only did so when there were no alternatives for those who deserved it.

Witnessing the pain of people who had watched their innocent loved ones die at the hands of terrorists had hardened Curly to become an executioner when the justice system failed to do the job. He practised the law of *an eye for an eye* (*lex talionis*), the ancient law of retribution, derived from three passages in the Old Testament of the Bible. Originally, the intent of this law was to ensure that the punishment corresponded to the crime. It actually formed the basis of legal systems in many countries. But in recent times many had replaced the death penalty with prison terms so even mass murderers and terrorists received the same punishment as more common criminals and were sometimes acquitted through lack of evidence or, if convicted, served only a fraction of their sentence before being released on parole. Curly wasn't opposed to the law, but his experiences in Northern Ireland and elsewhere, where known murderers and terrorists evaded the law, angered him. The victims of their crimes were usually forgotten and their human rights less respected than the criminals.

Curly considered himself a soldier in the war on terrorism so killing the enemy was justifiable. A soldier didn't have to provide evidence before killing the enemy.

Curly lit a cigarette while Alicia made some coffee.

'Now we can talk,' he said, patting her bare bottom as she walked past him.

She put two cups of coffee on the table, saying, 'I prefer to get dressed first.'

He gave her a longing look, suggesting he would like more, but she was satisfied and wanted to return to work. One session with Curly was enough for her.

Curly had eliminated most of the leaders of The New Order who had initially conspired with al-Qaeda to explode atomic bombs in New York and London on the eve of the millennium. But two had yet to be found and dealt justice.

Bin Laden, the most wanted terrorist leader, was still being hunted by the CIA and the FBI for the bombing of the US Embassy in Kenya in 1998 and the *USS Cole* in 2000 in the Yemen. These acts of terrorism were part of bin Laden's 1996 fatwa, declaring jihad against his own government of Saudi Arabia and the US government. They initiated his global jihad; the ultimate object of which was to create a global Islamic state. But first, he wanted to remove all non-believers from the Arab Peninsula. His increasingly powerful al-Qaeda network justified the killing of innocent people by a distorted interpretation of a thirteenth-century religious belief, based on the Hadith of the Prophet Mohammed.

Osama bin Laden was born in 1957, the seventeenth child of Mohammed bin Awad bin Laden, who, after working for the Saudi Royal Family, became a very wealthy Saudi builder. He died in a plane crash in 1967, but his son, Osama, continued to make the business prosper. In 1980 bin Laden junior went to Afghanistan to fight against the Soviet invaders. He became their funder, helping the Mujahedeen to acquire weapons to fight and eventually expel the Soviets. After the rise of the extreme fundamentalist regime, the Taliban took control of Afghanistan. Its form of Islam was similar to that practised by the Arab members of al-Qaeda, so it became a natural base for them. Al-Qaeda evolved from being a regional threat to US soldiers in the Persian Gulf to a global threat. Although led by Arabs, it was actually a coalition of disparate radical Islamic groups of different nationalities but with a common goal – the expulsion of non-Muslims from Muslim-inhabited lands, including Palestine.

Many al-Qaeda supporters were not religious; some hadn't even studied the Koran and, in Islamic terms, were morally corrupt. They were uneducated, unemployable and had been indoctrinated with those parts of the Koran that their masters wanted them to know. They knew little about anything and nothing about history of the wider world, so believed everything they were told. Young people growing up in a closed community were easily brain-washed. They could be compared to battery hens, bred for only one purpose, the killing of all non-believers. The more educated ones sometimes used the movement as an opportunity to become rich and powerful. They were quick to exploit the benefits from what was considered to be the decadent Western culture. For these it was a new world that offered the good life now instead of waiting for it in death. But for the more devout Muslims, obeying their religious masters and becoming suicide bombers was a way of achieving martyrdom and everlasting happiness.

Curly had traced some al-Qaeda members through contacts in brothels that were frequented by them. What concerned him and Alicia was the large number of field agents working for the CIA who were stationed outside the US. Some were double agents working for the terrorists, who paid them well. Most were employed by the CIA because of their language skills and knowledge of the Arab world before extensive checks had been made into their backgrounds.

Al-Qaeda had Curly marked out as a prime target with a fatwa on his head. He was greatly feared and known as Satan's Killer. By eliminating most of the leaders of The New Order who had betrayed al-Qaeda, he had done their dirty work. But for that, he didn't expect, and didn't get, any gratitude.

Curly was dismayed, however, when he discovered that Takaki Tobata, the Japanese member of The New Order, hadn't been killed when his private plane crashed in a field outside Tokyo. He had been warned that someone was going to kill him so he faked his own death by having an employee use his identity on the plane. The body was too badly burned to be physically identified. Tobata owned property and businesses in Queensland, Australia, and was thought to be living at a place called Noosa Heads under a different name. Tobata had been supportive of al-Qaeda's plan to destroy New York with an atom bomb. He sided with the Russian member, Boris Sudakov, who, unknown to the other members of The New Order's Cabal, secretly supported al-Qaeda. It was Boris who had switched the dummy atom bomb that was sent to London on the eve of the millennium for a live one.

Tobata saw it as retribution for the deaths of family members at Nagasaki. He would certainly support any future attempts of al-

Qaeda to destroy a US city. Sudakov was dead, but Curly had unfinished business to carry out in Australia, but that would have to wait. The question that vexed him was, did the Russian section of The New Order become re-activated under a new name and leadership?

Curly and Alicia had broken their own rules by becoming lovers. It had been going on for over a year. He was almost killed in a shoot-out with members of an al-Qaeda cell in Baltimore. Someone had betrayed Alicia after she sent him on the mission. The enemy had been pre-warned and had ambushed Curly. Fortunately, he escaped with only minor injuries. After the incident she nursed his wounds and, out of pity, spent the night with him. It had been a night to remember. The tall, strong, curly-haired, ruthless Irishman had awakened a latent passion in her; one she had inherited from her Italian father. Once released, there was no going back.

Now that Alicia was the director of the newly formed Counter Terrorist Unit (CTU), with no immediate operational boss, she was able to offer Curly assignments without having to obtain permission from anybody further up the chain of command. In the past, she had to obtain it from the CIA director, but now she reported directly to the National Security Advisor at the White House, who in turn reported to the Vice President. Both distanced themselves from operational decisions. Having her own hitman was risky, but it suited Alicia; it gave her power. She was a woman who liked control and power. If discovered, however, she risked prosecution and life imprisonment for murder. But Curly was a professional and would never be caught alive; they had that pact.

Curly listened to what Alicia had to say about bin Laden and al-Qaeda. They had stepped up their jihad against the West. The lack of effective retaliation by the US after the *USS Cole* and millennium bomb events helped al-Qaeda to recruit more supporters. Its global networks now posed serious threats to democratic nations. Curly had always been the hunter, not the hunted. A situation he now didn't like. He would have to be more careful about protecting his anonymity.

Alicia returned to the room fully dressed with her Glock placed firmly back in its holster. It had saved her life many times. It was her best friend. She felt exposed without it.

Putting on her bossy voice, she said to Curly, 'Sit down and listen. CTU has received intelligence that bin Laden had appointed a man named Khalid Sheikh Mohammed, also known by his initials KSM. But he has used many aliases to escape capture. His job was to provide planning and support to al-Qaeda cells in the US. He is the uncle of Ramzi Yousef and, with him, was the co-planner of the attack on the World Trade Centre in 1993. He is currently on the FBI's wanted list. We believe he is somewhere in the US, but, using his many aliases, has been able to travel around and avoid capture. He controls a number of couriers who have US and British visas enabling them to move easily between the two countries.

The man on the BA plane travelling as a Saudi businessman was named Abdel Malik. We believe he was going to Britain to establish a new terrorist cell. Large sums of money had been laundered through a British subsidiary of an Arab company in Dubai. It was to fund the cell's activities. We decided to track him to London to discover his contacts rather than arrest him in the US. Anyway we had no legal reason to arrest him since all his papers were legitimate.

Our intelligence may have been incomplete since we now know that he could have been one of the bombers or someone knew we had him under surveillance and decided to kill him. But blowing up a plane would be an extreme way of doing it. It's more likely he was on a suicide mission for al-Qaeda to punish the British for the millennium bomb failures. Blowing up an aircraft over London at the same place where the millennium atomic bomb would have exploded would be their way of retaliation. We don't know yet how and where the bomb was placed on the plane and exactly what part Malik played. The tragedy was that by coincidence the Canes were on the same flight.'

Curly was visibly shocked to know about the Canes.

'Were they killed?' he asked.

'I understand that Paul Cane is the only survivor and is

recovering in hospital in London. We owe a lot to Paul. It was his work that saved New York and London from the bomb. It's ironic he's now the victim of a terrorist bomb,' she said.

'Was he involved in any secret activity?' asked Curly.

'Not to my knowledge, but, before he went to London, Robert Carville called to tell me about the Canes being on the flight. He told me that while in New York he and Cane had a private meeting with a Sheikh bin Abdullah, a member of the Saudi Royal Family. It was at the Sheikh's request. Apparently he wanted Cane to contact me and the British to warn us about a new al-Qaeda terrorist plot. Cane didn't want to become involved so he chose to ignore the request. Sheikh bin Abdullah was leading a Saudi delegation at the UN's debate on Iraq. He seemed to be well informed about me and CTU. He also sees bin Laden and al-Qaeda as enemies.'

Alicia was worried that the Saudi knew so much about CTU.

'Perhaps I should check him out since he probably knows more about the al-Qaeda plot than he told Cane and Carville,' suggested Curly.

Alicia, looking even more worried, said, 'Now, CTU is in trouble because we didn't inform the FBI or CIA about having our two agents tracking an al-Qaeda suspect on the London plane. They didn't know that I had strict orders from the White House to keep the other agencies out of the loop until we had definite proof of Malik's intentions and knowledge of his contacts in Britain. When the CIA discovered bin Laden's location in Afghanistan last year, the president at the time refused to give the order to kill him. He and his cohorts were in the range of one of our drones, which could have removed them all from the earth. The president and his advisors had the strange idea that martyring him would increase al-Qaeda's support in the Muslim world. The death of the seventeen sailors on the *USS Cole* and numerous people in the East African hotel bombings seemed not to matter. This president, however, takes a different view and after the failure of the agencies to gather intelligence to prevent the embassy and *Cole* bombings and the near disaster of the millennium bombs,

CTU has been given the authority to act independently. Unfortunately, the identities of my agents who were killed on the plane were found by the British police and the FBI, so explanations are being demanded. Our cat is out of the bag.'

Looking puzzled, Curly asked, 'Where did the intelligence on Malik come from?'

'From a suspect captured in the Yemen. He was interrogated by one of our reliable Arab-speaking CIA agents, codenamed Eli. The suspect revealed the existence of an international network of couriers who were channelling funds for another large-scale terrorist act. Malik was one of the leading couriers in the US who had also been travelling around Europe.'

'So the CIA was aware of the identity of the man on the plane.'

'They knew Malik was in the US, but not on the plane. For reasons unknown, intelligence information was filed away by the CIA and no action was taken to find Malik. One of my agents picked up an encrypted email sent from the Yemen to the CIA in New York, presumably by Eli, which mentioned Malik as an al-Qaeda suspect who should be placed on the watch list. We discovered him when he used the internet to book a late first-class airline ticket to London on flight BA66. All foreigners booking seats on planes leaving the US are logged and their details sent to Langley for checking. When he arrived at Kennedy we placed him under surveillance and I put two of my best agents on the plane. Our only excuse is that, to our knowledge, the FBI or CIA didn't take any action to prevent Malik from entering or leaving the US. CTU is not under any obligation to inform them about its activities.'

Alicia was still worried. Had she failed on the first serious task that confronted the CTU? There was only one way to redeem the CTU's reputation. She had to find the people responsible for the bomb and bring them to justice. It wasn't necessarily an assassination job, but one that required Curly's skills and contacts. There was little time left to do it. She had to be careful not to lose any more agents or attract the attention of the CIA.

Things were further complicated because of the British

connection. Alicia had already had a telephone conversation with John Nicholas, Commander of the Counter Terrorist Unit in Scotland Yard. She had been guarded in what she told him, but had to admit to the reasons why her agents were on the plane, fearing that it might get back to the other agencies.

The White House contact hadn't called even though the President had spoken to the British Prime Minister. Alicia thought that to be very ominous. But sooner or later she would have to file a report. It was the reason why she had met with Curly. He was now the only person who could help her out of the mess.

Curly said, 'I need to speak to the CIA agent who gathered the information from the terrorist he interrogated in the Yemen or see a full copy of his report. It might give leads on others who were involved in the bomb plot.'

Alicia replied, 'I think the agent, Eli, may still be in the Yemen, but I should be able to get you a copy of his interrogation report. He speaks Arabic and is the best agent the CIA has in the region. I may be able to get you his secure cell phone number, but read the report first. I will get an encrypted copy from my contact at the CIA. I will send it to you.'

Alicia gave Curly a hug and left the apartment block through a rear door to travel back to CTU.

CHAPTER 6

Counter Terrorist Unit – Washington DC

On arrival at CTU Alicia was anxiously greeted by her two senior analysts, Pat King and Brad Walker. They had tried calling her, but failed to get a line because she had switched off her cell phone while with Curly so calls couldn't be traced.

Brad Walker had been recruited from the CIA. She had tried to get her old colleague and friend, Mark Brooks, but he wasn't permitted to transfer from the Agency. Like Alicia he was one of the few who had survived the shake up after the Senate enquiry of Project Whirlwind – the millennium conspiracy.

It had been Mark's intelligence work that had actually helped the police locate the London atomic bomb. Not wishing to lose him, the CIA had promoted him to the post of Director of Counter Terrorism and Intelligence. He was Alicia's eyes and ears in the Agency and a source of inside information. They had developed a strong brother–sister type of relationship while working together on Whirlwind. Mark was married with three children. After Whirlwind and the murder of his friend from the FBI, Gary Stevens, he took steps to ensure his family's safety by moving them to a secret location away from Washington. Alicia also wanted to tell him about the Canes with whom he had become close friends.

Brad said, 'I've placed an urgent report on your desk. The White House called. You need to call them back immediately. There's an angry man waiting to talk to you.'

She knew who that would be.

He also briefed her on the latest developments on the plane bomb investigation. MI6 were now involved and were intending to send over to CTU one of their best agents, codenamed Angel.

Alicia thanked him and went into her office to use the secure blue phone that connected her directly to the White House Security Advisor's private office.

'What the bloody hell is going on, Alicia?' ranted Rob Burger. He was the Security Advisor to the Vice President. Knowing the technique, she deliberately paused before replying. Attack with more rhetorical questions was the best response.

'That's what I want to know. Why was the intelligence flawed? What the hell were the CIA and NSA doing not stopping a terrorist boarding the BA plane? I lost two of my best agents. I need some answers and I need them quick.'

There was a long pause while Burger considered his reply. He didn't expect that response. In a less aggressive tone, he said, 'You had better come to the White House immediately so we can talk with the Vice President and President.'

But she was on dangerous ground. Both the FBI and CIA hated the existence of the CTU since it undermined their own authority. Only the National Security Agency (NSA) at Fort Meade shared the President's support of CTU. The NSA had a role similar to the British Government Communications Headquarters (GCHQ) at Cheltenham, providing their respective government agencies with global intelligence, but had to act under strict legal guidelines. The hierarchical structures of the CIA and FBI meant that only the director generals could access the President's Office so all reports went through a cleansing procedure before the Vice President or President saw them.

The turf war between the CIA and FBI was always present because the two agencies didn't respect the boundaries within which they were supposed to operate. Intelligence sharing was essential, but once outside the US, this often broke down. CIA personnel were trained in intelligence gathering not in interrogation techniques; that was the FBI's area of expertise. But when terrorists were captured in countries outside the US, the CIA assumed it was their prerogative to carry out interrogations of suspects. This often resorted in methods of torture outside US law, but permitted in the countries where the interrogations were carried out. The end result often led to bad intelligence and misinformation. Later, this methodology would prove to be very controversial.

Alicia knew that both agencies would seize any opportunity to denigrate the competence of the CTU. The agency directors would have already spoken to the President. He would have been embarrassed not knowing about CTU's actions. But she had to defend them. She alone had authorised the placing of the two agents on the plane. She really needed Curly to come up with some further intelligence on the bombers, but more time would be required. She was getting anxious when she flipped open the report on her desk marked 'URGENT – For Immediate Attention'.

In front of her was the answer. She felt a sense of relief. Her adrenaline rose and she became excited. Attached to the memo was a rare photograph of bin Laden with a bearded Abdel Malik faintly visible in the background. It had been taken in Afghanistan some months previously and placed on a website used by bin Laden to broadcast his messages to the US. The figure was hard to recognise at first, but after some computer enhancement, it clearly showed Malik.

Before entering the US, Malik had shaved off his beard and was wearing Western-style clothes. It was stated clearly in the English version of the al-Qaeda training book, known as the Manchester Manual, that all members travelling outside Arab countries must look like Westerners to avoid attracting attention. The book was discovered among papers captured by the police when they raided a house in Manchester, England, and arrested a man called Anas al-Liby, who turned out to be a senior al-Qaeda operative. It was an important find since it enabled interrogators to understand how prisoners would react when questioned. It offered insights into their mind-sets and behaviour patterns. Instructions on how to react when captured to torture and interrogation were included. Bin Laden had extensive training camps and facilities to train and brainwash those who were destined to carry out his fatwa against the West.

The photo proved what Alicia had suspected, that Malik was a high-ranking al-Qaeda member of bin Laden's inner circle. The memo showed a copy of a coded email sent from Afghanistan to Malik referring to a deposit of money into a bank account in Dubai for office equipment. CTU had done a good job in acquiring this evidence using the variety of encryption software they had for decoding messages; it justified their surveillance operation.

She called in Brad and his team and congratulated them on their work. This breakthrough would help sustain the credibility of CTU. But she still had to convince the White House.

Alicia shut the door, took out the laptop from her desk drawer and sent an encrypted message to Curly. She asked him to find out who Malik had been in contact with in the US, the UK and Dubai. The BA flight had been diverted to Amsterdam to pick up passengers from the BA plane from Dubai that had to make an emergency landing with engine trouble. Could the bomb have been loaded onto the London flight at Amsterdam? It was known that al-Qaeda had cells in that city and transferring luggage that had already been through security within the airport would have made it easy for a bomb already in the luggage to have been transferred onto the London flight. But someone employed by the airline had to help facilitate it. Alicia knew the FBI and British agencies would be checking out all airport personnel and passengers. She had to make sure that any relevant information was also made available to CTU. It then occurred to her that if the British MI6 agent really wanted to share intelligence, then this was her opportunity to do so.

Alicia sat back in a green leather chair and thought about the anguish that Paul Cane, lying in a hospital bed, would be experiencing. He would want to find and kill the people responsible for blowing up the plane and killing his wife. Alicia had never been in love, but she knew how terrible it must be to lose someone so soon after being married.

Finding all the people responsible was going to be difficult. They would be embedded in well-hidden networks, possibly spread across different countries. It was likely al-Qaeda members had infiltrated the security services and airlines. She believed that her CTU agents were clean. She had interviewed and vetted all of them. Working with the CIA and FBI she had learnt how to spot insurgents.

The phone on her desk rang. It was Burger.

'I'm on my way to see you now,' he said.

'Good. I have something to show you,' she replied.

She was relieved at not having to go to the White House. Burger would be on her ground. She knew he would have spoken to the Vice President, his political boss, and possibly, the President. Having unfiltered advanced intelligence gave the President and his National Security Advisor an advantage over the CIA and FBI. The director generals had often manipulated intelligence to gain political advantage. J Edgar Hoover, the founder of the FBI, had secret files on all politicians, including presidents, so he could exert pressure on his masters and influence their decisions. Presidents Truman, Kennedy and others had to endure his threats. It gave him power over them, which they knew he would use if they opposed his wishes. He did so, when the Kennedy brothers opposed him.

On the security monitor Alicia saw Burger and his two secret service bodyguards arrive in the lobby area of the CTU building. He showed his pass and, after proceeding through the eye and fingerprint scanner, was brought to her office by a security guard.

Burger was an impatient man and not given to niceties or small talk, so went straight to the purpose of the visit. He gave her a menacing look.

'The Vice President is furious with CTU for not being briefed about the surveillance agents on the plane. He had an awkward time explaining it to the President after his telephone conversation with the British Prime Minister, who raised the issue. Everyone is looking for someone to blame, so your explanation had better be good because you're in the direct firing line.'

Alicia was well prepared for Burger's performance. She let him finish ranting then, without saying anything, showed him the photograph and the analyst's notes. After giving him time to digest the information, she said, 'We believed that Malik was a key al-Qaeda operator and would have led us to important contacts in the

UK, which is why we put him under surveillance. The CIA and FBI knew he was in the US on al-Qaeda operations, but did nothing. No one knew that he was a suicide bomber or about the bomb on the plane. Again, it was gross failure of the FBI and CIA's intelligence, resulting in the worst ever terrorist bomb outrage and the loss of many innocent lives, including two of my best agents. We are now tracking Malik's contacts on both sides of the Atlantic and reviewing the intelligence report from the FBI agent in the Yemen that led us to Malik. I am convinced we are on to something big that al-Qaeda is planning beyond the plane bomb. Tell the President that CTU has made it a top priority to find those responsible and will report back immediately when we have something useful. But we must have access to any intelligence gained by other security agencies.'

Burger's demeanour changed. He was an ambitious guy who wanted to be on the winning side. Alicia had given him a good story to take back to the White House. He had personal reasons to hate the CIA and, although the Vice President and President had to take note of what it told them, having unbiased information from CTU helped in the making of better informed decisions.

Looking at Alicia, he made what could have been a well-rehearsed speech, demonstrating how much he had learned from the politicians.

'CTU has done a good job and taken the initiative, but we need results quick as international pressure is building, particularly from the Brits. We can expect them to take a leading role in the hunt for the terrorists since the bomb was meant to explode when the plane was over the Houses of Parliament. They see it as an attack on Britain, not America. I want you to work with their agents. Politically, it has to be seen as a joint operation. But CTU will have unlimited resources to find those responsible and uncover any other plots al-Qaeda are hatching. Remember, we are at war with a ruthless enemy, who has to be flushed out and destroyed, even in the mountains of Afghanistan. The President is also worried about Saddam Hussein and his possession of WMDs. We need to find a link between him and al-Qaeda.'

Alicia had concerns about the last statement, but knew she had succeeded. CTU and her position were safe. But she didn't trust Burger or the politicians. Project Whirlwind had taught her that it was necessary to be always one step ahead of them. She didn't underestimate the power and influence of the CIA. They were the organisation on which the US depended for its overseas intelligence. She had many good friends in the CIA. The Agency had given her good training and the opportunity that led to her existing job. But their recent failures were putting the US at risk. They had the best expertise and technical equipment available and vast resources, but their hierarchical and bureaucratic structures sometimes produced communication issues and allowed the creation of internal powerful groups.

Burger left the room with copies of the photo and notes and, followed by his bodyguards, drove away in his official SUV.

Alicia called a meeting with her senior staff to discuss their operations. Nobody knew about C5; he didn't exist, but he was going to be essential to CTU in the coming weeks.

It was time to call Mark at Langley and get a copy of Eli's report on the interrogation of al-Qaeda suspects in the Yemen. She could obtain it officially through Burger, but going through Mark unofficially wouldn't alert everyone that CTU was interested.

The phone rang for what seemed like an eternity before it was answered by another man. Alicia was on her guard. It was Mark's private number, so why wasn't he answering? She decided to take an official approach.

'Who is speaking?' she asked.

'Who are you?' was the cautious reply.

'This is the Director of CTU. I want to speak to Mark Brooks.'

'He is not in the office until next week, but I am Agent Bellini, can I help?'

Alicia took the risk and said, 'Do you have the interrogation report on the suspects responsible for the bomb that damaged the USS Cole in the Yemen?' A long silence followed, so she added, 'It's the one filed by your agent Eli.'

Again silence, but this time she could hear background noises on the line. It was supposed to be a secure line. Alicia switched on the recorder.

Then the reply came.

'Yes, we do have that, but we've boxed it.'

'What do you mean boxed?' she asked.

'It's been closed and restricted on the orders of the Deputy Head of the CIA,' he replied.

That immediately raised Alicia's suspicions so she decided to pull rank.

'We already know from a brief we received earlier that Eli discovered the names of people in an al-Qaeda network operating in the US, one was Abdel Malik, who was on the British plane blown up over London. Since all agencies are on alert to find those responsible, the sharing of vital intelligence is essential, so I am sending over a courier to obtain a copy of the report unless you can send an encrypted copy to me right away. Do I make myself clear?'

She hadn't wanted to go through the official channel since the request would now go into the system and require the CIA operations director's approval, but she couldn't wait until Mark's return.

Bellini must have already checked up on Alicia, which was the reason for the delay in response. He would know of her Italian lineage and, like himself, knew their kind didn't take no for an answer.

'OK, I can send it, but I shall need my director's approval first.'

'Let me know immediately if that's a problem because I have a direct line to the White House. Delays will not be tolerated.'

She knew that would be sufficient to dissuade any reluctant director from sending the file.

Ten minutes later the red alarm flashed on her computer warning of an incoming encrypted file. She knew from the code designation what software to use to decode the file. CTU had the best software experts and decoders in the US. They had a library of deciphering programmes.

The report made interesting reading. In March 2001, Eli had

interviewed a man named Abu Hathayfah al-Adani (AHA), a Yemeni, who had admitted being involved in the planning of the *Cole* bombing. He had been close to bin Laden, acting as a courier so was trusted with inside information. But after the *Cole* bombing, which didn't produce the exact outcome bin Laden wanted, he was accused of recruiting the wrong people to do the job. Bin Laden had promised to pay for an urgent operation required by his wife, but, because of the disappointing result, refused to pay. She died shortly after, leaving three children. This made AHA very angry and determined to avenge her death. Afterwards, he was traced and arrested by the Yemeni Secret Service. He agreed to be interviewed by the CIA on condition his family was given protection. The Yemenis refused his request, but, when assigned to the job, Eli persuaded General Yassim, the Yemeni Chief of Security, with whom he had developed a good working relationship, to agree to the prisoner's request. It proved to be a wise move.

Unlike other CIA interrogators, Eli, being a Muslim, understood the Arabic culture. He befriended the prisoners rather than bullying them with threats of torture so succeeded in extracting more reliable information. Al-Qaeda trained their operatives to deal with interrogators by telling them what they wanted to hear. They expected to be tortured and in most cases stood up to it. Prisoners were more worried about what would happen to their families, particularly their wives and sons, more than themselves. Eli used this knowledge by giving them assurances that they would be looked after and cared for if the prisoners cooperated. He even went to see the wives and children and befriended them, much to the annoyance of the other CIA interrogators. This had a dramatic effect on the attitude of the suspects, who saw it was in their best interests to truthfully answer questions.

In the case of AHA, he was willing to help since he felt nothing but hatred for his old master, the Sheikh. Many Yemeni Arabs didn't like the Saudis, but expected their word to be their bond. That was an Arab tradition. Bin Laden made a big mistake in breaking his word to AHA. Another CIA agent was often present at interrogations, but Eli insisted on leading the interview, even when the agent was more senior in rank. This caused some friction and occasionally the senior agent sent back negative reports to Washington and New York.

Eli was based in the CIA's New York office where he had the full backing of his bosses. His interviewing technique had been so successful that his department head had every confidence in him. But there were factions within the other departments that disagreed on procedures dealing with suspects. These were often as divisive as the rivalry that existed between the CIA and FBI. It may have been this that led to Eli's report being boxed since it proved that his interrogation technique brought results rarely achieved by other CIA interrogators who resorted to torturing their prisoners when more conventional legal techniques failed to bring results. There were some CIA agents who cast doubt on Eli's integrity being an Arab. Because he was an American Muslim, they suspected him of being a sympathiser.

AHA told Eli that a man named Khalid Sheikh Mohammed (KSM) was one of bin Laden's most trusted followers and was tasked with setting up a network infrastructure in different countries to provide bases for terrorist acts. Late in 2000, a meeting had taken place in a hotel in Kuala Lumpur, Malaysia, between six men known to be members of bin Laden's inner circle. KSM was thought to be one of those present. They wanted to strengthen their European, African and Asian networks. Something big was being planned for the US involving aircraft. This information was filed before the London plane bombing took place.

Abdel Malik was supposed to be an al-Qaeda courier. AHA gave the names of four other individuals who were at the Kuala Lumpur meeting. They were two Jordanians, Musab-al-Zarqawi and Yusuf Ibrahim, and two Saudis named Khalid al-Mihdhar and Nawaf al-Hazmi. He didn't know much about them except they travelled freely to the US so must have had visas. They had spent time training in Afghanistan along with others whose names he didn't know. Apparently large sums of money were being placed in bank accounts in the UK, US and Malaysia for funding whatever was being planned.

Alicia found the report a goldmine of information. She noted that for some reason certain passages had been underlined by someone. It did provide leads that could be followed up. She was curious why the CIA hadn't done it before the London aircraft bombing, knowing that al-Qaeda was planning terrorist acts involving aircraft. If Malik was a key element in the bombing and if CTU had been told more before they set up the surveillance, then he would have been arrested before getting on the plane. She only knew he was suspected of being a courier and could possibly lead to others in London. But why had the CIA not informed CTU about the full content of Eli's report earlier? She decided for the time being to use the information and pursue her own investigation.

It was important for Curly to see the report, but sending it to him even in a coded form was a big risk. If she was being watched then she could be found out. CTU didn't have all the clever people, even though most had come from the CIA and FBI. There were still people in the CIA who knew about C5, not by identity but by deed. They might assume she had continued to use him since CTU was now also a covert organisation. She needed to think carefully about how to protect Curly and herself. Now he was more than just her hitman.

Pat knocked on the door and brought in a coffee and some sandwiches just at the moment when Alicia needed them. The analyst seemed to read her mind. She gave the names of the two Saudis for her to trace. Alicia wanted to know if they had entered the US or any other country. Where were they? And who were their associates? These men could provide the link to the US network. It had to be identified and compromised before another terrorist act was perpetrated. Once she had that information she would send it to Curly. He would find them before anyone else and know what to do. He didn't use Eli's technique, but would get fast results.

The men responsible for the terrorist atrocity in London had the blood of over 349 innocent people on their hands and were likely to be planning similar acts; they had to be treated as mass murderers. They didn't deserve a trial. Anyway it would be exploited to publicise their misplaced beliefs. If necessary he would have no qualms about torturing or killing them to prevent more deaths. She knew Curly sometimes used others to do the work or arranged fatal accidents because he actually didn't enjoy killing people with his own hands.

Two miles away, a communications operator at Langley put a report on the desk of the Operations Director stamped 'Urgent CTU'.

Three thousand miles away in Hamburg, four men were meeting to finalise plans for the next big attack on America.

Three-and-a-half thousand miles away in the SIS building on the Thames Embankment in London, the Director General of MI6 was having a meeting with Jayne Clayton-Browne, alias Angel.

CHAPTER 7

Hamburg, Germany

Four Arabs met in a secluded flat in Hamburg to review the plan for the big attack on America. They were led by Khalid Sheikh Mohammed (KSM). These men were bin Laden's most trusted followers and would be key players in the plan.

Their original plan had to be changed owing to the new situation that had arisen after the blowing up of the British plane by another terrorist group who had duped their brother, Abdel Malik, into believing he was acting under orders from the Sheikh. The security agencies in the US and Britain were now on high alert and arresting people on their list of al-Qaeda suspects; that was making things difficult.

KSM told the men that two days before the flight, a package had been handed to Malik in New York by a man named Mohammad bin al-Zarak. In the morning on the day of flight BA66 he had been instructed to send a coded telephone message to Mullah Mohammad Omani in Kandahar, a southern city in Afghanistan. The message simply stated, 'The package was successfully delivered.' At the time of sending the message, bin al-Zarak didn't know that Omani had been arrested by the Taliban for criticising bin Laden and his Arab followers, and that his cell phone was in their possession. The Taliban leader immediately questioned him about the meaning of the message. But it was only after torturing him and the threat to kill his son that he revealed the conspiracy to implicate al-Qaeda in the terrorist act of blowing up the London-bound plane.

Omani knew revealing the plan was the signing of his death warrant, but he did it to save his son. The Taliban were not merciful to traitors and intended to kill him slowly anyway by cutting him up piece by piece. He was spared that painful death for a quicker one by giving the names of the two other conspirators. Bin Laden was informed of Omani's treachery by the Taliban leader, Mullah Omar. He ordered that Omani and his two fellow conspirators be brought before him and his followers at their headquarters in the mountains of Tora Bora. If he hadn't given that order the three men would have been instantly killed by the Taliban.

The three were driven over rough roads and mountain passes to finally arrive at bin Laden's headquarters. There, in the presence of the Sheikh, they confessed their betrayal and admitted they had been paid by a Russian who promised them and their families sanctuary in Russia. None of them knew the Russian's real name. To them he was known as DZ. Their plea for mercy was denied.

The package that had been given to Abdel Malik by bin al-Zarak in New York had bin Laden's forged signature on it. In it was a letter giving clear instructions on how to detonate a bomb that would be in a suitcase on the plane. Malik believed it was the part of the plot that had been discussed with KSM and unquestionably accepted his fate. The last sentence in the letter said that he had been specially selected for the task by the Sheikh in the name of Allah for the honour of being the first Arab to strike a devastating blow to the British and American unbelievers who had caused so much suffering to Muslims. The package also contained a watch with a miniature generator capable of sending a signal to a small radio transmitter that was to be hidden in the toilet nearest to his seat on the plane. It would transmit a signal to fire detonators attached to explosives in a suitcase concealed in the plane's luggage hold. This would be done when the plane was directly over the Houses of Parliament, located on the north bank of the River Thames. The watch had a built-in GPS receiver that would synchronise and set the watch time when it was ten minutes from the target. Then the countdown would start. There was a manual override, which he had to use if the automatic system failed. Malik was told not to sleep and keep the watch on his wrist at all times. He was given drugs to keep him awake.

Two Russians, looking through their binoculars from a mountain top, were horrified at the sight before them. Three Afghan men with their heads bowed and their hands tied behind their backs were kneeling before Osama bin Laden, or the Sheikh as he was known. He was reading something from a book and making gestures with his hands. To any Christians viewing, it looked like he was holding a baptism or funeral service. Standing beside the men was a tall man with a black turban, of the type worn by the Taliban. He was holding a long curved sword. One of the men was weeping and crying out for mercy, but his cries were falling on deaf ears. A crowd of men standing and sitting on rocks around the scene were laughing and chanting while others were holding their Kalashnikovs above their heads. A small group of women and children were held by ropes in a pen in full view of the men who were about to be executed. They were assumed to be their families.

The Sheikh finished speaking, turned and walked back towards a large cave, followed by ten armed bodyguards. At the cave entrance, he stopped and looked back briefly before entering the cave. It was the signal. Immediately the first man was decapitated with one stroke of the sword. It was the one making the most noise. A loud cheer went up from the onlookers, who fired off their guns. Shortly after, the other two men were dispatched by the swordsman whose skill in decapitation seemed to please the crowd. The bloody bodies were dragged to a nearby ditch and the heads thrown into a box.

The two observers had seen enough and walked swiftly away to a partially wooded area where they mounted a concealed motorcycle. It was the best mode of transport in that mountainous area of Afghanistan. After travelling for twenty miles to a village close to the Pakistan border, they abandoned the motorcycle for a Land Rover that was waiting for them with a driver. The vehicle was equipped with a satellite phone. The older of the two men dialled a number. A tape recorder, connected to a secure phone at an oligarch's mansion in the suburbs of Moscow, took the coded message. Translated it said:

'This is DZ, three of our Afghan helpers were caught and executed by the Taliban under bin Laden's orders. Al-Qaeda knows about the deception. Make all agents aware that al-Qaeda will be hunting them since we don't know how much the Afghans revealed under torture. At present the Americans and British are sure al-Qaeda is responsible for the aircraft bomb so their agents will be hunting al-Qaeda suspects, but we are now exposed so alert our people in the UK and the US.'

The vehicle crossed the border and disappeared on the busy streets of Islamabad.

The conspirators at the Hamburg meeting listened intently as their leader revealed the revised plan.

'The Americans will not expect us to carry out another attack on an aircraft. We should make them believe we are going for infrastructure targets, like nuclear power stations and rail networks. We will sacrifice some brothers by making sure they are caught attempting to blow up some bridges or small buildings. The infidels will interrogate and even torture them. They will be instructed to release information about other similar targets and create a false trail for their agents. Meanwhile other brothers in the US can continue with their flying training so when the time is right, they can hijack aircraft and fly them into US buildings and strike a devastating blow to the unbelievers and finally make their ultimate sacrifice for Allah. We will limit our operation and direct our attacks on New York and Washington, removing Los Angeles, San Francisco and Dallas from the plan because we don't have enough pilots. You all have the Sheikh's blessing to do Allah's work.'

They all chanted, *'Allahu akhbar*, God is great.'

Mohamed Atta, the most educated member of the group and one of the three who had personally met bin Laden at his hideout in Afghanistan, was given the job of leading the operations in the US and responsibility for selecting the pilots and teams who would hijack the planes. KSM would continue to provide the funding and liaison since he had a US visa, which enabled him to travel freely. He had also secured visas for most of those who had yet to go to the US. After the BA bomb incident, all visa applications from Muslims were being reviewed. But KSM had powerful connections in the Saudi Embassy that could be used if necessary.

Unknown to bin Laden, KSM had secured himself protection and a getaway plan since he knew the CIA would be actively seeking him after the attack. The hijackers would all be dead, but they would inevitably leave a path to his door.

He misled bin Laden into believing that after the operation the US wouldn't retaliate by attacking Afghanistan, claiming they wouldn't want another Vietnam situation. He believed the Americans were weak and wouldn't fight any more wars overseas. Bin Laden had to convince the one-eyed Mullah Omar, the Taliban leader, of this to allow him and his followers continued sanctuary in his country. It was bin Laden's money and Arab support for the Mujahedeen that had helped to expel the Soviets in 1999 and bring the Taliban to power in Afghanistan. Bin Laden also promised he would arrange for the assassination of Ahmad Sha Massoud, the leader of the national alliance movement, the main opposition to the Taliban. Knowing he would likely be sacrificed by his leader if the US and their allies sought retribution and invaded Afghanistan, KSM had already conceived his own escape plans.

There were Saudi fundamentalists who had no liking for bin Laden, but wanted the US out of their country. After the Gulf War, military bases were established mainly to protect US interest against Iraq and Iran. They did benefit from the oil revenues and other commercial interests so had to make sure the CIA or the Saudi government didn't know their identities. They were prepared to support bin Laden's attacks on America, but wanted him to stay in Afghanistan. KSM knew their identities; it was his insurance if things went wrong.

CHAPTER 8

MI6 Headquarters – London

Jayne Clayton-Browne, at thirty-four, was one of the youngest female field agents in the service. She had served in many countries, including Iraq, where she had established a chain of contacts and agents in the Middle East. A Cambridge graduate in Middle Eastern and Arab studies, she was a tall, attractive brunette with a sharp intellect, unlike the stereotype image people might have of a MI6 agent. To an outsider she could be viewed as the female equivalent of Ian Fleming's fictional character, James Bond.

Her father, Janusz Bronowski, came to Britain with his family from Poland in 1939 when a boy, just before the Nazi invasion. In the 1950s he set up and ran a successful building business before marrying Laura Clayton, an upper-middle-class girl from a wealthy mid-shires family. They met when his company was contracted to build an extension to the family's country mansion in Berkshire. After their marriage, Laura changed the name to Clayton-Browne, to make it sound more English. Jayne's father died of a heart attack just after she graduated from Cambridge. She had been close to him and was broken-hearted by his death. A year later, her mother married a wealthy London estate agent named Norman Goodfellows, whom Jayne didn't like. He was one of the senior partners in the Daton France Estate Agencies, a global company that had portfolios for some of the large properties in Mayfair and Kensington Palace Gardens, known as Billionaires Row. It was where many foreign embassies were established, including the Russian and Saudi embassies. Russian oligarchs, Chinese and Indian industrialists and Saudi princes also have properties on the Row.

Jayne's first-class degree in Middle Eastern studies made her a candidate for MI6 head-hunters, even before she left university. After a rigorous selection procedure, followed by extensive training and successful overseas assignments, she proved to her masters that she was an exceptional field agent with the right stuff, so was fast-tracked for promotion. She was given the operational field name of Angel, but to her colleagues she was known simply as JB.

The Director General, referred to simply as BS outside the office, offered Jayne a drink. His actual name was Sir Henry Barrington-Smith. Most internal staff used the term DG when they were talking about the office, rather than the man. She preferred coffee, but he offered all his visitors a drink because he wanted the excuse to pour himself a large Scotch. The ten-year-old malt whisky hidden in a locked cupboard behind his desk was only offered to special visitors, usually other DGs or ministers, but knowing very few would accept, since they wanted to keep their minds sharp when in his presence, he drank most of it himself. His exact office location in the interstices of Legoland, the nickname given by the intelligence community to the imposing building on the Thames Embankment near Vauxhall Bridge owing to its layered architecture, was known only to a few carefully selected people.

In the year 2000, terrorists fired a Russian-made missile at the building. It produced little damage and failed to kill anyone. At the time it was thought that BS was the target. After, extra measures were established to place senior staff in secure locations within the building. Legoland, or the SIS building as it was formally called, was purchased by the government of Margaret Thatcher in 1988 and refurbished for use in 1994. She had personally authorised its allocation to MI6 owing to the IRA threat. MI6 was geographically separated from MI5. The latter was established across the river at Thames House to ensure that not all the country's security services were in the same building, but it was thought at the time the PM may have had other reasons.

It was unusual for internal staff on lower pay grades to be invited to the DG's office. Jayne wondered why she had been summoned. It had to be related to the BA66 bomb. BS was highly respected and feared by all those who crossed his path. Unlike his female counterpart in MI5, his real identity was known only to a small number of senior staff members, military chiefs and certain members of the Cabinet. He should have retired after receiving his knighthood two years previous, but since there was no obvious replacement, the PM intervened and asked him to stay on. DGs of MI5 and MI6 were always invited to apply for the posts to avoid the laborious selection procedures. It was the best method of ensuring the right person was appointed. Strict checks had to be made to ensure no skeletons existed in the cupboards of candidates. BS took great steps to ensure that his were well hidden.

BS's retirement to his hereditary castle in Scotland was put on hold; even though his physical health was not good, his powers of judgement were still excellent. Being able to make the right decisions in a crisis was an essential quality for any DG. Since the millennium bomb, threats from terrorist groups were increasing.

BS was a bachelor. His life in the army and his later career had made married life an impossibility. Many women had shared his bed, but none stayed too long. He did want for a lasting relationship, but it didn't happen; so like many career men, he became married to his job.

Jayne knew that after the BA66 bomb, a crisis would be looming, but why had she been selected? There were more experienced agents than her in the field. But she had been told that he took an unusually strong interest in her career, particularly in the work she had carried out in Iraq.

Jayne was like the daughter he would have liked to have had. She didn't know that BS and her mother, Laura, had been lovers before she was born. At the time he was a young major in the Guards. After being posted overseas on a special assignment and failing to write, and then discovering he was seeing another woman, Laura ended their relationship. They didn't see each other again and went their separate ways.

BS gave Jayne a little time to relax and feel comfortable. He brought her a freshly-made coffee from the pot bubbling away on a table in the corner of the room.

They sat on the plush black leather armchairs that occupied about a quarter of the office space. He noticed how much alike she was to her mother. She had her mother's eyes and facial expressions.

'You will be wondering why I have asked you here,' he said.

Jayne remained silent and just smiled, trying to conceal her anxiety. He handed her two files, one was marked 'Top Secret' and the other 'Confidential'.

Speaking in a more demanding tone, he said, 'I want you to read these files before we talk.'

He then went back to his desk to read through some papers to give her time and space to digest the contents of the files.

She looked first at the confidential file. The first few pages contained a performance report made by her senior officer on the work she had done in Iraq. She was amazed and almost embarrassed at the positive remarks recorded and the recommendation she should be fast-tracked to promotion to a senior rank. She scored an *Outstanding Field Agent* marking. The only slight concern expressed by another senior colleague was the comment *tendency to take risks when acting alone*. But then he was a man she had rebuffed after making sexual approaches to her. Being an attractive woman, it was a problem she often faced, but had learned how to deal with it. Some men still carried the physical scars of their misdemeanours.

The top secret file related to a project called 'Operation Clearwater'. It was endorsed by the NCTC, so had the highest level of approval and priority. The objectives were to find and bring to justice those responsible for the destruction of the BA flight by all means necessary. All known assets were to be used and new ones put in place to ensure early success. It was to be given top priority and every resource needed would be made available. Parliament and the public's confidence in the security services had to be restored quickly.

The new security measures established after the millennium

bombs had proved to be ineffective since the enemy was able to blow up a civilian aircraft without any prior knowledge. Intelligence was often compromised by the infiltration of the enemy moles into their ranks. It was a matter of high priority for them to be found and removed.

All security services in Britain and the US were on alert and hundreds of people had been assigned to seeking out terrorists, but, like ants emerging from underground nests, when some were caught or killed, more took their place. Al-Qaeda was a main threat, but The New Order was believed to be still functioning with a possible new leadership in Russia. The relationship between al-Qaeda and The New Order, if any, was complex; they would now be enemies.

Within the notes on Operation Clearwater, there was a specific brief that stated SIS would work exclusively with the new Counter Terrorist Unit (CTU) recently set up in the US under control of the White House with the Office of the Vice President taking direct responsibility. The British Prime Minister and US President had agreed on an exchange of intelligence information between the two organisations. MI6 would have the most significant role since foreign terrorists were involved and the act was carried out on British soil. Alicia Garcia was named as the Director of CTU. She would work with a nominated MI6 agent. There was no specific mention of MI5, the counter-terrorist unit of the Metropolitan Police in Scotland Yard, the FBI or CIA. But these agencies would also have tasks in Clearwater, directed towards the same objectives.

Jayne read the papers with some trepidation. Was BS going to offer her the job? Before she had completed reading the papers, he came and sat opposite her, but just looked and said nothing. He wanted her unprompted reaction to the brief. She knew he expected her to say something.

'I want to know the real reason behind Clearwater. The brief must have been written by a desk agent instructed to satisfy a policy committee,' she said.

He smiled and nodded agreeably.

'Exactly.'

It was her turn to stay silent and wait for what she knew was coming.

'I'm giving you a secret assignment as our special agent working with CTU,' he said.

'What is the assignment?' she asked.

'You will find and eliminate the person who was responsible for the aircraft bomb, not the operatives; others will take care of those. You will work exclusively with Alicia Garcia, the Director of the CTU. You will report only to me. I will decide what is passed on to the NCTC. You will use your codename, Angel. No other agents in MI6, MI5, Scotland Yard's Counter-Terrorist Unit, who are also working on Clearwater, will know about your special role, except one.'

'You mean I have to find and kill the person responsible?'

'Yes, but there might be more than one person,' he replied in a soft voice, then added, 'You can use any method or means that is appropriate. It would be politically embarrassing to bring the culprits to trial. Can you imagine the complications of bringing a person like bin Laden to trial? I don't think, however, you need worry about bin Laden. It would be difficult to find and kill him at the present time. He has been the CIA's prime target for years and they are no nearer to achieving that objective now than they were after the bombing of the *USS Cole* in the Yemen. You are more likely to find your target nearer to home,' he said.

'What do you mean, nearer to home?' she asked.

He simply replied, 'Russians.'

'I am giving you one assistant. He will be the only person in MI6 who will know about your assignment and be under your control. How much you involve him will be up to you. He is waiting in the next room.' He handed her another file. 'In this file is a preliminary report on the BA66 plane bomb and all the information we have collated so far on potential suspects. Beware, this is more complicated than it appears. The evidence shows that al-Qaeda is unlikely to be the culprit. We believe the same people in Russia who were behind the millennium bombs set them up to take the blame. But intelligence reports from the CIA indicate that al-Qaeda is still our biggest worry because they are also planning something big. If that is true, then this latest aircraft bomb will worry them, since it will make further acts using planes more difficult for them to carry out.

'Your first priority will be to talk to John Nicholas and Paul Cane. They were some of the people who worked with Alicia Garcia on Project Whirlwind. But you have seen the papers on Whirlwind so you will know the background. John Nicholas has already spoken to Paul Cane, who is the only survivor from BA66. He is currently recovering in hospital under police protection. His wife, who was with him on the flight, was killed, so remember that when you speak to him. Nicholas will fill you in on the details. They may be able to provide some good leads. You should also fly to Washington to talk with Alicia Garcia. Politically this has to be seen to be a joint operation. There's one more thing. When required, I can provide you with a back-up. He is an ex-SAS highly trained marksman who occasionally helps us out.'

Jayne thanked BS for his confidence in her. She saw this as an opportunity to make a name for herself. But there were formidable obstacles to overcome. Her brief within Clearwater seemed unusual. It was dangerous and very political and could become murky. She was placing a lot of trust in BS, who she believed probably had his own agenda. Was she just a pawn on that agenda? It wasn't unusual for senior SIS members to recruit their own people who weren't on the staff to do their dirty work. But here was the DG giving her, an experienced staff member, such a task and the skills of a marksman.

BS made a phone call. A few minutes later a tall, fresh-faced, young man walked into the room. He was introduced to Jayne as Bob Bradley. Like Jayne, he was another one of BS's rising stars destined for higher things. She could see that he looked uncomfortable. Was it because he would be working for a woman or was it because he was ignorant of the operation or just being in the overpowering presence of BS?

BS gave him copies of the Clearwater brief and told him and Jayne to use another office to review the intelligence information.

As they were about to leave, he said, 'I have arranged for you both to see Alan Leeke later today. He is our firearms and equipment expert who trains agents on their use and briefs them on the latest gadget technology. He is known simply as AL. You both have a licence to carry your own pistols while on operations for protection purposes. But MI6 will not officially issue them. You know the rules of engagement. Don't break them, otherwise you will be in front of the judge instead of the terrorists.' Jayne noticed a twisted smile on his face as they left the room.

BS made a phone call to Lord Clifton Davenport, an old Etonian friend, to confirm a long arranged dinner meeting. Davenport had been a minister in the Home Office in the previous Conservative government and had once chaired the Security Review Committee. It was that committee that had put BS's name forward for the MI6 appointment. Davenport's existing seat in the House of Lords enabled him to keep abreast with current affairs and gave him access to the key government contacts.

Davenport was also one of Britain's most wealthy landowners with extensive properties in Scotland and in London's Belgravia. When a branch of the family moved to London in the nineteenth century, it became involved in the expanding wine trade, supplying fine wines to the wealthy growing business community of the city. In the early nineteen-eighties, Clifton Davenport, then a successful businessman, became an advisor to the Thatcher government. The Prime Minister liked to be surrounded by such people and persuaded him to take a safe seat at the next General Election. He lacked parliamentary experience, but, like so many others whom she liked, was soon elected and made a minister in the Home Office. After the Conservatives lost the election to Labour in 1997, he was given a seat in the House of Lords.

Local property owners and estate agents were delighted at the influx of the wealthy Russian exiles and Arab oil magnates since they pushed up property values. Local department stores such as Harrods and Harvey Nichols benefited when such people opened up accounts. In fact, the injection of millions of pounds greatly boosted the local economy. The downside was the increasing number of closed communities and secret clubs being set up raised suspicions that the Russians were generating their own self-serving community. Britain gave the Russians much greater freedom than they could ever have had in Russia. Over two thousand large London properties were owned by foreigners, twenty-five per cent of which were companies.

The Russian oligarchs had formed business relationships with a number of rich and influential people in the city of London to safeguard their investments. But many were afraid of being murdered by jealous rivals and political opponents in mother Russia.

Davenport's meeting was more than a social occasion. He had also invited one of the richest Russian oligarchs in London, who knew most of the powerful people in Russia.

Bob Bradley, a good-looking, fair-haired man, was at least five years younger than Jayne. Like her, he was a Cambridge graduate and because of his specialism in the Middle Eastern affairs he was also head-hunted by MI6. He didn't know that his father, Sir Thomas Bradley, was also an old army friend of BS. The DG of MI6 had a vested interest in the two people with whom he had entrusted the nation's secrets, but nobody knew about it. Even in 2001, the old boy network still existed at the highest levels of government, the military and the Civil Service; it was deeply entrenched in the system.

The two agents locked themselves in the room to ensure privacy. Bradley had done his homework and suggested the assets Jayne had established in the Middle East be used to help track down the people who the Russians had used to dupe Malik. The intelligence report showed that CTU had good assets in Russia. There was some evidence that The New Order could still be operating and controlled by a high-level person in Moscow.

The agents had a copy of a preliminary draft report from the accident investigators, who had worked non-stop since their call to the Thames crash site. It contained data taken from BA66's black box, from eye witness accounts and the examination of the wreckage. There was no message on the cockpit voice recorder after 6.30 am except for a hissing sound as the explosion destroyed the aircraft. Up to that point in time, the exchanges between the pilot and control tower at Heathrow were normal instructions for landing. On the recordings of the aircraft's communications there was a spurious radio signal not associated with the normal ones used by the responders for tracking the aircraft. For a few milliseconds just before the explosion it blanked out the aircraft controls. It was likely to be the signal that triggered the detonators of the bomb.

The explosion was massive and tore open the hold. The effect on the plane was increased by the large pressure difference between the aircraft interior and the outside air. The force of the explosion blew off the cockpit and front section, leaving an open cylinder that then started to disintegrate. Most of the passengers in that part of the plane would have been killed instantly. This took place in fractions of a second. A small part of the tail section was also blown off from the main fuselage with some passengers strapped to their seats. Some may have survived the descent into the muddy water of the estuary. There were only five eye witness accounts from people on the ground close to the crash site since it was early in the morning and locals, being familiar with planes flying low, took little notice until they heard the explosion. By the time they looked up, only burning parts of the plane could be seen plummeting in the river. It was all over except for fires burning on the river so they could add little to what was already known.

More interesting was the forensic report on the watch retrieved by Cane from the dead body in the river. The watch contained a timing mechanism and a signal generator, which, although not strong enough to trigger the detonators, could have triggered a more powerful radio transmitter used to trigger the bomb explosives. The watch showed a time of 6.40 am when it stopped, but the actual detonation time of the bomb was 6.30 am. If this was the original signal source then it proved the man sitting near Cane in first-class was the bomber. Identifying him could give a lead to those responsible, for what was being described by the newspapers as the deadliest terrorist act of all time. On the assumption it was the man in the seat opposite Cane, then his name according to his passport and ticket was Abdel Malik, the man under surveillance by CTU. Every other passenger was being investigated for links; all but three were dead.

Before arranging to fly to Washington to meet with Alicia Garcia, Angel decided she would need to speak to John Nicholas and Paul Cane.

CHAPTER 9

Victoria House, Belgravia, London

The phone rang in the basement study.

'Davenport.'

The caller knew the receiver would be at his desk at that time of the day. The phone was encrypted and the number known only to three people.

'We need to talk privately. Can you come to my house next Friday evening for drinks? BS will be present.'

When Davenport called, the Russian knew it was trouble, particularly when the name BS was mentioned. He owed everything to these two men. One day he knew the debt would have to be paid. He simply replied, 'Yes.' Any other reply would have been unacceptable. He amended his diary.

Oleg Detroski, one of the richest of the Russian oligarchs, had everything material any man could wish for, but like so many exiled Russians who gained their wealth from a variety of investments and nefarious activities, he constantly feared for his life. He had supported the opposition to the new Russian president so made political enemies in Russia. He thought it prudent to leave the country. One day he knew someone would come for him so it was necessary to have an army of bodyguards and keep a low public profile.

Britain was the most popular country to seek refuge in owing to the attitudes of its socialist government towards those who sought asylum from dictatorships. But the government had to be careful since it also wanted improved relationships with the new president. Detroski's vast fortune enabled him to enjoy a degree of seclusion. It also gave him access to the top levels of British society and with powerful friends in London. He was not alone; other rich exiles had similar advantages.

Detroski was of particular value to British Intelligence because he knew the names of many ex-KGB members. Some joined the new Federal Security Service of the Russian Federation (FSB) and the Foreign Intelligence Service, Sluzhba Vneshney Razvyedki (SVR), others worked for private Mafia crime syndicates that flourished during the former presidency. Some Mafia bosses became rich and were able to blackmail those politicians whom they had helped to come to power.

During the difficult days in Moscow, Detroski was supported by his friend and business partner Boris Surak, nicknamed Voss. He came to London and set up a number of companies. The Home Office also gave him a British visa as part of the package. Voss had worked as a courier for the KGB and after the fall of the Soviet Union joined a Mafia gang. He didn't commit any crime, but had inside knowledge of the structure of the syndicates. He was of particular interest to John Nicholas and MI6 because he knew people who had been close to Boris Sudakov, the deceased Russian member of The New Order's Cabal.

When Detroski sought exile in Britain for himself, his wife and Boris Surak, he was willing to share information with the police in exchange for citizenships. Equally important were his extensive shares in the Siberian oil and gas fields and his willingness to invest in Britain at a time when inward investment was high on the government's policy agenda. Davenport, although not in the government at the time, was influential in expediting his entry into Britain because of his business interests.

Detroski owned a block of apartments in Knightsbridge, where he accommodated many of his relatives and friends from Moscow, and a secluded Georgian house in Berkshire.

Before their other guests arrived, Davenport and Barrington-Smith had a private dinner together, something they did on occasions to update each other about current events. Since both men were bound by the Official Secret Act, they could exchange classified information, particularly at a time of national crisis. Their friendship went back to their days at Eton. They were from a generation when strong bonds made at public schools were life-enduring.

Detroski's chauffeur-driven Bentley arrived at the old Victorian house located in one of the fashionable squares in Belgravia. The wealthy Russian was accompanied by Voss, his friend and bodyguard. The two men were observed by two high-level security cameras positioned above the front door. It automatically opened and closed immediately after they were inside the building. They were met by Clare, Davenport's young PA, who took them to a large room at the end of a corridor. The pungent smell of cigar smoke drifted from the room as the door opened to a six-foot-six man who greeted them with a welcoming smile and firm handshake.

'Good to see you again. It's been a long time,' said Davenport, stooping down to shake their hands.

With a large glass of whisky in one hand, BS got up from an armchair and advanced towards them and also shook their hands. Noting their observation of a bottle of Beluga malt vodka on the table, Davenport asked, 'Gentlemen, would you like a glass of vodka?'

Expecting a positive reply, he started pouring the drink over ice cubes already cooling two glasses. The Russians took the glasses and made themselves comfortable in the brown leather chairs placed conveniently between their hosts. The large room was like a study. It was furnished with a mixture of modern and old Victorian furniture, the latter being more fitting to the architecture of the room and the building. A large traditional mahogany desk sat across one corner and well-stocked book shelves covered two walls.

First, taking a traditional Russian approach to drinking vodka, Voss downed the drink in one gulp. Davenport refilled the glass. Detroski was more subdued and just took a sip. He preferred the English way. Davenport looked seriously at the two men. As an ex-minister at the Home Office, he had learned the art of making a guest feel comfortable before asking for a favour. These particular guests owed him many favours and they knew it.

'Thank you for coming at such short notice as I know you are busy men. The seriousness of the matter forces me to come straight to the point. We need your help in finding those responsible for the blowing up of the BA plane. If the intended target had been reached then we may not be here today since extensive damage could have been done to our London properties and we may have even been killed. We believe it could be the same group who planted the millennium bombs in London. Current intelligence suggests it's not al-Qaeda. I'm sorry to say that means it could be a Russian group. We have no proof at this time, but agents on both sides of the Atlantic are working on that assumption.'

Davenport could see that Voss was getting agitated. BS, who had not spoken, put down his whisky and looked straight at Voss.

'We believe you might know some of the people involved.'

It was a veiled threat. The Russian knew BS was referring to his past activities in the old Soviet Union. He would have a file on every ex-member of the KGB. Looking astonished at BS's statement, the Russian retorted in a detectable angry voice, 'Why should I know?'

BS took out a photograph from an envelope concealed in a desk drawer and gave it to him. By the expression on the man's face, BS instantly observed that he knew the man in the photograph. Noticing Voss's hesitation in replying and coming to the aid of his friend, Detroski took hold of the photo and said, 'This man's name is Alexander Larinko. He is one of the Russian president's supporters and a senior officer in the FSB, and distant cousin to Gregori Seperkov, who runs among other things a private security service in Moscow.'

Unknown to Detroski, Gregori Seperkov was the half-brother of Leon Seperkov, who was killed by the Russian Mafia after the millennium bomb incidents at the same time as his business associate, Boris Sudakov.

'Do you know Larinko and Seperkov?' asked BS.

Detroski ignored the question.

'Are they your suspects?'

'No,' said BS.

Voss was looking very uncomfortable and sweating. Perhaps the vodka was having an effect or was it he knew too much about the man in the photograph? Seeing the conversation was turning into an interrogation and angering the Russian, Davenport intervened.

'Gentlemen, before we get into questions I want to give you my assurance that anything said in this room will be in strict confidence and not be revealed to anyone outside this room. The situation is politically complicated. The British government is under extreme pressure to find and bring the perpetrators to justice. But because they are almost certainly not British, this will be difficult. At the present time it doesn't want to worsen relationships with the new Russian president and government of Russia by making accusations or pursuing suspects in that country. We want Russian help in our fight against Islamic terrorists. The public believe the bomb was the work of al-Qaeda. Officially, the Americans are also making that assumption. If a Russian group is responsible, they also want people to believe it was al-Qaeda. But it's their real motives that concern us. There are a number of possibilities: a warning shot to you oligarchs who have left Russia and transferred billions of dollars to Western banks, money that some believe was robbed from Russian assets, or retribution for the failure of the millennium bombs.'

BS poured himself another whisky and topped up the Russians' glasses.

Before Detroski could speak, BS said, 'It's likely that an al-Qaeda senior operative on the plane triggered the bomb. We need to find the people who set him up and gave him the order. Al-Qaeda have already caught and executed three Afghans whom we think were employed by a Russian so they almost certainly now know about the Russian plan. Someone had to coordinate the link and be responsible for the whole operation; that's the person we want to find.'

Detroski, now looking pale and disturbed even though the vodka was taking effect, said, 'I will help you if I can, but we must make sure that none of the Russians living in London know about this because the terrorists are likely to have their own people living in the community. Each of us has private security, but no one can be trusted. We are some of the wealthiest people in the country and, as you know, Clifton, money can buy anything and open any door. I will make some discreet enquiries and let you know if anything useful comes up.'

BS gave Davenport a suspicious look, wondering if too much information had been given away. After some small talk about families, the two Russians left the house, but an uncomfortable feeling pervaded the room.

Davenport poured himself another drink.

'I think the Russians know more than they are telling us.'

'I'm sure they do, but I wanted them to know what we knew, to see how much gets back to Moscow. I have agents watching them and monitoring their communications. It's Voss I'm most worried about,' said BS.

With a smile on his face and colour in his cheeks brought on by the vodka, Davenport turned to his friend, who also had a happy demeanour after the consumption of the three large glasses of a twelve-year-old Glenfiddich. Speech was becoming slightly slurred.

'Tell me more about this new young agent you mentioned before the Russians arrived,' said Davenport.

'She is one of our bright rising stars, ambitious, highly intelligent and with a streak of ruthlessness. Her work in Iraq proved she has the right stuff to get results. I've given her a specific job that makes her less dependent on other agents. She will report directly to me.'

'Sounds like a report I once saw about you. Hope you're going to be objective and not use her to do the things you would like to do,' said Davenport.

BS smiled, knowing his old friend had summed him up.

'I might let you meet her privately one day, but she must remain unknown to the Russians. I am sending her to Washington to talk to Alicia Garcia, the new head of CTU, the President's own special unit.'

'How do the CIA and FBI react to that?' asked Davenport.

'Not too favourably, but after the millennium disaster and the number of moles discovered in those agencies, the White House wanted its own unit.'

'You crafty old sod, Henry. That's where you got the idea from, having a special agent under your wing. Why a woman? I bet she's a good-looker.'

Henry was visibly becoming embarrassed. His old Etonian friend had struck a sensitive cord.

'You actually know her mother, Laura Clayton-Browne. She's remarried now and her name is Goodfellows.'

Davenport looked surprised.

'Yes, I remember Laura; that's the beauty you had a fling with before being posted overseas. She was a beautiful girl. But then you messed things up as I recall when she found out about your womanising.'

'That was an unfortunate mistake, but it's a long story for another time. Soon after, Laura met another man, got married and Jayne was the result. I think she did it to make me suffer. It worked. We never saw each other again. I did keep track of Jayne's life and when I saw that she was a brilliant Cambridge graduate in Middle Eastern and Arab studies, I made sure she had a job offer that she couldn't refuse. At the time we were desperately short of people with her language skills and knowledge. Her mother never knew I was behind it, although she tried to persuade her daughter to stay on at Cambridge and take a PhD.'

'I'm surprised her mother never found out about your job,' said Davenport.

'It would have been difficult because, as you know, MI6 keeps the names of its staff secret.'

'I hope Jayne doesn't find out about you and her mother. It would place you in a very uncomfortable position.'

Changing the subject, BS told his friend that he was worried there was something more sinister going on behind the bombing. It wasn't just revenge or settling personal vendettas, there had to be a political dimension. Someone was ramping up the War of

Terror directed at the Islamic countries. Al-Qaeda, already the prime suspect, was being used to ferment the ambitions of others. Bin Laden, with his jihad against the US and their allies, was playing into the hands of those responsible. It was likely to be the Russians, but is there a British element? Could The New Order still be active under a different name and organisational structure? These questions bugged him.

After more drinking, the two friends agreed there was urgent work to do. They parted company and, although many points over the limit of alcohol for driving, BS drove back to his secret apartment in the south of the city. If he was stopped and showed his special ID, no policeman would dare arrest him.

CHAPTER 10

Knightsbridge

Paul Cane had been in hospital for two months before he was discharged. He had recovered from most of his physical injuries, but still required the use of a walking stick. But he was a man who had lost everything that really mattered. Friends had rallied around to give him support and Robert tried to get him some journalistic work to occupy his mind. Frequently he woke up screaming after nightmarish dreams of the plane crash. Memories of that morning haunted him daily. He couldn't adjust to the reality of what happened. Valerie's premonitions before the flight actually made things worse. It was as if she knew something terrible was going to happen and he had ignored it. He felt guilty for missing the signs.

Why did he go back to New York?

Why did the terrorists choose that particular plane?

Had some evil curse been cast upon him to deny the happiness that he had waited so long for?

The only woman he truly loved was gone. He treasured the short time they had had together. He wished he'd gone with her. Why did he survive? Cane was a rational man, not religious and had no strong views on God, but what had happened to him during the last two years had shaken his belief in normality. Was there something driving his life beyond his understanding? There were so many questions that needed answers. But there was one feeling that consumed him beyond any other. Those responsible for the terrible act had to be found and punished. Countries went to war over such acts, but unfortunately that punished more innocent people and those directly responsible. He vowed this time to seek retribution, even if he had to do it himself. He knew the law wouldn't agree, but the enormity of such a crime was beyond the law. He was the lone survivor. He'd believed that his life had been spared so he could find justice, not only for his beloved wife, but for the other innocent people on the plane.

Cane looked out of the window of his apartment in Knightsbridge and thought back to how excited he was when he first brought Valerie to it just before Christmas in 1999. She had changed his life and given him a new dimension. Now his life was empty; it had lost its meaning. He was drifting into a state of depression from which he couldn't escape. The eerie quietness of his surroundings was suddenly shattered by a piercing shrill of the telephone. Once the telephone was his friend, his constant companion, but now it was a threat to his closed world. In anger, he lifted off the receiver and slammed it down, cutting off the caller. A few seconds later it rang again and again. An inner voice told him to pick it up and escape from his self-destructing world. Obeying his inner voice, he lifted the receiver again, but before he could speak, a woman's voice said, *'The debt is almost settled. Now you know how it feels to lose someone you love.'*

The caller rang off before Cane could speak. The phone display showed the number to be unknown. Very few people knew about his loss. Whoever it was could be a lead to those who had carried out the terrible act or they were attempting to make him believe that. The call made him angry, very angry and increased his determination to find those responsible.

Before leaving hospital, Cane had received a second visit from John Nicholas. The policeman told him to call any time he felt the need. John had become a good friend since the millennium bomb incident. Cane knew his team were working hard to track down the terrorists. Nicholas promised to keep him informed of any progress. It was time to tell him about the phone call. Cane dialled the secure number he had for Nicholas, who replied immediately.

'Hello, Paul. How are you?'

'John, I need to see you urgently. Can you come to my apartment? I've just received a telephone call, which I think could have been from Christine Hunter. Can it be traced?'

Sensing his friend's distress, Nicholas replied, 'I'll see what can be done. If it's from a public phone box then it's more difficult, but not impossible to trace. I have a meeting this morning, but will come this afternoon. I will give two sets of three rings on the phone when I arrive so you will know it's me. Don't answer any other calls before.'

Rupert Arnold had already arranged for Angel to meet with John Nicholas since MI6 was already working closely with Scotland Yard, but they didn't know about her special assignment. As far as they were concerned she was one of the many agents working on the case. After reading the report about Paul Cane's key role in Project Whirlwind and being the only person who had seen Malik up close, she believed he might have valuable information. Much was in the statement that Cane had made, but sometimes things come back to the memory long after the event.

Past experience had made John Nicholas wary of MI6 agents. Distrust between security agencies still existed. They liked their autonomies, which were rigorously protected by their director generals. Since the IRA problems and the Gulf War, governments had demanded closer collaboration between all the security services, but traditional loyalties and the structures under which they were established made it easy for them to maintain the status quo.

Angel wasn't like any agents Nicholas had previously met. Being physically attractive with a friendly demeanour that masked her sharp intellect and inner ruthlessness, she was immediately able to gain the attention of any man who was expecting to meet a blue stocking type of woman. Nicholas knew little about her apart from the briefing Arnold had given him concerning her knowledge and experience of the Arab world. She was fluent in Arabic and a number of lesser Middle Eastern languages including Pashto, one of the tribal languages of Afghanistan. Nicholas wondered whether it would be wise for her to meet Cane in his present state of mind.

The two met in a secure office at Scotland Yard, but to enter the building Angel disguised herself with a grey wig and padding to make her look plumper and twice her age. It even fooled Nicholas, until in the security of the office she removed the disguise to reveal a young, beautiful, dark-haired woman in her early thirties. Nicholas, who was not married and took little interest in women, on seeing Angel felt his hormones becoming active. He was always a little worried about his sexuality, but the sight of this woman gave him an assurance of his heterosexuality.

They discussed the recent intelligence from the US related to al-Qaeda's activities. It indicated that a Russian group was most likely behind the attack and had duped an al-Qaeda operative into believing it was ordered by bin Laden. But that was unconfirmed since it came from a dubious source in Afghanistan obtained by a CIA agent. Angel told Nicholas of her intention to fly to Washington to meet Alicia Garcia as she wasn't sure they were being told everything. The White House had its own political agenda and controlled the intelligence information it would share with Britain. Nicholas agreed it was right to meet Alicia and work closely with CTU. He told her that after the millennium incident he and his colleagues had a good relationship with the CIA and FBI. He reminded her that it was a CIA agent who discovered the location of the bomb on the Thames barge. Angel was one of the few MI6 agents who had been told about the bomb's true nature.

John Nicholas related the anguish felt by Paul Cane after the death of his wife and the horrendous experience he had gone through as a survivor of the plane explosion. He told her that Cane had just received a phone call from a woman he believed was Christine Hunter, indicating she knew he and his wife had been on the plane. She could have only known that from people who were involved. Angel had already read the files on Hunter and The New Order and her attempt on the Canes' lives. She was now even more eager to meet the man she had read so much about.

Nicholas told her that Cane had called early that morning and asked to see him. He suggested Angel accompany him in the guise of his assistant because it wouldn't be wise to tell him for whom she actually worked. Angel agreed to go, but told him that she couldn't sit in front of him disguised as an old lady. She told him that she had read the files on Project Whirlwind that covered Cane's exploits in the US and in London. Angel thanked Nicholas and agreed to meet him at the Knightsbridge apartment in the afternoon. She returned to her office at SIS and drafted a memo to BS. He immediately responded and sent her some briefing notes on the meeting at Davenport's house with the Russians.

On leaving hospital, Cane was advised not to drink since he was still taking medication for his damaged leg and ribs, but the temptation was too great to resist. He had already consumed two glasses of brandy when the phone rang three times, stopped and rang again. He pressed the buzzer to open the front door to the apartment. Nicholas was already known to Henry, the apartment block security guard, who let him and Angel proceed to the inner door since Cane had already notified him of the expected visitors. Angel had a specially made pass indicating she was a Detective Inspector at Scotland Yard.

On opening the door, Cane was surprised to see two people. Nicholas greeted him with a hug and introduced Angel.

'This is Detective Inspector Clare Angel, my new assistant. Hope you don't mind me bringing her along, but she is helping us in the hunt for Christine Hunter.'

Angel smiled and shook hands with Cane. Their eyes locked onto each other for a split second, her smile, her facial expressions were familiar. She was dark and different-looking, but her manner was the same. It was uncanny, almost surreal. She could be Valerie in a different body. John Nicholas noticed the brief interaction between them.

Still staring at Angel, Cane said in a stuttering voice, 'Pleased to meet you, Clare.'

He held out his hand to her while supporting himself with his stick with the other. She responded and shook it. Her hand was soft. It lingered in his longer than normal. It was the point of contact through which emotions can unconsciously be transmitted. He felt it, just perceptively. She had waited for the moment. She was excited at meeting him. Before their hands unlocked, he looked her straight in the eyes. But her eyes showed no emotion, no recognition. Her training was good.

'Angel – that's an unusual name,' he said.

He noted that she didn't follow up on his remark. She walked into the room. He beckoned the two visitors to sit on the settee.

'Would you like a drink?' he asked.

They both answered, 'Yes, coffee please, no sugar.'

The percolator was already in action so he was able to quickly provide two cups of steaming coffee.

'I'm glad to see you're up and walking about without your plaster, Paul. How do you feel?' asked Nicholas.

'Great. I'm walking as much as I can and the exercise is helping. I use the park opposite a lot, but have to be careful to avoid the runners, who increasingly seem to be taking over the footpaths. I want to thank you for the protection. Your policeman keeps his distance, but does keep a watchful eye on me.'

Angel took out her notebook like a true policewoman would be expected to do. With her irresistible smile she looked at Cane.

'Paul, do you mind if I take some notes?'

'No,' he replied, already starting to believe she was no ordinary policewoman. The notebook was new and she fumbled to find a pen. It was her eyes that gave her away. Behind those dark brown eyes an intelligent brain was at work. He had noticed her looking around his apartment taking in the books on the shelves and the papers stacked up on the desk.

Observing his books and papers, she said, 'I see you study Arabic and the Middle East. That was also my subject at Cambridge,' smiling for the first time. Wishing to avoid talking about his job, Cane quickly changed the subject.

'I hope John doesn't give you too much deskwork to do,' he said, in a slightly sarcastic way.

'No, I'm out with him most of the time. I was only recently assigned to this case. I have read the case notes and know about the attempts on your life.' She was careful to avoid mentioning Valerie.

Nicholas, clearly wanting to interrupt the conversation, said,

'Paul, following up on the phone call you received this morning, I have some news for you. We enlisted the help of GCHQ to find the geographical location of the call. It was tracked to a public phone box in the East End. They can now access all public phone box calls, but the criminals still believe calls made from them are undetectable. At this moment videocam footage of the streets in the area is being examined to see if the person who made the call can be identified. The caller, if it's Hunter, knew about you being on the plane. That means she's likely to have had access to secure information about the flight since we had kept both your names off the official passenger list and nobody knows that you are one of the only two survivors. The official communication to the press was about the other three, of which only one is still alive, but he's in a coma and not expected to live much longer. The question is, how did she know about you? Are you sure that apart from me and the hospital staff, Valerie's parents and your friend Robert, nobody else came to see you at the hospital?'

'No, I can't, because most of the time I was asleep, but I assumed the room was secure,' he answered.

Angel, who was writing in her notebook, looked at Nicholas and said, 'There is another possibility. Many people were involved in retrieving bodies from the river. What about those who actually placed him in the air ambulance. They would know that there were four survivors not three as stated in the media. Remember, we are dealing with people who are well connected and have unlimited resources. Money buys almost everything. There are probably people in the police, the security agencies or in the hospital who could have been bribed if the money was right. Those responsible for the bomb want al-Qaeda blamed and will do anything that leads us in that direction. If they know Paul is alive and being protected then they will assume he knows something. Added to this, his nemesis, Christine Hunter, still blames him for her mother's death.'

Cane now knew that Clare Angel was no ordinary police inspector. She knew too much and her demeanour shone through her disguise. But why would Nicholas, his old friend, want to hide her real identity? Cane decided for the time being to play their game.

'Do you suspect that al-Qaeda isn't to blame for the bomb on the plane?' he asked.

Nicholas felt it was time to tell Cane what he knew.

'We know that al-Qaeda has not admitted to carrying out the act. If they had, then they would want to use it as propaganda for their jihad against the West. There was no mention of it by al-Qaeda on Al Jazeera television, always used by them to make announcements. It was just reported as a news item with no blame attached to anyone.

'We also know from US intelligence that three Afghan members of al-Qaeda were executed for working with the Russians in Afghanistan. We believe that some ex-members of The New Order may be active in Moscow. They may be working under a different name, but their old intentions are similar. It may not be a global organisation, but just a Russian group. This time Russian politics and commercial interests are involved. Many oligarchs have been imprisoned and others fled to Britain, bringing with them vast amounts of money to invest in industry and infrastructure. The President wants to stop that, so various intermediaries, some of which have powerful connections to the criminal fraternity, are being employed to discourage suspected dissidents. The Russians want retribution on bin Laden and his Arab followers for helping the Mujahedeen to remove and destroy the Russian army's occupation of Afghanistan.

'We know the richest oligarchs have property in London. They employ private security firms for protection, but we have placed some of them and their associates under surveillance. Many foreign embassies are located in the Kensington area and have official police protection. That was established after the siege of the Iranian Embassy in 1980. We believe some of the privately owned mansions may be unknowingly sheltering criminals or even terrorists, since most of the houses and compounds are sealed off as private property.'

Angel knew that her boss BS had recently met with the wealthy oligarch Oleg Detroski, but that information was not to be shared. The possible connection of Christine Hunter to the émigré Russians in Kensington was an interesting one she would need to follow up independently of Nicholas's police. If Hunter was involved, it would take the investigation in the direction of the Russians. But why would they want to blow up a British plane over London? What possible motive could they have? Was it to accelerate the hunt for bin Laden and the destruction of al-Qaeda? She had to find a way of penetrating the Russian group; perhaps Hunter was the gateway. First, she had to find out why Hunter was back in England and where she was located. Paul Cane was obviously still on her hit list so he might be the bait. Her only problem was John Nicholas. Hunter was his prey and he didn't know about her MI6 assignment, but he had the resources and contacts to find her.

Angel was still thinking about the situation when Nicholas's cell phone rang. He walked out of the room to answer it. Cane studied Angel's face. He was disturbed by her similarity to Valerie, not so much a physical similarity, but it was her facial expressions and the way she looked at him. She could have been her darker sister. He noticed she was looking at a photograph of him and Valerie on a desk in the corner of the room, but said nothing. The silence was broken when Nicholas came back into the room.

'We have a videocam image of a woman in a hooded coat coming out of the phone box and getting into a grey Mercedes. It was driven away towards the West End. The car's driver was a young man, but unfortunately, although the licence plate was recorded, it proved to be false. The team is scanning all the footage in cameras across London to track the car. Once we have that we can set up surveillance on the building where the car went.'

Cane shouted out excitedly, 'This could be the breakthrough we've been waiting for. I want to catch this bitch who has caused me so much grief.'

He remembered those eyes looking at him. They were menacing and full of hate. He decided to tell Nicholas about that brief encounter in the hotel in Switzerland and apologised for not mentioning it before. He hadn't been certain it was Hunter so kept it to himself. Now he believed it had been her and, after seeing him, she was being true to her name and, once again, he was her prey.

Nicholas returned to the BA66 flight and asked Cane more about the man whose name was known to be Malik. It was now certain that he was the person who used the Casio watch to detonate the bomb. Cane couldn't add much more than what had already been said except what Anne, the air attendant, had told him about another Arab who had boarded the plane at Amsterdam and was asking if Malik was on the plane.

'That could be useful,' said Nicholas. 'He may have been an accomplice. I will re-check the Arab passengers who boarded at Amsterdam. We believe the bomb was in a suitcase loaded in the luggage hold at Schiphol. Someone at the airport switched suitcases after they had been through security.'

Nicholas then remembered that the man, who was in the tail of the plane and died at the hospital, was an Arab.

'We do have his passport, but may not be able to prove he is the person who knew Malik. But it's a possible lead.'

Nicholas was becoming excited with the progress being made. Cane could visualise it being a hive of activity now they had some leads to follow up.

The excitement was beginning to rub off on Cane. He noticed the so-called Clare Angel keeping him under close observation. They were both acting out their parts and neither was going to let their guard down and show it. After his past experiences, Cane felt more like an agent than a journalist. He had learned a lot while working with his CIA and FBI friends in the US, and now had a desire to seek out the terrorists himself and serve his own form of justice. He still had the Beretta that Alicia had given him. It had saved his life in Martha's Vineyard. Since he didn't have a British gun licence he could be prosecuted for illegally possessing a weapon, but now was not the time to hand it in to the police; he might need it.

Nicholas's phone rang again. This time he received the news that the grey Mercedes was seen going into the grounds of a mansion house in Kensington Palace Gardens. It was within a private gated community close to the Russian Embassy. The building comprised of three floors of luxury apartments. The camera couldn't show the occupants leaving the car and no one left the building. Nicholas gave orders for the building and its occupants to be placed under top priority surveillance. That meant twenty-four hours of non-stop observation using all the latest technology. Normally this would entail placing cameras and microphones in the apartments. To do this meant someone had to enter the building and carry out the installation. Fortunately, the latest microminiaturised technology enabled bugs to be inserted into small cracks or even flown in through windows or ventilation systems. The plans and layouts of all the buildings in the area were well documented and possessed by the police and the security agencies since it was the most protected area of London.

Cane's potential assassin had now given them a valuable lead. She had led them to the home of Russians, who were now the prime suspects. But these were people who had left Russia out of fear of persecution and after scrupulous screening had been given British citizenships. Why would they be involved in an attack on London?

Nicholas told Cane that he would have round-the-clock police protection and to immediately report any further contact with Hunter. A tap would be put on his phone.

As they left the apartment, Clare Angel gave Cane one of those looks that told him she wanted to see him again. It was similar to the look Valerie had given him after their first meeting in Washington. Cane gave Clare his cell phone number in case she ever needed to speak to him about Christine Hunter. It was just an excuse to make sure she knew how to make contact. But he thought she probably had it anyway. She seemed pleased and placed it in her book. As she left the apartment with Nicholas, she turned, looked back and smiled. It sent a cold shiver down Cane's back. It was exactly what Valerie did at their first meeting in Washington.

After they left, Cane poured himself a triple brandy. He knew it was against doctor's orders since he was still taking medication for his injuries. It wasn't the finding of Hunter, raising the possibility of at last removing an old adversary, that raised his adrenaline, but the meeting of Clare Angel or whatever her real name was. She had unsettled him. Cane was sure she worked for MI5 or MI6. She was about the same age as Valerie and therefore young to be a field agent, if that was her job. He would find out by checking her out through his contacts at Cambridge. Her one mistake was telling him she was a Cambridge graduate in Arab studies. He knew all the academics in that field. The old boy network would tell him what he needed to know.

Cane was still grieving for his beloved wife, but, for reasons he didn't understand, Clare Angel had tapped into his emotions. She had excited him. It was as if his dead wife's spirit or Karma had been transferred to another woman. He didn't believe in Buddhism or re-incarnation, but after recent experiences he was beginning to believe in the supernatural. Valerie was a very spiritual person. Her premonitions had come true. How could that be explained? She had physically vanished from his life. But there was no body to lay to rest. No last words or anything he could keep at the moment of her death. Did her spirit still exist and was it trying to find him? He was beginning to believe it was and it frightened him.

It was a strange coincidence to meet, so soon after her death, a woman who could have such an effect on him. Was it, however, just him wanting Valerie back and seeing what he wanted to see in another woman who just happened to possess some similar characteristics? He was still in a state of shock and having bad dreams. The medication he was on might be contributing. It was too soon for closure, but he knew that one day he had to move on. Bringing to justice those responsible for the destruction of BA66 would be the first step to closure. He owed that to his wife and to all the passengers. He knew what had to be done.

Cane looked out of the window to Hyde Park. It was a strange feeling knowing that at the opposite end of the park, not more than a mile away, was a woman who had tried to kill him and Valerie and, in some way, might be connected to the terrorist group. There were many assumptions being made. He needed to know more about the Russians living in their protected enclave. He picked up the phone and dialled Alicia's private secure cell phone number. There was a delay and various noises could be heard before it rang, but to his immense surprise, she answered immediately.

'Paul, what a pleasant surprise. How are you? We have been worried about you. We were all devastated at what happened in London. Robert has kept me informed and said that you were now out of hospital and back in Knightsbridge.'

Cane knew she had his number and that Robert had been in contact with her.

'Thanks, Alicia. I was glad to know that your position is secure after the loss of the two agents on the plane. There have been some developments here and I need your help. Let me first say that I'm not working for the police, MI5 or MI6, but just convalescing. But you will understand that once again I find myself in the middle of a crisis. I seem to attract them. Christine Hunter has appeared here in London and made a threatening call to me. Fortunately, John Nicholas's people traced her call and eventually found an address where she could be located. Ironically it was in a road in Kensington, close to Knightsbridge. Nicholas has placed the building under surveillance, but we need to know the names of the Russians she is associating with and if there is a connection to the terrorist group. It could be an offshoot of the Moscow section of The New Order. I know you have intelligence on those people and contacts in Moscow. Also we need to know who in the group duped Malik into believing his orders came from bin Laden. Nicholas says the information about al-Qaeda executing the Afghans who were working for the Russians came from CTU. Also have you had any contact with a female British MI6 agent who is working on the case yet?'

There was a long silence. Cane realised that he may have said too much not knowing what Alicia already knew.

'Paul, as an old friend, who wants to see you recover from the horrendous experience you have gone through, I would recommend that you don't get involved in this. It's very complicated and dangerous. I know you personally want to see the perpetrators caught and dealt justice, but leave it to the professionals. CTU is working with John Nicholas's counter-terrorist unit and MI6 and the agent to whom you refer is coming to see me. We do know the Russians are involved and at this moment have someone following it up. Please let us handle the investigation and we will find those responsible and you will be the first to know. I really am concerned about your well-being and you trying to become James Bond. Remember what happened in Martha's Vineyard.'

Realising he wasn't going to get any further, he thanked Alicia for being so frank and assured her he would be careful and ended the call. He realised she was right. But he was Christine Hunter's prey, so couldn't sit back and do nothing.

Cane called up an old friend, Richard Leach, who was a professor of Arab studies at Cambridge. He knew nothing about Cane's experiences. They had last spoken before his marriage to Valerie.

'Hello, Richard, hope everything is OK with you.'

'Nice to hear from you, old boy. Last time we spoke you were about to get married to that beautiful woman you found in Washington. I didn't hear any more. Did you tie the knot?'

'Yes, we did, but sadly she was killed in a car accident.'

There was a long silence.

'I'm so sorry to hear that. When did it happen?' he asked.

'A few months back, but I don't want to talk about it now if you don't mind. I'm ringing for some information about a young woman who graduated in Middle Eastern and Arabic studies about twelve years ago, named Clare Angel. Do you recall her? She is tall, good-looking with dark hair and brown eyes. I think she took a job with the police in London or some security agency.'

'I don't remember any woman by that name. Why do you want to know?'

'A friend of mine is trying to trace her, something to do with a family inheritance. He thought I studied at Cambridge instead of Oxford and might have some information.'

'I'll check my files and get back to you since I'm not in my office. I do, however, remember a Jayne Clayton-Browne who might fit your description. She was a top-level student and got a first, but we couldn't persuade her to stay on for a doctorate. Someone came along and offered her a job with good prospects and, as you know, at the time the political situation in the Middle East was getting worse and there was a demand for graduates who could speak Arabic. Her parents weren't keen on her taking the job and asked me to talk to her about staying on at the university. They were wealthy business people and were prepared to pay for her to continue.'

'Do you know who made the job offer?' Cane asked.

'No, but my guess it was those people at Vauxhall Cross.'

'Incidentally, do you know where her parents live?'

'Somewhere in Buckinghamshire, I think.'

'Thanks, Richard. We must get together some time for a drink.'

Cane had been careful not to say too much as he knew Richard was inquisitive and might want to find out why he was asking the questions. He didn't like lying about Valerie, but it was necessary to avoid anyone knowing they were on the fated plane. At least it confirmed his suspicions about Clare Angel. She was Jayne Clayton-Browne and worked for MI6. It would explain the alias, but even that was probably bogus. It seemed strange for such a young female agent to be placed on such an important high-level investigation. Perhaps John Nicholas hadn't been told about her identity since he wouldn't be too pleased to have MI6 involved.

If there was a Moscow connection to the plane bomb, then it would be within the jurisdiction of MI6. Clearly, Alicia had been trying to put him off from getting involved since she had her own private agent and hitman.

Cane fantasised that perhaps he could have a similar role with an MI6 agent. He had learned that all intelligence agencies had their own inner groups and contractors; it was like webs within webs that were almost impossible to unravel. The danger with such structures is that they can be easily infiltrated with enemy moles and become corrupted. Cane was reviewing his options before deciding what he would do. He then remembered the meeting with

Sheikh bin Abdullah in New York and pondered on whether to call him. Was he involved? Did he know about the Russian plan? The Sheikh certainly classed bin Laden and al-Qaeda as the enemy of the Saudis. They were the friends of the West and were unlikely to sanction blowing up a British aircraft.

Cane made the call. An answering service replied so he left his name and message that he would call back. It was a relief because he still had some uncertainty in his mind about the wisdom of making the call. He would wait to see what happened. Meanwhile, there was work to do.

CHAPTER 11

The Messenger, New York

Alicia's phone rang. She knew from the secure number who it was. 'Please come to New York now. Meet me at Winnies,' he said. That was the codename for a safe house owned by CTU. It was located on the beltway five miles outside New York.

The call sounded urgent and being so soon after their last rendezvous, she knew Curly must have important news.

She took the next flight to Kennedy, hired a SUV and drove to the house.

Being at least a mile from the nearest inhabited building and the same distance from a main road, the building was well hidden. The narrow, winding dirt-track leading up to the house made it only accessible with a four-wheel drive vehicle. It was late evening when she arrived. She parked at the side of the house next to a similar black SUV. She dialled a number and after three rings it stopped. She re-dialled. After six rings it stopped again. It was the signal to enter the house.

Curly gave her a cup of black coffee. This time he wasn't offering the usual invitation for sex. She was not disappointed since the crisis of the last few weeks had taken its measure. He put his cup on the table, gave her a kiss, squeezed her bottom and said, 'I brought you here because I want you to meet the man who gave Malik the signed letter purported to have come directly from bin Laden. I had to rough him up a little to persuade him to cooperate.'

'You mean he's here in this house?'

Curly pointed to the door leading to a room at the back of the house.

They entered a dimly lit room. Alicia saw a man bound and

gagged on a chair. His shirt was torn and soiled with dried blood from a cut on his face. His swollen eyes showed fear when Curly walked towards him holding his Glock 22.

'He hasn't talked much yet and won't tell me his name,' said Curly. 'I thought if you sent a photo back to CTU they might be able to identify him.'

'Where did you find him?' asked Alicia.

'Drinking in a New York bar, spending his blood money on drink and girls like all bad Muslims do when they find that life is better in the real world.'

'But how did you know he was in New York?' she asked.

'I have trusted contacts everywhere. I placed them all on alert after our last meeting. My New York one, who happened to be in the bar at the time, overheard him talking to a woman about the British plane bomb and condemning al-Qaeda. The plane bomb was the topic of conversation in the city. It was being assumed by everyone that al-Qaeda had carried out the act. The man was drunk and flashing lots of money about, which interested his woman companion. She beckoned over two men who were sitting in the corner of the bar. The two men rose from their seats, manhandled the Arab and took him outside. My contact followed them into an alleyway where he saw the man being beaten up and robbed. He rushed up to the men brandishing his pistol, shouting 'Police'. The two men ran off.

The Arab was shaken up, but seeing that his rescuer was of Middle Eastern origin, thanked him profusely. When my contact told him he wasn't a policeman but a sympathiser, they both went off to a coffee shop. He told him how pleased he was to meet someone who was against al-Qaeda. The man said he had worked as a courier for an Arab whom he now believed might be working for al-Qaeda. That statement rang alarm bells. He was clearly afraid for his own life.

My contact wanted to know more so told the Arab that he knew someone who could offer him protection. Still under the influence of alcohol and filled with fear, the man agreed to the suggestion. My contact called me. Since I was in New York at the time pursuing my own investigations and only ten minutes away, I drove to the coffee shop.

'By the time I arrived the man had sobered up and was getting suspicious of the strangers who were offering him help. He became agitated so I knew it was time to act. I surreptitiously injected him with a strong, fast-acting sleeping drug. Before it took effect we pushed him into my car, which was parked outside. I thanked my contact and paid him off. I drove the Arab to this safe house since it was the only one I knew we had in the vicinity. It took some time to remember where the key was hidden.

'I had to tie him up before asking him some questions. So far he hasn't been very cooperative. He could be the link man to the Russians if he was paid to be their contact person. He didn't have any identification as his wallet was stolen by the men who attacked him in the alley, but there was a phone number scribbled on a piece of crumpled paper in his pocket.'

Curly gave it to Alicia, who scanned it into her PDA. She also took a photo of the Arab and sent it to CTU asking for an identity check to be made and asked for the results to be sent back immediately.

Alicia looked at Curly. 'What are you going to do next?' she asked.

'Nothing until your people send a reply; then we'll have something to start with. If this man knows more than he's telling then we might be a step closer to knowing who was responsible for the blowing up of the plane, but we want all those involved, including the leaders.'

Alicia was aware that time was running out to find these people. The politicians were under public pressure for results. It was going to be a delicate balance between what was in the public interest and what the politicians wanted for political expediency.

The poor wretch tied to the chair listened to his captors and wondered about his fate. Mohammad bin al-Zarak had heard about the American torture techniques and what to expect when captured. He was not a devout Muslim, but had been educated in the Koran and initially believed in bin Laden's jihadist beliefs.

Bin al-Zarak had brought his family to New York from Kuwait after the Gulf War under an agreement between the US and the

Saudis because his home and business had been destroyed during the Iraqi occupation. At first it had been difficult to find work, but he eventually found part-time employment as a tourist guide for an Arab travel company in New York. The pay was poor, so living was hard. It was when escorting a Saudi group that he was approached by its leader, a man they called Mokhtar. The man offered him some private courier work, but it had to be kept secret from his employer. He was given a cell phone only to be used for the job. People would be sending him instructions by text, which he had to obey. He would be paid in cash for collecting and delivering sealed packages.

During the days that followed bin al-Zarak delivered them to hotels in Manhattan. The packages were addressed to room numbers; no names were written. Each hotel receptionist handed him an envelope containing money in exchange for the package. He didn't see the faces of any of the people who left or collected the packages or again the Arab who had first approached him. He was given two hundred dollars for every delivery. The financial rewards were too good to lose, so he did the job without asking questions. He had been warned by Mokhtar that if he told anyone about what he was doing his family would be punished. It was a form of blackmail. He knew the people who were requiring his services were capable of anything. He suspected they were involved in some sort of money-laundering crime syndicate. It was only later that he thought they might be part of a terrorist network. That worried him, but times were hard and he needed the money. The Americans had been kind to his family and had liberated his country so he felt guilty about what he was doing. But he was in too deep and feared the worst for his family if he went to the police.

Bin al-Zarak was particularly worried about the last package he was asked to deliver. It was larger than previous ones and had been brought to him a week before the ill-fated BA flight by a man whom he had not seen before. The man had sent him a text asking for a meeting in Central Park. He called himself Mohammed. He told bin al-Zarak that Mokhtar had given him the package because it contained valuable materials and had to be handed personally to a man in Room 17 at a hotel in downtown Manhattan. Mohammed insisted that bin al-Zarak telephoned a confirmation of delivery on a particular date. It was the date of flight BA66. He was given a special number to use, prefixed by a mixed alphabetic code. Believing the package might contain a bomb, bin al-Zarak resisted the temptation to open it. He was given a thousand dollars as a down payment and told that another thousand would be sent to him on completion of delivery. Clearly the package was special. He obeyed the instruction and duly went to the hotel address with the precious package. A tall, well-dressed Arab opened the door, accepted it and thanked him without saying another word. He noticed a first-class ticket for a BA flight on a table in his hotel room.

Malik had already been informed by KSM to be in New York at a given time and expect to receive a package for a special assignment. He was therefore expecting the package brought by bin al-Zarak, unaware it had been switched.

As agreed, bin al-Zarak made the call to the special number using the cell phone given to him by Mokhtar. It took a few minutes before the dialling tone stopped. An Afghan voice answered. Not knowing Pashto, he spoke in Arabic saying the package had been successfully delivered. After what happened later, bin al-Zarak was too afraid to tell anybody in fear for his family. But it confirmed his worst fears: that he may have unwittingly contributed to the worst terrorist atrocity in the history of aviation.

It wasn't long before Alicia received a message from CTU confirming the identity of the man who was tied to the chair. She confided in Curly. They decided to first try the friendly approach. Normally Curly's captors didn't get afforded that privilege.

Sensing that the woman who faced him knew his name, bin al-Zarak saw no point in not answering their questions.

Curly did the talking.

'You have two choices. You give us true answers to our questions and we shall be kind to you. If you lie, then we will punish you. Do I make myself clear? Nod if you understand. I am going to remove the gag, but not the blindfold and ask you some simple questions. I shall know if you lie.'

Interrogators test whether the prisoner is lying by first asking questions to which they have the answers.

'What is your full name?'

'Mohammad bin al-Zarak.'

'Who do you work for?'

'A tourist agency.'

'Are you a member of al-Qaeda?'

'No.'

'Let me ask you again.'

'Are you a member of al-Qaeda?'

'No, but I may have unknowingly worked for them.'

'Can you explain your answer?'

Bin al-Zarak decided it was his chance to tell the truth and prove he wanted to help his interrogators.

He told them about his part-time work for the Arab group and gave a detailed account of the last assignment.

'OK, we believe you, but we want to know more about the deliveries and to whom and where they were made.'

Bin al-Zarak hesitated, then replied, 'I am willing to tell you everything I know. I hate al-Qaeda and what they did to that plane over London, but I want a guarantee that you will protect my family.'

'We will do that if what you tell us is the truth.'

Bin al-Zarak asked, 'Who are you people? Are you FBI or the cops?'

'We can't tell you that. I am going to remove the blindfold and untie your hands, but if you try to escape, you will be shot. Do you understand?'

'Yes,' he replied.

Curly stood behind, so the prisoner didn't see his face, removed the blindfold and untied his hands.

He and Alicia stood in the shadow of the darkened room. The only light was directly on bin al-Zarak. They wanted to see his facial expressions when answering the questions. Curly offered bin al-Zarak a glass of water, which he eagerly drank, and a cigarette, but he didn't smoke. Curly started the interrogation while Alicia took notes using her PDA.

'OK, bin al-Zarak, why do you think you're here?'

'Because you think I'm a member of al-Qaeda,' he replied.

'And why should we think that?'

'Because I was talking about it and the recent terrorist act on the London plane.'

'Can you describe the man who first contacted you in the group?'

'He was short, fat and balding, clean shaven, although there were remnants of a beard. He wore a black Western-style suit. One person called him Mokhtar and he carried a cane marked with the initials KSM.'

Alicia almost cried with delight at the mention of the letters. She said to herself, *We've found him at last.*

'What did he ask you to do?'

'Just to act as courier to deliver small sealed packages to addresses in New York for $200 per delivery. I needed the money so didn't question the deal, which seemed an easy way to make a buck. He gave me a cell phone and told me it was only for receiving instructions on where I was to collect the packages and the addresses to where they were to be delivered.'

'Do you know what the packages contained?'

'No, but I think it was money.'

'Were you not tempted to open them since you say you needed money?'

'Yes, but I believed I was being watched and was warned that if I didn't obey the instructions then my family would suffer.'

'Did you ever see any of the people who gave you the instructions or who received the packages?'

'No, the messages were all text messages of the addresses at hotels in Manhattan. I just handed the packages to the desks at the hotels. They were well sealed and impossible to open without the recipient knowing.'

'How many packages did you deliver and over what period?'

'About four in total, but the last one was different; it was given to me personally by a man who called himself Mohammed who I have already told you about.'

'Do you have the cell phone? It's important we have the phone since it contains the code that may enable us to identify the callers.'

'No, it was stolen together with my wallet by the men who attacked me in the alley where your friend came to my aid. At the time I thought he was a cop; so did my attackers, who then fled with my property.'

'Can you give me the name of the woman you were with in the Blue Parrot Bar and would you recognise the men who attacked you?'

'I was drunk at the time, so everything is a little hazy, but I probably could. They were in the bar when I saw the woman beckon them. That was before they took me outside.'

Alicia made some phone calls.

'My people are on the way to the bar so we will need you to come with us to identify them when they are caught.'

Alicia looked excitedly at Curly.

'Can you describe the man at the hotel where you saw the airline tickets?' she asked.

'Yes, he was a tall, clean shaven Arab; smartly dressed in a dark blue business suit.'

Alicia clicked open her PDA and brought up a photograph.

'Is this the man you saw?'

'Yes, that's him without a doubt,' he said.

'It's Malik,' she said to Curly, who was looking at the screen. Immigration had photographed him at the airport and had copies of his passport when he had entered the US some time ago. Without his beard he looked younger, but the photo of him with bin Laden was conclusive. She also now had confirmation that Mokhtar was probably Khalid Sheikh Mohammed, the uncle of Ramzi Yousef, the bomber who attempted to blow up the World Trade Centre in 1993. He was one of bin Laden's key followers and thought to be behind the planning of most of al-Qaeda's bombing attacks, including the *USS Cole* and the hotels in Asia.

Bin al-Zarak was beginning to feel pleased that he had given his captors leads to the terrorists.

'What happens next?' he asked.

'That depends on you,' said Curly. 'For your protection we are keeping you under arrest for the time being.'

'What about my family?'

'Don't worry, we will see they are protected,' said Alicia, who was once again on the telephone.

Another SUV arrived at the house and bin al-Zarak was, to his surprise, handcuffed and taken away.

Alicia looked at Curly and could see a glint in his eye. 'Sorry, Sean, but we have much work to do. Lock up your passions for now and let's get the job finished. I'll put you on a promise for later.' That didn't really satisfy him or her, but they both knew what had to take priority. Bin al-Zarak had given them the best leads so far. Alicia suddenly looked worried.

'Sean, we are missing something here, something obvious.'

Looking puzzled, he said, 'What do you mean?'

'What we've just heard are two plots. Al-Qaeda is clearly planning something in the US and KSM, being their senior distributor of funds, is using money to set up a cell in New York. Malik, who worked for KSM, was part of that activity, but was duped into believing it was for the bombing of the BA flight. The package must have contained instructions and whatever else was required for that purpose. He must have thought they had come from KSM and bin Laden. Whoever is behind that found out about bin al-Zarak's courier service and used it. We need to find out the identity of Mohammed and his masters. If it's the Russians, then we have our proof.'

Curly smiled. 'The name Mohammed is like Smith and it's probably an alias anyway, so we need more than a name.'

Alicia said, 'Since cameras are everywhere in Central Park and on the roads going through it, let's see if there is any videocam footage of his meeting with bin al-Zarak.'

CTU had the authority to ask the police for any information so Alicia could demand to see any video footage in the interests of national security.

Alicia didn't want to bring in the FBI yet until she was sure about the facts, but now she was faced with a dilemma. Her special brief covered the BA terrorist attack and finding those responsible. But if a wider terrorist plot was being planned in New York or any other city then the FBI would have to be told. It was her duty to inform the Vice President, who would have no option but to invoke all the security services.

The videocam picture was not clear, but showed the man, Mohammed, giving the package to bin al-Zarak. His hooded head only showed part of his face, but it was enough to make comparisons with photos of known terrorists. The gigabits of information being processed on CTU's computers showed no matches with known persons.

Intelligence sources indicated that the man who could be behind the plot was Mullah Mohammed Omani, a well-known Taliban leader in Kandahar. He was known to be an al-Qaeda supporter and had fought against the Russians during the occupation. It was well known that many Afghans didn't like the presence of the Arabs under bin Laden in Afghanistan and sometimes, with the support of local chieftains, plotted to have them removed.

Alicia said, 'Omani couldn't have entered the US undetected so must have used a local supporter – the so-called Mohammed, to make the contact with bin al-Zarak. But others must have helped since the planners must have known about KSM's courier activities in New York to have been able to fool Malik. Perhaps after the London plane bomb, al-Qaeda found out about the Russian plot and their Afghan associates. It was likely that Omani was one of the three arrested and executed by the Taliban. It was possible that his Russian masters had left Afghanistan so the trail would now be cold. Perhaps someone in his village would know. There must have been some physical communication between them.'

Alicia realised that she would need the help of the CIA since it had contacts in the region who could find out. But that meant CTU would lose control because they would certainly do things their own way and claim any credit. There must be another way forward. While she was racking her brains, a call came through from one of her agents in New York. They had found the men who had beaten up bin al-Zarak. They were petty criminals known to the police and had been arrested. The agent had bribed them into handing back the phone if they confessed, thus saving court time and having a reduced sentence. Knowing the importance of the phone, he was bringing it back to CTU.

Alicia called Curly, who had booked in at a local hotel, and gave him the news.

'Why don't you come over until the phone arrives? We can spend an evening together. I will get a takeaway,' he said.

Leaving her options open, she replied, 'I'll let you know later.'

It was the first time Curly had actually asked her to his room. Usually it was a convenient rendezvous when they were working. She knew what was in his mind. Part of her wanted to go, the other part was the worry their relationship was moving beyond just sex.

KSM had become well known to the FBI and CIA. But his many aliases made tracking him difficult even with their large computer networks. However, the tiniest footprint could now be detected. His fingerprints and DNA had been left in many places and were in their possession. New analytical equipment made the analysis of DNA matching much faster and in that respect was now comparable to conventional fingerprinting, but more accurate owing to its uniqueness. Some clever analyst only had to match these up with an al-Qaeda terrorist act and they would have enough evidence to arrest and convict him.

While KSM pondered that, he suddenly realised he had left the phone with bin al-Zarak, who also knew the hotel addresses where the recipients had stayed. They hadn't used their real names at the hotels, but may have left their DNA and fingerprints. That had been a bad mistake. All hotels had cameras in their reception areas. The packages containing money for Mohamed Atta's four trained pilots had been received, so bin al-Zarak had done a good job, but he was now dispensable and posed a threat if the FBI or police found him. It was a task for the New York cell. But no trace of a body must be found. KSM didn't know it was too late.

In view of KSM's vulnerability, bin Laden decided to replace him with another Arab who wasn't on the FBI's wanted list. He was a wealthy businessman who had lived in the US for many years. He accepted the job on the condition that his identity was never revealed to anyone, even to KSM. He was given the codename Ali Baba, shortened to AB. His first task was to communicate with the leaders of al-Qaeda cells in the US to check on the plans and funding arrangements needed for the planned hijackings. He was satisfied that the New York, Washington and Boston cells had their plans well advanced.

All the cell members involved, except one, had passed through immigration without any problems. Concern was raised about the rejection of Ramzi Binalshibh in Florida because it had alerted the immigration authorities. It could have placed the whole mission in jeopardy. But slow bureaucratic systems in the US often meant different agencies in different states weren't linked up to a common database. Many Arabs and Asians had been refused entry because their paperwork wasn't in order. In Florida, thousands of Mexicans and Cubans were turned away every year with forged passports so the authorities were always overloaded. They didn't worry too much about one Arab's papers.

The diversionary plan was for two cells to carry out attacks on power stations in California. They would leave a trail so that the FBI would easily find them. Under interrogation they would eventually break down and say they were part of a campaign to disrupt US power networks and that attacks were planned in other states. The object was to make the FBI divert resources to guard the thousands of power stations and national grid lines. The intelligence agencies were expecting more attacks after the London plane bomb so al-Qaeda wanted them to believe that these were the targets and not aircraft. The FBI wouldn't be expecting al-Qaeda to attack another aircraft again so soon after London, particularly when tighter security now existed at all airports. If the diversion worked, it would help Mohamed Atta's nineteen aircraft hijackers to continue training without raising suspicion.

Alicia returned to her office at CTU in the morning after another night to remember with Curly. She enjoyed the sex as usual, but had to make it clear to him that she had no intention or desire to have a serious love affair. It would affect her job and, at present, that came first. Curly agreed, but told her when it was all over he would make her a proposition. She wasn't sure what he meant, but decided not to pursue it. She didn't understand how he possessed so much sexual energy. Most men were usually satisfied with one, and always after two sessions, but he wanted four, so she had little sleep and woke up the next day exhausted. She left him in bed and drove back to her office to be greeted by her PA with the comment, 'What happened to you, Alicia? You look like you've climbed a mountain.'

She smiled and ignored the comment but thought, *If only she knew how true that was.*

Her thoughtful colleague brought in a cup of strong black coffee.

Brad Walker, her senior analyst, knocked on the door with papers in his hand. Without saying a word, he wasn't a man of words but actions, he placed them on her desk.

They were marked: '**Analysis of bin al-Zarak's Cell Phone**'.

Noticing Alicia's tired face and rather dishevelled hair, he asked, 'Are you OK?'

'Yes, I had a late night,' she answered.

Looking briefly at the papers, she remarked, 'Have you been working on these all night?'

Feeling embarrassed, he replied, 'Not all night.'

He certainly looked better than she did.

'Bin al-Zarak's telephone arrived last night so I immediately had it checked for fingerprints and DNA and then analysed the calls it made. I'll let you read the results, but suffice to say they provided us with a goldmine of information. I've asked the team to follow up on some of the findings because they suggest we have a major terrorist activity being planned on US soil. You may need to consider talking to the Vice President.'

'Thank you, Brad, I will read it now,' she said, feeling bad about spending the night being bonked by Curly while her staff were analysing serious data. But she had to put that behind her now and get to work.

She started to read the report.

Attempts had been made to delete all previous calls on the cell phone, but the basic data was still stored in the memory. Digital cell phones had similar memory discs to those used in computers. The team at CTU simply plugged the phone into one of the specially programmed computers so it became an extension of the computer's hard disc. Every item of data was accessible, including every call ever made. It wasn't difficult to fill in the gaps when the outlines were discernible. It was like colouring a picture once the figures were drawn.

The team of analysts found fragments of calls made on the phone to other Arabs in the US. They were encrypted, but since CTU had some of the best crypto-analysts in the country it didn't take long for them to determine where the calls were made. Three names repeatedly came up: Mohamed Atta, al-Mihdhar and al-Hazmi. They all had US visas and were thought to be in the country. The link to KSM meant they were al-Qaeda suspects. But what where they doing in the US?

Many people had handled the phone. The fingerprints and DNA would take some time to analyse, but the most important information came from the prefix code given to bin al-Zarak by Mohammed for him to make the call. It had been identified as similar to the one used by the Russian members of The New Order that had enabled the CIA to track telephone calls during Project Whirlwind.

Brad dialled the same number bin al-Zarak had used. To his surprise it was answered by an Afghan woman. She spoke Pashto. He pressed the record button. He took a chance and asked to speak to Omani. She understood the name and started crying, muttering something he couldn't understand except for the words 'Taliban' and 'Russians'. Then he heard what sounded like a plea to help. She kept repeating the same phrase. Clearly she was too distressed to ask who was calling.

Using his basic knowledge of Pashto, Brad asked, 'staa num tsa dhe?' (What is your name?) There was no answer, he then said, 'ta da kom zaee ye?' (Where are you?)

He could faintly hear place names with the words 'Khan' and 'Kandahar', then the phone went dead. But he had collected enough information for the translators to work on. All CTU agents had been taught some basic Arabic and Pashto, but not enough to speak it fluently. Analysts were not required to speak languages, only to interpret them. That was the job of field agents.

Using intelligence, the interpreters concluded that the telephone conversation could have been with one of Omani's relatives, maybe a wife. She lived in Khan, a small village near Kandahar in Afghanistan. The telephone call went through a satellite receiver so it was likely the Taliban military were in the area. Bin Laden had spent millions of dollars setting up such receivers, but when he found out how easy it was for the US to track him, he abandoned them to the locals to use in return for human messengers.

Hundreds of telephone calls were made during the days following the London plane bomb. The whole Middle East was full of chatter. Using the codes and after a search through many hundreds of calls, CTU tracked one made to a house in Moscow from a satellite phone close to the Pakistan border. CTU's contacts in Moscow quickly came back with valuable information. They believed the house was located in the wealthy suburbs of the city and owned by a Gregori Seperkov.

Local intelligence also told them the Russians had spies working in Afghanistan. But was Seperkov behind the plane bomb? Gregori Seperkov had been a colonel in the Russian army and had served in Afghanistan at the time bin Laden and his followers helped the Mujahedeen push them out of the country. Many of Seperkov's fellow officers were captured after being ambushed in a mountain pass and butchered by tribesmen fighting with bin Laden, so had good reasons to hate the Arab Sheikh. He would also have good reasons to want to take retribution for the murder of his half-brother Leon by the CIA.

The team had also checked out the hotels where bin al-Zarak had made deliveries of the packages. They had the names of those who had received them, but none were in the CTU database. That wasn't surprising because they were all aliases. Al-Qaeda cell members used a wide range of aliases. The photos obtained from the hotels' videocam recordings were useful, even though they were hazy. All the hotel receptionists were interviewed and able to identify them against the video photos. Photo fits against known terrorists didn't reveal any suspects.

Slowly a picture was building up. It confirmed Alicia's suspicions that the Russians were responsible for the London plane bombing. They had tried to make it look like it was part of an al-Qaeda plot.

Two courses of action were now required. Alicia's own brief extended to working with the British MI6 and the police on the London bomb and eliminating the leading Russians involved. She would have to report the intelligence gathered on al-Qaeda's suspected US plot to the Vice President, who would have to involve the FBI and CIA since national security was once again at stake. The failures of the past could not be repeated.

Alicia spent the whole day drafting her report for the Vice President, but she made it clear that she wanted CTU kept in the loop. She expected the Vice President and the President to agree, but the President would have to deal with the complex politics involved; unfortunately, it was something in which he lacked experience. In the current administration it was the Vice President and his advisors who held the power and made most of the decisions.

It was the end of the day. Alicia had just finished her report when Curly called. He had just received news from an old MI5 colleague that an IRA man, named Paddy O'Grady, whom he had helped convict, had just been released from prison after serving part of a life sentence. He had told a mate in the prison that when he got out he was going to find and kill Sean O'Brien and his two sisters for shooting his brother. The man had murdered Sean's mother and father in Belfast back in the 1980s. O'Grady didn't know where to find Curly, but did know that his two sisters, Tracey and Maria, worked at a London West End night club. He intended to use them as bait. Curly told Alicia he had to protect the only two remaining members of the O'Brien family so was flying immediately to London.

Alicia briefed Curly about the Russians and the possible al-Qaeda plot in the US. She told him that it was likely CTU would have to work with the CIA and the FBI since the US was under threat from a group outside the US. She asked him to stay on in London after he had dealt with his personal business since there could be a London connection to the Russians and suggested, if he had the time, to call and see Paul Cane. Curly wasn't sure about the wisdom of revealing himself to Cane, but told her he would keep it in mind. He booked a business-class ticket to London with American Airlines under the assumed name of Patrick Ryan.

CHAPTER 12

The Plan

Alicia called Angel at MI6 using a secure telephone line and updated her on the latest intelligence on the Russians. She told her about a possible al-Qaeda attack being planned in the US so would be working full-time with the CIA and FBI. It was therefore decided that Angel would follow up the leads on the Russians through her own contacts and not travel to Washington. She didn't mention that Curly, her own unofficial secret agent, would be in London. Angel saw it as a message that the US were handing over the work to MI6.

Angel called BS.

'We need to talk immediately,' knowing that whatever BS was doing, he would give her priority. It gave her a sense of power over a man that most feared. She enjoyed it.

BS beckoned Angel to sit down on his favourite black settee and offered her tea and biscuits. Nobody else was given such treatment, but she was special. The more he looked at her, the more he realised how much she resembled the woman he should have married. Angel started to brief him on the information from CTU.

He listened intently and said, 'So the Americans want us to handle the London plane bomb investigation. It makes sense since the plane was destroyed on our soil. It looks like they are more worried about their own al-Qaeda threat. Alicia Garcia is very politically astute. She knows her President has to be seen helping us, but also knows we will do things our own way.'

Angel interjected, 'She has given us some good leads so has made her contribution.'

'That's true, but we already have our own intelligence on

126

Seperkov. We've had him under surveillance in Moscow for some time. Last week, however, he disappeared. He was last seen going into the Kremlin and didn't come out. We had him placed on our watch list owing to large cash transfers he'd made to a UK bank. There were suspicions he might be planning to secretly enter the UK so we put immigration officials at airports and ports on alert. Seperkov and his cousin Alexander Larinko are known to frequent the Kremlin. It could easily arrange for Seperkov to enter the UK through diplomatic channels.'

'But why would he want to come here?' she asked.

'That's a good question. I can only assume he might feel safer in England in some disguise. Very few people actually know what he looks like and, of course, he is unknown here. He has many enemies in Russia and if he or his organisation were responsible for the London bomb, then he will know al-Qaeda and our agents will be out to get him. There would be no better place to hide than in the enemy camp. Our intelligence provided conclusive evidence that his half-brother Leon Seperkov and Boris Sudakov had acquired a number of stolen suitcase bombs from the Ukraine just after that country broke away from the old Soviet Union. Together, they set up a small factory on the outskirts of Moscow to modify and service the devices. It was an illegal operation, but with high-level protection no one bothered them. We know two of these were the millennium bombs smuggled into London in December 1999. One had been converted into a miniaturised atomic bomb, but then you know about that from the top secret report I gave you. If there is a link with Christine Hunter through a reincarnation of The New Order, then Seperkov might want to see her. Catching them both would be a bonus. She could, however, prove to be his Achilles heel. As you know we haven't seen Hunter since she vanished into the house in Kensington Palace Gardens.'

BS noticed Angel looking thoughtful.

'I have a problem. The house is named Kensington House. I found out it's owned by a Russian company and the three floors are rented out to individual tenants. My stepfather, Norman

Goodfellows, owns the company contracted to manage the tenancies. The company, an estate agency, manages many of the large houses in the area that have been rented or leased to overseas clients. If Goodfellows or my mother find out that I'm involved then the game's up for me. She thinks I work as an interpreter for an export company in the city. As you know, it's one of my fronts. My mother and I haven't seen much of each other since she remarried. I loved my father. He was a good man. When he died my mother gave me little comfort. She was soon out and about and eventually met Goodfellows. I disliked him right from the start. It was the way he looked at me. Once he tried it on and I kicked him hard in the groin. He never tried it again. Hopefully it ruined his sex life. I told mother, but she didn't believe me so that was it. I had just started to work for MI6 in the back office so it was easy to disappear from her life.'

BS felt even more uneasy now he had heard about the family rift and said, 'I'm sorry to know about you and your mother. Are you sure you want to continue with this mission?'

'Absolutely, I'm taking Bob Bradley with me to give him some field experience. He will use the alias Alex Newman. He will take the lead and, to keep a low profile, I will be his assistant. Bob has arranged with the Borough Council and the police for us to make an official visit to Kensington House to check on security arrangements for a forthcoming foreign royal visit to the nearby palace. It really comes under the domain of the special police unit that guard these residences, but since Kensington House is privately owned, then it's not strictly part of their job.'

'I didn't know about any royal visit,' he said, looking rather surprised.

'No, it's fictitious, but the residents don't know that and I want to get into the house and plant some bugs. Being one of the few private residences located near to the embassies, it's one in which we don't yet have any electronic surveillance.'

'Be careful – you know it's illegal,' he said.

'I know, but since when has that been a problem for MI6?'

BS admired her initiative, but was beginning to worry about

the chances she might take; but he had given her the job so had to live with the consequences.

'OK, but keep me in the loop. Do you have all the resources you need?'

'Yes,' she said, and was about to leave the room when she turned back.

'There is one other problem: John Nicholas's people. I thought they were keeping the house under surveillance. Shouldn't we inform them about what we are doing?'

'Leave that to me. I will talk to Nicholas since they tracked Hunter to the house. But don't get caught, otherwise it will cause us great embarrassment.'

Angel nodded, but didn't believe BS would talk to Nicholas.

BS did call John Nicholas at Scotland Yard and explained Angel's plan. He wasn't pleased that such a decision had been taken without consultation. After much argument, Nicholas agreed to help, but wanted the agents to be wired with cameras and microphones and to use the control centre set up in a SUV positioned on Kensington Palace Road. It was to be a joint operation.

Officially BS knew the police should be involved, but was still worried about enemy moles. The people they were chasing were likely to be members of the so-called Billionaires Club, who could buy or blackmail anyone they wanted. They knew they were above the law – that's how they survived. Sending them to prison was not an option. The only option was elimination. They all knew that, so their survival stakes were high, which made them dangerous. Christine Hunter had already proved she was determined to continue her mother's ruthless criminal activities and relationship with the Russians, so was on the wanted list.

BS had an instinctive feeling that things were going to get nasty. He was in the job because of his instincts. It was an inherent quality, not one that could be learned from any training manual. He had stuck his neck out by thrusting a relatively young woman into a dangerous assignment. Had he done it for personal reasons?

A number of suspects lower down the chain were under surveillance. Two baggage handlers at Schiphol Airport and three members of an al-Qaeda cell in London had been arrested, but so far none had revealed any useful information about those further up the chain of command. People lower in the chain usually commit criminal acts for money.

BS was fortunate because he was a beneficiary of a society that was structured to give advantage to the rich and powerful. Twentieth-century socialism did force the state to provide benefits for the poor and raised the living standards for millions of people. But it created a large middle class, which in turn fed an enlarged upper class. Everybody aspired to have what the rich land-owning classes possessed. But once they achieved wealth, they joined the club and cared less for those below; that was human nature.

Capitalism created the wealth that ultimately provided the tax revenues to government, thus enabling it to support the welfare state. But a large share of the revenue came from overseas investors. It was why members of the so-called Billionaires Club were welcomed into the country and allowed a degree of freedom. The Russian criminal elements were now exploiting that freedom. But when they attempted to destroy the very environment and infrastructure enjoyed by the rich, they became the enemy. The London plane bombers had done just that, so the culprits had to hide even from people who would have normally given them sanctuary.

Now, at the dawn of the twenty-first century, the governments and security services were faced with a new threat – the rise of religious fundamentalism based on early century ideologies. It was not only a threat to democracy, but also to those rich and powerful groups who prospered under it. Powerful countries like the US and Britain have well-established police, law enforcement and intelligence agencies to combat them. Afghanistan, Pakistan, the Yemen, Somalia and others have corrupt systems that became vulnerable to the fundamentalists. Iran and Iraq had already succumbed.

Eastern Europe, now free from communism, already had many countries where Mafia-like gangs were operating freely. They had infiltrated the police and the Civil Service. After the collapse of the Soviet Union when poverty drove many people to crime, ex-KGB members saw their opportunity to set up the secret infrastructure to protect Mafia gangs. These quickly spread to old Soviet bloc countries.

The only way to break up the growth of such gangs in the UK was to find and remove the leaders. But BS wasn't naive enough to believe he could completely eliminate them from the world, but at least he could try to stop them from operating in the UK. It would mean using all his trusted political contacts and old friends to do it.

BS called his old friend Clifton Davenport and briefed him on events. Davenport agreed to speak to Oleg Detroski to find out more about the tenants of Kensington House, but would warn him to not involve Voss. Further checks carried out on Voss's past criminal connections had raised concerns.

CHAPTER 13

A Busy Day
9 am, 2 June

Sean (Curly) O'Brien used one of his many aliases and a fake passport to enter Britain. He was now Patrick Ryan, a wealthy Irish businessman. His initial reluctance to go to London was overcome by the serious threat made to the two remaining members of his family, his sisters, Tracey and Maria. He knew that Paddy O'Grady, the man who had made the threats, was a ruthless republican, who would stop at nothing to get his revenge for the killing of his brother, even though, at the time, it was justified. Strong family bonds existed amongst Irish Catholics. Curly knew this was a personal vendetta – it was going to be a one-to-one encounter.

It was a bright, clear June morning when the taxi left Heathrow and took the M4 to London. Some years had passed since Curly had set foot in what was considered to be the most vibrant city in the world. Watching the cabbies manoeuvring around the streets of London, the shoppers and tourists enjoying the city sights, made even an Irishman feel homesick. Eventually the taxi arrived at the door of the hotel. He was greeted by frocked doormen, who were surprised to see he only had carry-on luggage that he wanted to keep in his possession. Patrick Ryan booked in at the Connaught Hotel in Mayfair, one of the most expensive and prestigious five-star hotels in London. Being located in the heart of Mayfair, it was close to the White Flamingo Casino Club; a fashionable venue for the rich and famous, where the O'Brien sisters did their nightly show.

Curly had telephoned his sisters before he left Washington. They hadn't seen him for five years. Back then, it had been during a brief visit to Belfast when they were making their names as singers in local hotels and pubs. He didn't know their home address in London so had to call them at their club to let them know when he was arriving. They knew his visit meant trouble. Having not seen their brother since he left the army, they always assumed he did some kind of security work. Curly didn't make social visits. There had to be a good reason for him to be coming to London at such short notice. He had hinted on the telephone that someone from Northern Ireland was searching for him and might try to use them as bait, so to be careful. He gave Tracey, the older of the two sisters, his coded cell phone number. Remembering the horrendous murder of their parents by the IRA and its aftermath, they guessed it had something to do with the man their brother had shot for the crime. It was one of the reasons why they had left Belfast. Since their husbands didn't want to leave the city, the sisters eventually divorced them and started new singing careers in London's theatre land and clubs. Currently they shared an apartment in St John's Wood, partly paid for by the club. Tracey gave Curly her cell phone number and her address, but asked him not to go there, but to meet somewhere else in private. The sisters didn't want men seen at the apartment. It was one of the conditions imposed by their employers. There was a strict security system in place to protect the women. Curly agreed, but was worried that the man who wanted to kill him might have already found out where they lived. It was important not to involve the police, since it was a personal matter and incumbent on him to deal with it. After taking a shower, Ryan made a phone call.

'When you arrive, come straight to Room 467 on the fourth floor of the Connaught Hotel.'

Still dressed in his bath robe, Ryan opened the door to a tall man of aristocratic stature. Without saying anything, the man went into the room carrying a small black case, which he placed on the bed. He opened it to display a modified Sig Sauer P228 revolver, complete with bullets and a silencer. It was a small light-weight gun that could easily be concealed under clothing. Curly gave the man an envelope containing £2,000 in old untraceable bank notes.

He smiled and left the room as silently as he had entered it. Firearms couldn't be brought into countries, so when required, Curly used secret arms dealers whom he trusted, who, for exorbitant prices, sold weapons to order. There were limitless supplies of guns in most countries if the right money was available. Like drugs, it was a ruthless but profitable trade for the dealers. The few policemen who managed to penetrate the trade had short lifespans. The dealers protected themselves and always used well-disguised couriers. Their clients had to be rigorously identified and money collected before handing over the weapons. Guns were always imported and not traceable or ever returned. They were not available to street gangs or petty criminals.

Curly liked the P228. He had used it when in the SAS. Instructors taught their pupils to fire at the enemy's mouth; doing so blew out the spinal cord and instantly prevented the brain from sending messages for the rest of the body to react; important, if the enemy had a loaded gun or was about to detonate a vest bomb. Its short range meant the bullet usually stayed in the body and didn't harm anybody close or behind the target. Special bullets that explode on impact were often used, but they made a sickly mess of the body. For Curly, using a gun, even with a silencer, was the last resort because it was obvious the victim had been murdered. Whenever possible, he made the death look accidental to minimise any police investigation. Hit-and-run road accidents or falling off high-rise buildings were favourites if they could be arranged. This time he knew his assailant would want to see him at the point of death. He was dealing with an ex-IRA soldier who faced and embraced death almost as much as the jihad fanatics, so his choices would be limited.

Curly decided first to get some rest and then find a way of visiting the Mayfair club to see the girls. He wanted a discreet service so went to the hotel concierge for help. The flash of a bundle of hundred pound notes and a gold American Express card always softened attitudes should he find them uncompromising. For the purpose of gaining entry to the club he would become Patrick Ryan, Head of Security for Sheikh Armani of Qatar. The concierge would make the calls and travel arrangements for their VIP guest.

2 pm

It was a hot sunny afternoon when the black BMW passed through the security gates of Kensington House on Kensington Palace Gardens Road and drove up to the ornately panelled wooden front door. A voice at the gate had raised the barrier, obviously expecting them. The council had sent a letter to Goodfellows explaining why security checks on the property had to be carried out.

The door was opened by a well-dressed man who introduced himself as Robert Palmer, the Estate Manager. Bob Bradley introduced himself as Alex Newman, a senior council official, and his assistant Pamela.

Palmer told them that all the tenants were out of the country and the house had been unoccupied for some months, but they were welcome to review the property. His statement immediately raised Angel's suspicions since she knew Hunter's Mercedes was seen entering the grounds. Noting Angel's raised eyebrows, Newman asked if any persons other than the tenants and his own company staff had access to the property through the security gates.

After a short, but noticeable, delay in replying, he answered, 'I'm not aware of any permission or access codes being given to persons other than those you mentioned.'

'But could any of the tenants give such permission?' Alex asked.

'No, we would have to be informed. That was part of the contract,' he replied.

'We would like to look around the grounds at the rear before we go into the house,' said Angel.

Palmer smiled. 'Be my guests.'

The two agents walked to the ornate gardens at the rear of the house. The garden was surrounded by high wooden fences, in front of which were tall conifer trees. Security cameras and lights were mounted on poles at the edge of the lawn. There was no easy way

135

to enter or leave from the outside without being seen. Angel noticed the level of the patio and lawn was raised above that of the ground floor of the house. It looked odd and didn't fit with the architecture of the building. At the side of the building was a large annex, presumed to be a double garage. Newman walked over to it and peered through the window, but no cars could be seen. Nicholas had told them the grey Mercedes had been seen entering through the front security gate and had not left. So where was it now?

They saw Palmer looking at them through the window with a camera in his hand. Angel had put on a blonde wig and spectacles. It wasn't the most brilliant disguise, but would help fool anybody looking at a photograph. She knew the house would be surrounded by cameras. Newman had also covered his fair hair with a black wig and stuck on a very amateurish-looking moustache. They pretended to be making notes about the lights and cameras in the garden when Newman told Angel about the garage.

Turning her back so Palmer couldn't see her talking, she said, 'There is something not right about this building and its garage. Can you ask Palmer if we can look in the garage?'

They strolled back to the front of the house. Palmer was waiting at the door.

'What exactly are you looking for?' he asked.

Newman put on his official government voice. 'You must have seen the letter sent to your company by the council, explaining the reasons for our visit.'

Not wishing to show his ignorance, Palmer simply said, 'Yes, of course, but if there is something you are specifically looking for, then I may be able to help.'

'Can we look in the garage?' asked Angel.

It was the first time she had spoken as she wanted Palmer to believe she was the underling, the assistant to Newman. She enjoyed watching him take a leading role. He clearly liked it.

'It's empty. There is nothing to see,' he snapped.

His polite manner suddenly changed. He thought, who were these civil servants poking their noses into his clients' private property? What were they really looking for? Why hadn't they asked to see the inside of the house? All these questions raced through his mind. He knew his boss, Norman Goodfellows, would want a full report. He made sure the perimeter cameras were on to record the movement of his visitors. He didn't know what was in the garage.

Angel detected a slight air of suspicion in his voice. They had to be careful, but she wanted to see if a car had recently been in the garage. It was also an opportunity to plant a miniature videocam with a high-powered transmitter. She checked that her personal one was working and sending signals back to the hidden SUV.

'We are getting everything clear,' said an excited voice.

The guys in the monitoring vans loved their jobs. They had all the gadgetry available and could communicate with the outside world in warm comfort knowing they were rarely in danger. They were very often the life-savers to agents out in the field if back-up was urgently required.

Palmer activated the electrically driven door. It slowly moved upwards showing an unusually clean, empty garage. There was no sign that anything had ever been stored or placed inside. Most strange for garages where cars were supposed to be kept.

'When was the garage last used?' asked Newman.

'Not for years. The tenants, when they are here, use chauffeur-driven cars.' That immediately flashed up a red flag in Angel's mind.

Palmer stood outside while Angel walked around the interior. She noticed a small gap between the sidewalls and the concrete floor. Fitted to the end wall was a wooden panel that stretched across its whole length. The floor also seemed soft for solid concrete. She was convinced there was something underneath, perhaps another floor. She made her suspicions known to Newman, but whispered to him not to say anything to Palmer. He either didn't know or, if he did, was concealing something. She took some photos of the fittings around the walls and scraped up, what looked like, soot from the floor and placed it in a small polythene bag.

Newman thanked Palmer and asked to see inside the house. The furniture in the ground floor apartment was very basic and looked as though it hadn't been used, almost like a show house. They looked around the apartments on the other two floors and saw a similar sight.

'How often do the tenants live in these?' asked Newman.

'They are two Russian families and a Hungarian family who only use them for their few visits to London each year,' replied Palmer.

It seemed strange that these people, who were obviously wealthy, didn't use hotels. The agents saw no cameras, surveillance devices or telephones in the house. Angel was able to fix a micro-videocam into a light fitting in one of the bathrooms. It was so small that only a specially designed scanner would detect it.

Before they left, Palmer asked again why it had been necessary for them to make an inspection of the property. Again they referred him to the letter sent to his boss, which he clearly hadn't seen. Palmer was obviously suspicious. If he was concealing something then those involved would soon know about it. The agents would have to work fast if they were to find out the secrets that lay beneath the garage floor.

Their first task would be to check the plans of the house at the time of building and the local council approval of any subsequent structural alterations. Many of the houses in that part of London were listed buildings and changes were rarely approved. But the owners were very rich so could buy anything they wanted, including council officials.

Christine Hunter's Mercedes never left the property, so the only place it could be was underground and the garage was the most likely point of entry. They had a decoder to bypass the gate security if they wished to enter the garage unseen at night. A plan was already formulating in Angel's mind.

3.30 pm

Bradley drove the car away from the house and parked in a side street. Angel called BS informing him of her suspicions and told him she intended to go back into the house in the early hours of the morning. BS told her to hold back and await further instructions since there were political implications that had to be dealt with before further actions could be taken.

BS looked at a report from Davenport relating to his conversation with Detroski. The Russian believed Kensington House could be a safe house for wealthy illegal immigrants. It was owned by a Russian company registered in Moscow with connections to the Kremlin. He was more worried about its close proximity to the Russian Embassy. Under diplomatic immunity, people could enter the country through the embassy and migrate out into London. The Foreign Office was supposed to be informed, but it was doubtful if everybody was tracked.

Detroski was used to daily death threats, but recently they had stopped. It was this sudden change that worried him. His bodyguard, Voss, was also acting strangely, suggesting that his boss should consider leaving London and staying at his country mansion, Riverside, located on the River Thames in Berkshire. It was a secluded retreat very few people knew about, almost a safe house, built in the eighteenth century for one of Queen Anne's favourite courtiers. Unfortunately, Mrs Detroski didn't like it; she preferred London, so rarely made a visit.

Davenport told BS that Detroski had people in Moscow making discreet enquiries. It had been established that small metal fragments salvaged from the London plane's luggage section matched samples found from one of the millennium bombs. There was no doubt they were manufactured at the same place – Seperkov's factory. It was believed they came from bomb containment casings. In the violent explosion, the casings were blown apart so quickly they didn't melt. Using electron microscopy, forensic scientists were able to match micro-sized particles. They were also able to pinpoint the location of the bomb in the aircraft hold. It had been loaded at Schiphol Airport. The confession to the loading of the extra case by a baggage handler arrested at the airport also confirmed it.

After checking that their camera photos and videos had been processed successfully, the two agents went back to their respective apartments. Angel was disappointed that the counter-terrorist unit at Scotland Yard had to be involved. It placed her in a difficult position. The finding of Christine Hunter and any Russians involved was her project. She could take the initiative and go to the house alone, but it was likely that whoever had been in the car would have already been warned by Palmer or Goodfellows if they were involved.

4 pm Knightsbridge

Just a few miles away in Knightsbridge, Paul Cane was contemplating how he could get into Kensington House. He didn't know about Angel's visit that afternoon. He was about to take a walk to Kensington Gardens when Alicia called him on his cell phone. Fortunately, it was the one item he forgot to take to New York so it was saved from destruction. He had lost everything else on the plane, including his precious laptop computer. Fortunately, all his files were backed up on his desktop.

'I hope you are well, Paul, and getting plenty of rest. I am calling to let you know that one of my people, whom you've never met, is in London on private business. I have asked him to look you up so don't be surprised if you receive a strange call. He has to keep his identity secret so may have to do security checks before he will meet you. You have common enemies who may not be far away. He is fully briefed on the terrorist situation and knows all about the Russians. Remember that you're not James Bond and I don't want to see either of you taking unnecessary risks.' Before he could say anything, she abruptly rang off. Cane suspected it was for security reasons.

He detected an unusual tenderness in the last remark she made. Was the person she mentioned more than just her hitman? Cane knew she had a soft spot for a man known as Curly. If he hadn't met Valerie, he wondered if they might have made it together. Suddenly, Cane's frustration was replaced by a feeling of excitement. It took the phone call to bring it on. Could he team up with Alicia's man and find the Russians responsible for the bomb? It was clear that MI5, MI6, the CIA, etc. and John Nicholas's people had no intention of involving him. Even if they wanted to, they couldn't, since he had no official position. Anyway he was classified as unfit and a protected witness to the nation's worst terrorist crime. No one would want him involved in the investigation. The recent act might be linked to the millennium bombs, but very few people knew about it.

Counter terrorism was now big business, both for the perpetrators and the seekers. It was estimated that in Britain and the US more than ten thousand people were working directly in the security field and many more indirectly. The biggest problem still remained. How was all the intelligence being gathered to be used and by whom? Most of the terrorist groups in the world were fragmented. Al-Qaeda still presented the largest threat. They needed success against the US, who they deemed the Evil Satan, to prove to their supporters that they could deliver jihad and so attract more followers. But as history showed, success attracts people who will often use it to further their own aims. While he had been speaking to Alicia, Cane noticed a light flashing on his apartment phone signalling that a text message was arriving. He eagerly switched on the screen to see the text.

It read: *'If you want to find Christine Hunter, then go to the gates of Kensington House at 7 pm.'*

Cane couldn't believe what he had just read. Had someone been listening to his conversation with Alicia? Was it a hoax? Was someone trying to get Hunter caught? Was it a trap? Should he call Nicholas? He was in a state of confusion. His journalistic instincts prevailed. He would go alone. But he had to shake off his protection officer. After his conversation with Alicia, he realised that would be unwise, but he had to do it.

Nicholas received a call from his observation unit that a grey Mercedes was leaving Kensington House and heading south out of London. All units were put on alert and a helicopter fitted with an infrared camera was scrambled. Information was channelled through to Scotland Yard's control room. As agreed, a feed was relayed to the MI6 building and BS was immediately informed.

Angel's phone woke her up from a shallow sleep. She switched on her computer and connected into the Agency's secure system. It wasn't long before clear pictures appeared on her screen. They were of a car containing the heat signature of two occupants, racing toward the M3 motorway. It was accompanied by the helicopter observer giving a running commentary. This was not the expected discreet surveillance operation, but the full blown police operation one saw on TV programmes. It was exactly what BS didn't want, but knew once Scotland Yard got involved, all hell would break loose. The helicopter was a bad move. It wasn't exactly a silent observer. Those in the car would know they were being followed. Someone had devised the diversion. Angel soon realised this and guessed what had happened. Her presence at the house had been reported to whoever had something to hide. That implicated Palmer and Goodfellows. Had they tipped off the owners of the car? The runaway car was a decoy. They knew they were being watched and had devised an escape plan. But billionaire criminals and terrorists didn't need to act like gangsters who had just committed a bank robbery.

Most of the intelligence information and observations gained were based on assumptions and speculations. Since the first sighting of the Mercedes in Central London, no faces had actually been seen. The police were chasing ghosts.

Soon after the Mercedes had left the house, Nicholas ordered a SWAT team to enter it and the grounds. Some went to the garage and the others into the house. As expected they found the garage floor could be lowered to a basement area that extended under the house. The area had living accommodation and an office. The grey

Mercedes had been parked under a false floor when the MI6 agents made their visit. The rooms in the house had been swept clean and little evidence was found of who might have been occupying it. The most disturbing fact was a long partially-lit passage, which led from the underground garage to another property on the far side of the road. That property was the Russian Embassy. This gave access for people to move between the embassy and the house.

The Russian Ambassador was contacted by the Home Office in the early hours of the morning, who, after knowing the facts, gave permission to the police to come onto the property and search the grounds. The search revealed an entrance to a tunnel under the floor of a garden storage shed located about seventy metres from the house. There was evidence that someone had recently used the tunnel. An immediate denial of knowledge of its existence was made by the ambassador, who then offered maximum assistance to any investigation. A message was immediately sent to Moscow.

Tracking the Mercedes continued for thirty minutes until it left the M3 and took the road to the town of Guildford where it disappeared into an underground car park just outside a shopping centre. Unable to be seen by the helicopter, the two occupants abandoned the car and scattered in different directions. The police arrived within minutes and barricaded the entrance and sealed all the exits, but failed to arrest anyone. They had the Mercedes, but its occupants had just vanished without a trace. A massive hunt was mounted of the surrounding area, but no one was found. The operation had been well planned and executed. It was embarrassing for John Nicholas. Everything had gone wrong and the one opportunity of catching one of the most wanted criminals had been lost.

As Angel watched the failure of the operation, it reinforced her own belief that Hunter and the Russians were probably still in the London area and had escaped through the Russian Embassy. She called BS, who agreed with her assumption and immediately ordered all the CCTV footage taken on all the roads leading from the embassy during the last two days to be requisitioned and sent to him personally. It was time for MI6 to sort out the mess. He knew questions would be asked by the PM and the Home Secretary at the NCTC meeting called for 8 am the next day. The Russian Ambassador was also summoned to the Foreign Office to explain why he didn't know about the secret passage hidden in the grounds of his embassy. Things were made worse when the media learned about the car chase and wanted answers to questions. The police promised that a statement would be made later. Everything now depended on the outcome of the NCTC meeting.

6 pm

Armed with his camera and the cell phone Alicia had given him in the US, and with some trepidation, Cane set off across Hyde Park walking in the direction of Kensington Palace Gardens Road. The summer sun in a clear sky had made the air dense and uncomfortable, but it brought out walkers to the park. Theatres were setting up for summer shows and a carnival atmosphere pervaded. The traffic was heavy on Kensington Road and through the park. People were queuing to buy tickets for the Albert Hall summer shows.

Cane's leg was reminding him there was still some way to go before he would be fit enough to do any strenuous work. Robert had suggested a holiday in France using the Euro train, since flying might be off the agenda for a while. Cane hated being dependent on anybody so wanted to wait until his body had healed before travelling again. What was now happening made it impossible for him to relax. His active brain was in control of his body.

Within walking distance there were possibly people who wanted him dead. He went through the secure gate at the entrance to the Kensington Palace Gardens Road. After passing an armed protection officer standing outside one of the embassies, he made his way along the tree-lined avenue. It was the location of many foreign embassies and the Royal Palace so photography was forbidden. Cane noticed the many black SUVs with darkened windows parked in and around the embassies. They were used by the security police and private firms for moving their charges about. No markings could be seen so most vehicles were indistinguishable. The big question was, would Christine Hunter show herself? He started to think it was someone's idea of a cruel joke, but why ask him to go to a specific place? He wished he had brought his Beretta, but if the police stopped him, he would be in real trouble since he didn't possess a licence.

Kensington House where the Mercedes had been tracked was just a few hundred metres in front of him. On the opposite side was the impressive building of the Russian Embassy. Walkers were not encouraged to stop and stare. Everyone was being watched by security cameras. Looking at the large impressive houses he could see why it was called Billionaires Row. Cane was tempted to use his camera, but didn't want the police descending on him asking a lot of questions. Looking at the house where Hunter's Mercedes was seen to enter, he wondered how difficult it would be to find a way into the house. He had been walking with the aid of his stick for over an hour and needed a rest. He had convinced himself that exercising his leg muscles was the fastest way to accelerate the repairing process for his broken leg. He was no medic so it might actually be doing the reverse. He scanned the area outside the embassy, but couldn't see any sign of the so-called Christine Hunter. But he wasn't sure what he was looking for and began to realise what a fool he had been to believe the text. Was he the subject of a cruel practical joke? The time was exactly 7 pm. He walked further along the road, noticing there were few other people out walking. He suddenly felt vulnerable.

Hearing footsteps from behind, Cane turned around just in time to see a man coming towards him. Seconds later the man knocked his arm. He heard a muttered apology from the man, who continued walking. Cane couldn't see his face, but thought little of it until he felt a pain in his left arm. It progressed into his left side producing a numbness. He looked up, but no one was to be seen. The man who hit him had vanished. Several people could be seen in the distance on the other side of the road and two others, a man and woman about twenty metres in front.

Cane began to feel dizzy. He wasn't sure why he did. Perhaps it was a panic reaction. He used his stick to steady himself. Without knowing why, he fumbled in his pocket for his cell phone and switched it on. He pushed the panic button, which Alicia had installed on the phone for him to use on Project Whirlwind. It sent a signal to base when immediate assistance was required. But it was designed for use in the US. He didn't know if it would work in the UK. He didn't know what else to do or why he did it.

He saw a car come out of the Russian Embassy compound and turn onto the road towards him. It passed by and stopped just a few metres ahead. His head was now spinning. He felt like he was falling into a bottomless pit. Then everything went dark and he passed out. Before he hit the ground two figures emerged from the car and bundled him onto the back seat. The car went towards Kensington town centre. It happened so quickly that the few people on the road hadn't noticed anything.

7.10 pm

The black SUV left London on the M4 and headed west. Slumped on the back seat, Cane was slowly regaining consciousness. He was covered by a blanket and felt the presence of someone else on the seat next to him. He felt in his pocket for his cell phone, which still had the red LED glowing. It was transmitting to the satellite. It was surprising that nobody had bothered to search him, but everything happened so quickly. He remembered falling to the ground and feeling someone dragging him into the car. Alicia had taught him well, but the US cavalry was unlikely to come to his rescue.

2.10 pm CTU, Washington

A vigilant operative at CTU saw a red alert light on her screen. She wasn't sure what it meant, but someone who had one of their special cell phones needed immediate assistance. They were only issued to operational agents, but this one wasn't on her list. She highlighted the spot on the screen and noted it was coming from London. She immediately sent a message to Alicia's computer. The name on the tag was Paul Cane. Alicia was surprised his cell phone's panic mode hadn't been deactivated after so long. She had called him on that particular phone earlier in the day so knew the phone was active but not the coded emergency call system. Paul wouldn't use it unless he was threatened. The emergency button had to be manually unlocked before it could be depressed so accidental use was extremely unlikely. Alicia told her operative to track the signal and estimate where the source was heading. The satellite sending the signal would give an accurate GPS reference of all the places it passed through and record them.

Alicia was about to call Nicholas, but hesitated. This was an MI6 matter and CTU had an agreement with Angel to exchange all information relating to Operation Clearwater. She knew that Paul Cane wasn't supposed to be part of the terrorist investigation, but it looked like he was caught up in it. She called Angel on the secure line. She was re-watching the videos from the Mercedes car chase.

Angel saw the secure number ringing on her cell phone and immediately picked it up to an anxious American voice.

'Angel, I am sending a video to your PDA on our secure channel. The tracking signal is from Paul Cane's cell phone. He initiated the emergency signal thirty minutes ago and we picked it up immediately. Nobody else can see it since only CTU has the encryption code. The signal started in London near Kensington and is moving out of London on the M4 motorway. But you can see this for yourself when I transmit the decoded signal, but protect it with your system. We assume he is in trouble and travelling in some sort of vehicle.'

'I will switch on my PDA,' said Angel.

'It may take some minutes before you get it.'

'Why was Paul Cane in Kensington Palace Gardens Road?' asked Angel.

'I don't know, but I told him not to get involved, but he thinks he's one of us,' said Alicia.

'I am now getting the tracking signal,' Angel said.

'It looks like your bad guys have abducted Paul in a car and are travelling out of London. The fact that the phone is still working means the abductors haven't yet found it so you may have to move fast before they do and we lose the signal. I will try and get a visual from the satellite.'

Angel's suspicions were confirmed. She told Alicia about her visit to the house in Kensington Palace Gardens Road, prior to the Mercedes leaving it. It was obviously a decoy.

'Thanks for the intel, Alicia. Looks like we've all been fooled. I'll inform BS immediately. He's getting all the stored data from the video cameras in the area where Paul was abducted. I'm not sure why he was in that area. But it doesn't surprise me. He's hell bent on a personal vendetta for what happened. Until we know more, I'm keeping Scotland Yard out of the loop.'

Angel knew BS would want it that way. Now it was MI6's job again. Clearwater could start to operate. She called up BS and briefed him on CTU's tracking of the car.

He told her that he was preparing a report for the NCTC meeting in the morning requested by the Prime Minister because of the discovery made at Kensington House. The Russian Ambassador would be summoned to the Foreign Office to explain the tunnel in the embassy grounds linking it to the house.

Alicia called Curly, disturbing him from a relaxing nap so he wasn't in the best of moods.

'We believe Paul Cane has been abducted by either the Russians or Christine Hunter or both. I'll keep you updated. There is one more thing: it looks like Gregori Seperkov has left Moscow. He might be in England. There is no entry in immigration records, but he might have used the diplomatic route. I have someone checking. You know he's sworn to seek retribution for the killing of his brother. I don't know if he knows it was you.'

'I'm sure someone would have told him, but if he is on the run after being responsible for the London bomb, then I want him anyway, but I have to deal with my personal business first, so keep me posted on developments,' said Curly.

He thought it ironic that there were now two men seeking him for killing their brothers.

Alicia didn't tell Curly she had called Angel since it was important they never met, otherwise it would jeopardise his security status.

Alicia drank her late afternoon coffee with a troubled mind. There were too many strange coincidences and happenings going on in the UK. She didn't like to admit it to herself, but she was worried about the two men in her life who were supposed to be just friends. That meant they had moved onto a new level in her emotions.

Terrorist suspects seemed to be able to freely enter the US without checks being made as to their whereabouts. CTU was desperately short of good field agents to track them. She needed to talk to the Vice President and get some arses kicked. She also found it strange not to be able to communicate with her friend Mark Brooks at the CIA. It was unusual for him not to return her calls. The big question she faced was whether there was a link between the London bomb and the Russians and the new al-Qaeda threat to the US. It was different to the millennium conspiracy or Project Whirlwind that doomed the last presidency. This time the Russian terrorist group had failed to implicate al-Qaeda so they were now the enemy. But for the US, al-Qaeda was still the main threat.

Alicia called Burger at the White House and asked him to arrange a meeting with the Vice President and his security advisors.

2 am, Next Morning

Goodfellows and Palmer were arrested in the early hours by a squad of armed police and taken to Scotland Yard for questioning rather than to their local police stations. Goodfellows had already told his wife, Laura, that he believed her daughter, Jayne, had paid a visit to Kensington House and was behind the police raid. She was furious and decided to find out the truth. She knew little about her husband's business dealings with the Russians and the Arabs except their offshore accounts were growing at an alarming rate. Her life was about to change.

CHAPTER 14

Riverside House

Cane decided not to move and pretend he was still drugged until he knew where he was being taken. He could just reach the cell phone in his coat pocket. The red LED indicated it was transmitting. Just being able to reach the inclusive small keyboard with his fingers, he typed:

'*Was drugged, am in car with three people, on road.*'

Before he could type any more he heard a woman's voice speaking in Russian.

'Ivan should be waiting for us at the house. Is our passenger still asleep?'

The man sitting next to Cane pulled back the blanket; Cane kept perfectly still.

'Yes,' he answered.

The SUV turned onto a tree-lined gravel drive and arrived at the front of a large country house set in private grounds. Tall trees and bushes obscured it from the road.

Riverside was an eighteenth-century Georgian house. Its walled gardens extended the property down to the banks of the River Thames, close to the village of Henley in Berkshire.

Owned in the past by a number of wealthy English families, it had become too expensive for the last owner. A few years back he had sold it to a Russian oligarch.

Two men were standing outside the entrance of the house. The woman, whom Cane assumed was Christine Hunter, had her back to him so her face wasn't visible. He would never forget the mean, penetrating, evil, dark eyes that he had seen in the hotel in Switzerland.

Cane tucked the cell phone well back into his inside pocket, making sure it was still sending the emergency signal. He thought it strange that his captors hadn't taken it from him. On the floor of the vehicle was his stick. His hands weren't tied so the mystery deepened. Who had sent him the message about Christine Hunter? Why was the vehicle coming out of the Russian Embassy? He overheard the woman telling the men in Russian to take him into the house.

'Better give him another shot so he doesn't wake up until we're ready for him,' she said. The blanket was pulled back. Cane kept very still. He then felt a sharp pain in his thigh as the needle went in. Before he passed out he managed to see the face of the woman who had given the order. It wasn't Christine Hunter. The woman had blue eyes, fair hair, was short and plump, and of Slavonic appearance. Who was she? His thoughts went hazy and he faded into oblivion.

3 pm CTU, Washington

Alicia was tracking the SUV on the computer screen when the signal showed it had stopped at a location near the village of Henley-on-Thames. A text appeared just before it stopped.

'Paul Cane is alive,' shouted Alicia.

'Should we send him an acknowledgement? It would tell him that we've received his message and know where he is,' said Bradley, who had been also looking intensely at the screen.

'Not yet. If his abductors see it, they'd know we've discovered them and that might put Cane's life in danger.'

'Angel, are you seeing the tracking path?' asked Alicia.

'Yes.'

'Good. I just sent you a copy of a text we received from Cane's cell phone.'

'Yes, I have it. I am checking on the name of the house, which shows up on the map as Riverside.'

SIS Headquarters – The Director's Office

BS was also receiving the information and checking up on the house ownership. It didn't take long.

The name Oleg Detroski immediately came on the screen. He immediately called Davenport and briefed him on events.

'I will phone Detroski immediately,' said Davenport.

Detroski's PA answered the call, as she often did when anybody rang Detroski's private number.

'I want to speak to Oleg urgently,' said Davenport.

'Mr Detroski is not here at present,' she replied.

'Can I ask who's speaking?'

'I'm Susan, his PA.'

Davenport detected a nervous intonation in her voice.

'You know who I am. Where has he gone?' shouted Davenport in an authoritative tone.

'Sorry, Lord Davenport, but I cannot tell you. I have specific instructions.'

'This is a matter of extreme security. Unless you tell me, I shall have to call the police.' There was a prolonged silence.

'He has gone to Riverside, his country residence, for a few days' rest,' she replied. 'But please don't reveal that it was me who told you, otherwise I'll lose my job.'

'OK. Is his wife with him?'

'No, I think she's in Spain. Mr Surak is accompanying him.'

Davenport thanked her and called BS.

'Detroski left for Riverside a few days ago with Voss.'

That information was enough to set alarm bells ringing. BS immediately took out a notebook from his desk, scanned the telephone numbers and made a call.

Sergeant Major Bill Simpson was enjoying a Madras curry at his favourite Indian restaurant in Regent Street while eyeing up a blonde with a pair of the largest breasts he had seen for a long time, accentuated by her almost anorexic figure. The young man with her, who was obviously a banker from the city, would be paying a week's wages for her company and a lot more for an all-night session.

Simpson, now in his forties, had sampled his share of such women over the years in every theatre of war; the last one being

Iraq. That had been the most difficult mission and had nearly cost him his life when the squad he was leading was ambushed in the desert. The mission had been to kill Saddam Hussein and as many of his top generals as they could, before the war actually started. But the intelligence was flawed and the squad was attacked by the Iraqis soon after they disembarked from their helicopter. There was a fire fight and only three of the eight-man team who survived were rescued. After Iraq, he left the SAS, but being a crack marksman, his services were unofficially made available to the head of a certain intelligence service. He was too good to be just another security officer working for some profiteering company.

BS had been contacted by Simpson's CO, an old army friend, and told that his best man needed a job. Over a drink in a pub, an approach was made by AL, one of BS's trusted aides and expert trainer. At first, Simpson took some convincing, but shooting was in his blood. Once an SAS man always an SAS man. The money was too good to pass on. It was agreed that he would only be called when an emergency situation arose, but would be kept on a monthly retainer.

Simpson's cell phone buzzed and the unmistakeable message appeared 'Spear', that was his codename, and a signal that a job was on the line. Instructions would follow, but he had to re-load some encryption software that was locked securely away in a safe in his flat before they could be read. He finished the meal, paid the bill and took a taxi to his modest abode in Victoria.

BS sent Angel a message:

'Go to Riverside and find out what's going on. I'm sending Spear to give you some muscle. Remember, this is our special part of Clearwater so make sure no one, except Bradley, knows. Keep him in the office for now. It's your show.'

He knew he was taking a big risk not informing John Nicholas about Riverside, but he didn't want SWAT teams rushing to the house until he knew more about what was going on. On receiving the text, Angel became excited. At last she had a mission of her own. It was thoughtful of BS to give her protection, but she preferred to work alone. She checked her Walther P99 and placed an extra magazine of sixteen bullets together with a camera, other equipment, boots and clothes in her bag. It was the one semi-automatic weapon she liked. It had been given to her by a man in Kuwait where she had a cause to use it. The original owner had been an ex-policeman who was employed as a security guard when he was shot during a bank raid in Kuwait City.

Officially MI6 didn't issue its agents with pistols. It was too risky because any death would have to be explained and fit within the rules of engagement. They were similar to the guidelines issued to the police. Agents were given a special licence to use their own weapons of choice, but had to take responsibility for their actions. AL had given Angel some extra training, but she actually knew more than he did. He soon discovered that she was a crack shot. Shooting at a target was like punching someone you hated in the face. Maximum determination and force were required. Since the brain controlled every action, it had to be fully engaged. The old saying always applied – *She who hesitates is lost.* AL also gave her some boots with specially designed gas capsules concealed in the heels. They were for protection should she lose her other weapons and were less likely to be detected if she was captured.

CHAPTER 15

The White Flamingo Club, Mayfair
9 pm, 2 June

Curly went to the concierge of the hotel. Out of sight he placed a hundred pound note into his hand in exchange for services. Various phone calls were made. One was to the manager of the White Flamingo Club telling him to expect a very important visitor.

A black Mercedes arrived. A smartly dressed man in a chauffeur's uniform introduced himself as James. Curly shook his hand and jumped onto the back seat. The car had been hired for the occasion from a company who guaranteed a discreet service to its clients. James was familiar with the discretionary needs of guests at the hotel.

The door of the Mercedes was opened by the doorman of the White Flamingo Club. The exclusive club offered its members almost anything they wanted. They had to be at least millionaires and vetted before they could join. Amongst its facilities were a casino, private bars and rooms, and a two-hour cabaret. Hostesses were provided if required. The cabaret had two acts: one was the O'Brien Singing Sisters who were the resident performers; the other act changed every week, depending on what celebrity was available in London.

Curly had spent some time on his disguise and rehearsing his alias. The Sig Sauer P228 revolver was well concealed in its holster tucked under his arm. Patrick Ryan was the Head of Security for the Sheikh Armani of Qatar, one of the world's richest men. The Sheikh always had his people check out any venue he wanted to visit in advance.

At the club's reception, Ryan was met by Antonio Benito, the manager of the club, a tall, handsome Italian. They shook hands. Benito introduced Ryan to Ricky, obviously an ex-boxer, who was the club's security man and chief bouncer. They all went to an office annex. Ryan produced his card that contained a phone number. He knew Benito would be doing a check on him and would use the number. Both men looked suspiciously at Ryan and noticed the bulge in his suit.

'Mr Ryan, no guns are allowed in the club. I will need you to leave what you are carrying with us until you leave. I will place it in my safe.' Ryan was unhappy with that arrangement in case he had to leave quickly. He decided to go on the offensive.

'Sorry, I have to keep my weapon with me at all times. It's a rule imposed by my boss. If that's a problem, then I will leave now and advise the Sheikh against visiting the club.'

Knowing that would be bad publicity for the club and its owners, Benito agreed on the condition that the bullets were removed from the gun and placed in a safe. It was the best deal Ryan could get, so he agreed, knowing he had concealed some bullets in the lining of his jacket so he wouldn't be rendered defenceless. He emptied the pistol not allowing the two men to see much of it. They took the bullets and placed them in a wall safe.

'Mr Ryan, can I ask you why we haven't been informed of the Sheikh's interest in visiting the club before now?'

'Yes, he made a late change to his schedule and is only stopping over for a few days in London to complete a business deal and wants a night out to relax. Your club was recommended, so he asked me to make the necessary arrangements and check out the security for his visit.'

'We can assure you that we have the tightest security here and entertain the most notable businessmen and showbiz celebrities.'

Ryan decided to take a hard line. He frowned at Benito and said in a loud voice, 'Can I remind you that Sheikh Armani is a very rich man, who is coming to London to discuss investments with top city businessmen. He takes nothing for granted and only trusts his own hand-picked people. I would now like to see the club and look at your security if you don't mind.'

Benito beckoned to Ricky, who was still eyeing up Ryan suspiciously.

'Ricky will show you around the club before our show starts. You are very welcome to stay as our guest and see the cabaret.'

'Thanks, I would like that,' Ryan said with a smile. It was exactly what he wanted to hear.

Ryan followed him and Ricky into the club. He was given a seat at a private table, out of sight of the main guests. It gave him a panoramic view of those in the club. He scanned the faces. There were many Arabs, Asians and men who looked like Russians. Their bodyguards were noticeable. It was unlikely that O'Grady was among them, but he could also be disguised to throw off any police who might have him under surveillance.

Benito shook hands with Ryan and left him with Ricky. 'Bleep me on this if you need anything and when you wish to leave,' said Ricky.

He left what looked like a small bleeper on the table, but Ryan believed it was something else. He knew Benito would be making a call to Qatar. The man receiving the call would give every assurance being sought.

Ryan knew it would be impossible to talk to the Sheikh or any of his close associates, but it was a risk if Benito actually knew someone close to Armani. The Sheikh was well known in business circles, but, being a private man, kept a tight security around his private life. He would know within the next few minutes. Ryan slipped his hand into his coat pocket and took out a clip concealed in the lining and carefully loaded it into the Sig. Ten minutes later an ice bucket arrived with a bottle of champagne so Ryan relaxed, knowing, at least for the present, his deception had worked.

The lights were dimmed, the music started and the cabaret was about to begin. He wondered if his sisters would recognise him. They knew he was going to the club and would be in a disguise, but were told not to treat him any differently from other guests.

The two sisters came on the stage, dressed in short red skirts and tops and black fishnet stockings with high stiletto-heeled shoes. They started to sing songs from the hit show Chicago. Ryan's table was at the side of the stage and out of direct line of sight of the sisters. He didn't want them to recognise him during their performance. After the show the two sisters moved amongst the audience to talk to the guests under the watchful eye of Ricky and two other bouncers. Some of the men who had been drinking heavily and were becoming too friendly were spoken to by the bouncers.

Tracey and Maria eventually came over to their brother's table. Tracey looked into his eyes and recognised him immediately, but was discreet enough to show no recognition. She squeezed his hand before leaving the table. He took the opportunity to pass her a note saying he would be following them back to their apartment in a black Mercedes.

After the show, Ryan called James to say he was leaving. He thanked Benito for the hospitality, retrieved the bullets and left the club. He made sure the doorman saw him get into the Mercedes that arrived just at the right moment. He told James to wait on the road near the club because he needed to follow a taxi.

The club had a contract with a taxi company to take the sisters home every night. Tracey told Maria that Sean would be following them in a black Mercedes. As usual their taxi arrived. They sat on the back seat. After some minutes they realised it was not taking the usual route back to their apartment. Tracey questioned the driver who said he was new to the job and was taking a short cut. He had a cap pulled down over his face and was looking at them in the mirror. She froze. He was not like their usual taxi driver. His demeanour made her suspicious. Was he O'Grady? Maria saw that her sister looked nervous. Tracey took out her cell phone and sent a text message to her brother using the number he had given her.

'We think our taxi driver could be O'Grady. He's taken a different route back.'

The Mercedes was at a safe distance behind when Sean received the message. Now the next move would be for O'Grady to make. He didn't have to wait long. O'Grady turned into a private underground car park and stopped the taxi near a wall on the far side. He had seen the Mercedes following and knew Sean O'Brien had taken the bait.

The sisters, now knowing they had been abducted, were

terrified of what might happen next. Maria wanted to jump out, but Tracey held her back. The taxi driver turned to them, took off his cap and with a broad Irish accent said, 'Do exactly what I tell you and you won't get hurt.'

He reinforced the command by taking out a pistol and told them to get out and stand against the wall. Tracey noticed him nervously looking at the entrance. He was clearly expecting someone. It was the anniversary date of the death of his brother. Sean had already warned his sisters that he might strike on that day. It was why he had decided to go to their club that night.

O'Grady had waited outside the club in a taxi he had stolen earlier. When the sisters came out he drove it to the entrance. They assumed it was the taxi sent by the company they always used so didn't hesitate to get into it. He had been watching them leaving on previous days so had been able to plan the action.

While waiting for the sisters, O'Grady noticed a man being picked up by a chauffeur-driven Mercedes. The man didn't look like Sean O'Brien, but he had a similar build and walk. Since the car didn't move and the man was watching the club entrance, O'Grady was convinced it was O'Brien. Everything was playing into his hands. He would take the sisters to a quiet place and wait for the man he wanted to kill. When he saw the car following, he knew his plan had worked.

Curly saw the taxi turn into the car park so told his driver to stop near the entrance. He left the car after instructing the driver to park a few blocks away to avoid being seen.

'I will call you when I need to be picked up.'

There was a risk that the night club owner might talk to the police about the unexpected visitor. So the matter had to be resolved quickly. His main concern was for Tracey and Maria. He had to get them away from O'Grady since he now feared for their lives.

Curly walked slowly into the underground car park, keeping to the shadows. It was very dark so he was able to take cover behind parked cars. It was then he heard O'Grady shouting, 'O'Brien, I know you're there. If you don't show yourself I will shoot one of your sisters. You know I'm not bluffing. I just want to make sure you see it happen. Unlike my brother, whom you shot from behind, she will know when it's coming.'

Curly could see that O'Grady had his gun pointing at Maria's head. Tracey was standing against the wall. He moved closer and positioned himself behind a car to within about ten metres from where O'Grady was standing. He knew that as soon as he showed himself O'Grady would shoot Maria. The only chance she had was for him to shoot the pistol from O'Grady's hand before the trigger was released. It was a great risk. He was just within range, but would have only one chance, one shot to disarm O'Grady. He needed O'Grady to be distracted for just a split second so his brain couldn't send a signal to the hand holding the gun. In situations like this, Curly's SAS training demanded a head shot, preferably in the mouth to sever the spinal cord, but since he was side-on to the target such a shot was not possible. He had to destroy the pistol and the hand holding it. Curly had re-loaded a magazine containing explosive bullets into the Sig. They would blow up the target, but he had to hit the right spot. A few centimetres' error either way would kill Maria. There was a chance she would be injured by the blast but it was one he had to take.

Tracey's agitation watching their abductor getting increasingly angry and pressing the gun to Maria's head because he wasn't getting the response to his calls was clearly visible. Time was running out; Curly had to act. But he needed a distraction. Then he saw Tracey take off her stiletto-heeled shoe. It looked like she intended to throw it at O'Grady, who noticed her movement. His concentration momentarily lapsed. The Sig was aimed at O'Grady's hand. Curly's finger was on the trigger. He squeezed it hard. The gun was fitted with a silencer so only a soft pop could be heard. But a loud clatter was followed by a scream that filled the air as the bullet found its mark. The gun in O'Grady's hand shattered into many fragments taking with it some of his fingers. The scream was from Maria, who thought she had been shot when her face became spattered with blood from O'Grady's hand.

It was time to show himself. With the Sig in his hand, Curly walked from behind the car that had provided him with temporary cover to a very surprised Irishman who was holding up a half-severed hand dripping with blood. Turning to face his adversary, O'Grady shouted, 'You bastard.'

Everything happened within seconds. At that moment Tracey threw her shoe at O'Grady. The pointed steel heel struck him straight in the eye and embedded itself in his skull. He fell backwards screaming, clutching the shoe, but it was too late. Blood spurted out from the wound. Holding his face, he screamed and writhed in pain for a few seconds, then fell and lay motionless at their feet. It was a very lucky throw.

Maria ran crying into Tracey's arms, thinking that she had been shot. Her face was covered in O'Grady's blood but not seriously damaged. Curly went forward cautiously with the gun in his hand. He bent down to feel O'Grady's pulse; but there was none. The man was dead; killed by a stiletto shoe. Tracey couldn't believe what she'd just done and was shaking in a state of shock.

'I didn't mean to kill him. I didn't mean it,' she said in a high pitched voice.

Curly went over to comfort his two sisters. They flung their arms around him.

'Sean, how did you know it would be tonight? How did he know where to find us?' Tracey asked.

'It's a long story and there's no time to tell you now. We have to get out of here and make sure nobody sees us,' he said. 'But first, I need to clear up this mess.'

He pulled out the six-inch heel of Tracey's shoe from O'Grady's head; it was a gruesome sight. The heel had blood and brain tissue stuck to it. He dragged the body onto the front seat of the taxi, collected up the gun fragments and other debris, wiped any fingerprints from the body and made sure nothing was left behind. The Sig had done its job, but it was Tracey's shoe that had saved them and dealt the deadly blow to their enemy. When the bullet hit the gun it was only about five centimetres from Maria's head. Fortunately, its forward momentum pushed the gun away and she only received minor cuts to her face from flying fragments. Curly examined Maria's face, wiped it with his handkerchief, being careful not to let any of her blood touch anything. It was important to leave no evidence that the girls had ever been at the scene. He had to think quickly. Someone might have heard the commotion in the car park.

He tried to calm the girls, who were both crying and in a nervous state. He grabbed their hands and said, 'Now listen to me. I want you both to walk to the entrance of the car park, turn left and walk slowly down the road. A black Mercedes will pick you up. The driver's name is James. He will take you to your apartment. Behave normally as though nothing had happened. James won't ask any questions, but will make sure you're safe. Call me when you arrive at your apartment.'

'What are you going to do?' asked Tracey, still looking bewildered at the man she had just killed.

'I am going to get rid of the body and the taxi. Don't worry, everything will be OK. Now go,' he said.

Curly made a phone call.

'James, pick up my two sisters who will be walking along the road from the car park entrance in a few minutes.'

Although Curly had removed the blood and cleaned it up, Tracey reluctantly had to put on the shoe that had saved her life. The girls walked hand in hand out of the car park and onto the street.

Curly dragged O'Grady onto the back seat of the taxi and covered him with a blanket he found in the luggage compartment. Checking that there were no blood stains or anything else left at the scene, he drove the taxi out of the car park. Fortunately nobody had appeared so there were no witnesses to the shooting.

It was 2 am and for London the narrow road in front was unusually clear. Nobody was walking along it. Taxis were a common sight in London in the early hours so he wouldn't attract any attention. He headed for the East End, which was being prepared for re-development. The government had allocated

163

millions of pounds to encourage developers to make that part of London a desirable place to live. Most of the river sites had already been sold and expensive new apartment blocks were now looking out across the river. Little attention had been given to those further away.

The Mercedes pulled up alongside the girls. The window moved down and a smiling James said, 'I believe you ladies need a lift home.'

Without saying a word they got into the car. It then sped off to St John's Wood. This time they hoped the taxi driver was friendlier.

Curly's knowledge of London streets was limited so he kept close to the river, circumnavigated the Tower of London through Smithfields and headed towards Wapping. He found a building site in the early stages of development so security hadn't been established. It wasn't difficult to break through the flimsy gate at the entrance.

The radio in the taxi had been disconnected so its owners would have already informed the police. Hijackings were not uncommon in London, but because a terrorism alert was in progress, the police were extra vigilant and would be looking at every street video camera. It was why O'Grady had attached false number plates, but Curly wondered how he had disposed of the driver. He knew it was only a matter of time before the cab would be identified. He drove the taxi alongside a shed. He was in luck. It was full of building materials, including wood. He had already considered the only possible option: to burn the taxi and its contents. It would have a full tank of petrol. The Sig's explosive bullets would once again prove their worth. He found the location of the petrol tank. He screwed on the silencer and was about to fire the Sig when his cell phone rang. It was Tracey saying that they had arrived home safely and thanked him for saving their lives. He told her to hide the phone and not attempt to contact him again since he was going undercover, also to ignore what the newspapers reported and to say nothing to the club management about the rogue taxi.

Curly was pleased with the unexpected outcome of the night's work. He stood back and put a shot into the taxi's fuel tank. There was a slight flash when the bullet hit the metal of the tank, but no explosion. The tank was protected with a thick outer casing. But the bullet had punctured the tank and petrol started dripping onto the ground beneath. He waited until a large pool had collected. He took off O'Grady's coat, soaked it in petrol and placed it back on the dead man's body. Standing some distance away from the vehicle to avoid being ignited by the petrol vapour, he fired another shot into the pool of petrol. This time a huge flash resulted and the whole taxi became engulfed in flames. He knew the shed and the wood would increase the fire's intensity. Once he saw the body was burning he started to walk away.

There was no visible street camera nearby, but Curly knew that once the fire was detected any camera in the area would direct the police to the scene. At first, it would look like just another fire on a building site. It would take some time before they discovered the body. Hopefully, O'Grady's body would be incinerated so badly it would be impossible to know what actually caused his death. A detailed autopsy might discover the truth. Paddy O'Grady's DNA, teeth and other physical characteristics were on record. His crimes were also well known. Knowing this, the police wouldn't be too vigorous in their investigation and assume he had been the victim of a revenge killing. To make sure, Curly made a call. After a delay, while the encryption software kicked in, silence followed. It was the signal to leave his message. The recipient would know who was calling. In a soft voice he said, *'Subject eliminated. Take care of body in burning taxi at Wapping.'*

He walked back along the river bank and then took a route to the West End, where possible avoiding street cameras. Sean O'Brien hoped his long-time MI5 friend would understand his message. It was the friend's warning about O'Grady's intention that had brought him to London.

Patrick Ryan arrived back at the Connaught Hotel at about 4 pm. The concierge gave him a wry smile as he walked past him in the foyer, conscious of the smell of petrol on his clothes. Ryan showered and changed his clothes. It wasn't long before he was overcome by the oblivion of a welcome sleep in a comfortable bed. Before he drifted into another world, Alicia's message came into his mind. *Paul Cane has been abducted. We believe Gregori Seperkov is in London.* But that was tomorrow's job. What mattered now was that the O'Brien sisters were safe from an IRA maniac. Luck had played its part, but then it always did.

CHAPTER 16

A Bad Day
7 am, 3 June

Cane woke up in a comfortable bed. Sunlight was seeping through the partially drawn curtains, casting shadows on the walls of the bars on the windows. As he became increasingly aware of his surroundings, his memory came flooding back of the events of the past day. The text message to meet Christine Hunter, the walk along Kensington Palace Gardens Road, the man crashing into him, feeling dizzy, being pulled into the car, being drugged, sending a text to Alicia, being taken out of the car, seeing a woman and hearing Russian voices. Now where was he? In the house, he supposed. Someone had taken off his clothes since he was only in his underpants. They were laid out neatly on a chair in the room. It was then he noticed a camera mounted on the wall opposite. He was being watched. He decided to act normally and went into the en-suite bathroom.

The house was of Georgian design with high ceilings, but had been modernised with luxury fittings. Whoever owned it was wealthy. The effects of the drug had completely worn off. In fact, he felt invigorated. He was obviously a prisoner. The next move would be made by his captors. But unknown to him, the house was under observation.

Located in thick woods about one hundred metres away, binoculars were focused on the rooms of the house, observing its occupants, some of which could be seen through one of the downstairs windows. Angel had driven from London early in the morning before most people would have arisen and parked her car off the road in a clearing close to the wood that overlooked Riverside.

She put the binoculars down and from her bag took out a camera with a 300 mm lens attached. Steadying it on a bipod, she took a series of pictures. One was of a woman who just happened to look out of the window at the right time. Using the camera's wireless facility, she sent the photo directly to her PDA and then forwarded it to BS. He was having breakfast at his apartment when his PDA bleeped, signalling an incoming mail. He knew its origin by the information Angel had provided. Angel asked if the woman could be identified and if it was Christine Hunter. BS sent an urgent request to SIS's face recognition department. The problem was that only Paul Cane had seen Hunter in the last year, so the files only had a description of her. The initial results showed no known match. A few minutes later a new message flashed on the screen. A match had been found. The photo was of a Katrina Vasalov. She was a Third Secretary at the Russian Embassy in London and had only been in the post for less than a year. A footnote indicated that she was a suspected SVR agent. BS hurriedly dressed and drove to his office at SIS. In the car he pondered. What was a Russian diplomat and suspected SVR agent doing in a house owned by Oleg Detroski? Where was Detroski? He sent Angel the following text:

'Keep the house under observation. Try and photograph other residents and await further instructions. We need to find Detroski.'

Sitting on the grass next to her was Spear, who had arrived just a few minutes previously. BS had given him Angel's address so he was able to follow her car to Henley and Riverside. She didn't know how much the grey-haired, ageing SAS man knew, or was supposed to know, about why they were there. At first she was angry that BS had sent someone to protect her when she didn't need protecting. His manner was gentle, almost fatherly. She thought he might even be old enough to be her father. SAS killers usually looked like ex-boxers with rugged features. This man had a refined face, intelligent eyes and was clearly a professional; the kind of person who could keep his head in a crisis. He also had an attractive demeanour. BS hadn't told her anything about the man or what he was supposed to know. Was that deliberate or was she expected to brief him?

'How much do you know about the mission?' she asked.

'Very little, but I don't need to know much since I'm only here to protect you and give firearm support. I understand the people in that house are Russians and have abducted an agent and possibly others whose lives may be at risk,' he replied.

She showed him the face of the woman on the camera. 'My orders for the time being are to keep the house and its occupants under observation. This is Katrina Vasalov, a Third Secretary at the Russian Embassy. She is also an SVR agent. The house is owned by Oleg Detroski, one of the richest oligarchs in England. He is supposed to be in the house, but as yet not seen. The man you call an agent is Paul Cane. He is not one of our agents. Being the only survivor of the BA plane that exploded over London, he was given our protection, but, for reasons that we need to discover, has been abducted by the Russians. We believe these people are connected with the terrorists responsible for the destruction of the London plane. I cannot tell you any more, but it's only right you should know why this mission is so important. We may be dealing with ruthless people.'

Spear had listened intently and, without displaying any emotion, responded with a grin. 'Sounds like we're going to have an interesting day.' Pointing to a black case resting on the ground beside him, he added, 'I may need Oscar. It's my tool kit.'

Angel guessed it was a sniper's rifle.

Cane washed and dressed, noticing that his cell phone was missing from his coat pocket. Fortunately, the messages he made were encrypted so couldn't be interpreted without knowledge of the code that only CTU possessed.

He heard a key go into the door lock. A tall man, who had all the appearances of a butler, brought in a breakfast tray containing an assortment of food and fresh orange juice. Without saying a word, he placed it on a table in the corner of the room, left and re-locked the door. Knowing he was being watched, Cane wasted no time in enjoying the free meal. He had developed a hunger and a thirst.

Thirty minutes later a phone rang. At first Cane couldn't see where it was, but eventually found it tucked away in a drawer beside the bed. He picked it up. A woman with a distinctly Russian accent said, 'Good morning, Mr Cane. Hope you slept well and enjoyed your breakfast. You will be wondering why you have been brought here in rather an unconventional manner.'

Cane immediately realised by her excellent English and manner that his captor was an educated person. She was no common criminal and certainly not Christine Hunter.

'Let me first apologise for drugging you, but it was necessary. The drug is harmless and will not have any long-term effects. You will naturally be wondering why this has been necessary; that will be revealed later. Meanwhile you will not be allowed to leave the room or communicate with anybody. Please don't attempt to try since, as you will have noticed, we can see you on camera. Incidentally, this phone is only internal and not connected externally. There are some books on the shelves for you to read. You will know more in due course.'

'I demand to know where I am and what you want,' shouted Cane. But the phone call ended leaving him confused but slightly relieved that his captors didn't intend to harm him, at least for the time being.

Something was being planned, but he could do little but wait. He had hoped that Alicia had received his messages. She would know what to do and inform the British police or security services. There was no way a SWAT team was going to suddenly descend upon the house with guns blazing; he wasn't that important. The fact that his cell phone, as the Americans called it, hadn't been taken from him when he was in the car, still bugged him. These people were professionals and didn't make such fundamental mistakes. Then it occurred to him. Could they have monitored any calls he had made or messages he had sent? But those sent to Alicia would be impossible to understand. The smart phone Alicia had given him could be used in the same way as any other phone, but by activating the concealed button it was changed to operate in an encrypted mode that only she and certain CTU staff could interpret. His text messages had been sent in that mode so were coded.

The big question was, whom did she contact? He wondered why his protection officer hadn't seen him being abducted. By now he would have reported back to Nicholas.

Like all prisoners, his first thoughts were how to escape. The friendly voice on the phone was re-assuring, but didn't fool him. Rooms in large old country houses were difficult to completely seal off. He thought about secret passages and priest holes, but that was the stuff of novels. The house had been modernised so such places would have been discovered and sealed up long ago. He had to find a way out. It worried him that Christine Hunter was involved as she wanted him dead. But where was she?

Angel and Spear discussed their strategy. They believed that only BS knew they were at Riverside. What they didn't know was an Irishman, codenamed Curly, was on his way to Riverside on orders from his boss, Alicia Garcia, the Director of CTU.

Curly had arisen late owing to an eventful and difficult night. After checking that his sisters were alright, he told them to go to work as normal and try to forget the events of the previous night. He assured them everything had been taken care of. He had other business to carry out, but told them he would call again before he returned to the US.

It worried him that O'Grady might have had accomplices, but it was unlikely. If his friend in MI5 had done what he promised then last night's incident wouldn't be reported and would go unseen as though nothing had happened. A clean-up gang would see to that.

Curly wasn't pleased to have been woken up earlier by Alicia, who checked if he had finished the private business and was available to go back to CTU work. Using their secure line she briefed him on the situation at Riverside. Curly had the same encrypted phone that Cane possessed, but their operational codes were different, so they couldn't use the phones to send each other coded messages. He told her he would see what could be done when he had finally completed his other UK business. He actually meant he wanted some more sleep and went back to bed. After taking a late breakfast at the Connaught, he asked the concierge to order him a hire car. Fortunately, it was a different man on duty who was unaware of the previous night's activities so no questions were asked, particularly when a fifty pound note passed between them. A new, blue, three-litre, automatic BMW duly arrived.

While waiting, Curly called Alicia, knowing she was up early.

'I'm on my way to Riverside. Any updates?'

'No, Cane's cell phone has gone off-line. Looks like his captors may have found it. Suggest you be careful. We cannot be sure Seperkov is in the country and even involved. But the MI6 agent believes he may be after Oleg Detroski, who is reported to be at Riverside – his secret country retreat. He had recently stopped receiving the usual threats which worried him so was advised by his bodyguard to go to Riverside. Very few people know that he owns it. The photo Angel sent was of a woman named Katrina Vasalov, who works at the Russian Embassy and has been identified as a possible SVR agent.'

'Who is Angel?' asked Curly.

There was a long silence, while Alicia realised she had given away Angel.

'MI6 insisted on appointing one of their agents to pursue the plane bombers. She is keeping the house under observation. If possible, don't identify yourself to her, otherwise things will be complicated. Your mission is only to find and rescue Paul Cane and find out what's going on in that house,' she said, knowing that Curly didn't take orders. It was more difficult for her now their relationship had changed. For the first time in her life she feared Curly getting hurt or even killed. It was a problem she had to face when he returned to the US.

Curly set the GPS on the BMW and drove towards Henley and

Riverside, not being quite sure what he would do when he arrived. He had his Ryan alias and box of disguises and a fully loaded Sig. He didn't want to make any contact with MI6 agents or the British police, but, since they didn't know him, he could be mistaken for a bad guy. He felt sorry for Paul Cane in view of what he had recently endured, but surprised that he had allowed himself to become involved.

Curly had been told that Gregori Seperkov blamed him for his half-brother's death. He didn't actually kill the man himself, but contracted one of the Russian mafia gangs to do it. It was only after the event that Curly discovered their family relationship. Their father had divorced his wife and re-married when Leon Seperkov was a young boy. Gregori was the product of his second marriage.

Alicia believed that Seperkov had left Moscow and was heading for London. But she had to find conclusive proof that he was behind the London plane bomb. Her agents were trying to find the Russians who set up and controlled all the other people involved. If they could be linked to Seperkov then that would be sufficient. It was known they had escaped from Afghanistan to Pakistan, but then the trail went cold.

Angel told Spear that she was going to the house and, using her police identity card, would ask to see Detroski on the pretext that she had an important confidential message from the government to deliver to him. She was going to try and get into the house and plant some miniature wireless microphones to pick up conversations. They had a range of over three hundred metres so could easily be received from their position in the woods. Spear didn't think it was a good idea as she would be going into the lion's den not knowing who inhabited it. But his job was to protect her and not ask any questions, so he assembled his sniper rifle, placed it on a portable rest and aimed it at the door of the house.

He had a clear view of the front door, the courtyard and the windows in the front of the house. He could take out any target he wished without revealing his position because of the silencer. No flash or sound would emanate from his position. The infrared laser rangefinder worked at day and night and gave his rifle sub-millimetre precision.

Angel opened her large sports bag and took out a range of items. She checked her pistol, put on a bullet-proof vest and the boots, specially adapted by AL. She gave a communicator to Spear so they could speak to each other. She now had to act as a plain clothes police inspector. He looked surprised at the transformation taking place before his eyes and the way she handled the gun. In his day, the SAS didn't train women for combat. They usually ended up operating a radio link or providing medical care. She was a beautiful woman and being armed for combat added to her sex appeal. But her piercing dark-brown eyes showed a ruthless determination to succeed. Spear had seen women like her before, but unfortunately they usually ended up dead trying to prove they were better than their male counterparts. He was old school and believed women were better suited to the roles that nature had intended. But sometimes he had been proved wrong.

'You've done this before,' he said, with a broad smile on his face.

She smiled back at him. In her new commanding role she said, 'Don't do anything unless I give a command. Contact BS if things go wrong and I can't get back. If Detroski and Paul Cane are in the house, it will be difficult for their captors to conceal them. When they know I'm from the police it will put them on their guard because police never send anyone without back-up located nearby. They will have to produce a plausible explanation for being in the house.'

Spear wished her luck, but told her that he wouldn't hesitate to fire on anyone who put her life in danger.

Unknown to Curly, a black SUV was following him at a safe distance. The driver was receiving a constant signal being emitted by Curly's cell phone. The man in the back seat smiled to himself. The plan was working like a Swiss clock. Soon he would have all his chickens in the same coup and, at last, a final retribution could take place. The Russian had waited a long time to avenge the death of his half-brother. That was a personal mission, but his main one was to remove the man his friends in Moscow considered to be a criminal and a traitor to mother Russia. A man who had become very rich at the expense of others. He had stolen Russia's assets and traded them for protection in a country that many still considered the enemy.

Seperkov had no remorse for the hundreds of innocent people killed in the BA plane. The Islamic jihadists had killed many more in his own country and committed atrocities to Russian soldiers in Afghanistan. He wanted all al-Qaeda followers blamed and hunted down. It was unfortunate that his men in Afghanistan were discovered and executed after revealing the plan. But many still believed it was al-Qaeda. Governments wanted that so they could devote more resources to hunting them down before they committed further acts. He had support from certain people in high-level government positions in Saudi Arabia and America. The reincarnation of The New Order was still on his agenda. He owed that to those Cabal members who had been savagely murdered by Sean O'Brien at the bequest of the bitch Alicia Garcia and her CIA murderers. He was pleased to have a mole in CTU who provided the encryption codes. At first she had been reluctant to cooperate, but the threat to the lives of her grandparents in Russia and exposure to the FBI of her real identity forced her to pass over the cipher codes embedded in Curly and Cane's cell phones.

Spear was looking through the small telescopic sight fitted on top of the rifle and by chance saw a face looking through a barred window. He switched the laser to red and aimed it at the face. The owner of the face soon realised he was being targeted and quickly moved away from the window.

Cane knew there was someone out there who had seen him. Was it a friend or an enemy? Did it mean a rescue attempt was to be made? Only a sniper would have a laser sight on his rifle and because he didn't fire then he must be a rescuer. That deduction made him feel good. But it could mean dangers ahead. Cane had counted at least three men and the woman. More were expected.

The muffled cry and a knocking sound he had heard earlier started up again. It sounded like it was coming from the next room. He was about to knock on the wall when he heard sounds of voices outside. Someone was on a cell phone saying, 'Yes,' to whoever was calling. He could just see four men through the bars; two were getting into a car, which sped away along the drive, and the others went back into the house. Ten minutes later another car pulled into the drive. It was then Cane held his breath when he recognised the woman emerging from it. It was the black hair and brown eyes that first caught his attention. Clare Angel had found him. Was he having a wishful dream? Perhaps the drugs were playing tricks with his brain. She went to the front door and disappeared from his view. But he could just make out people talking.

The doorbell didn't work, but the cameras had caught the visitor and showed her on the monitor. It brought a burly man to the door. He opened it cautiously.

'I would like to speak to Mr Oleg Detroski. I believe this is his house,' she said, noticing the shocked look on the man's face when she showed him her identity.

'Inspector Clare Angel from the Metropolitan Police. I have a special letter for him from the Home Office that he needs to sign before it can be released. It's very important that I see him now.'

'He's not here at present,' said the man in a Russian accent.

His facial expression belied his disbelief.

'Please wait a minute.'

Leaving her at the door he went back into the house. He didn't immediately return so she stepped inside finding herself in a large hall with a passage and a staircase leading from it. She could hear a faint knocking noise coming from an upstairs room. Angel took the miniature bugs from her pocket and placed them under the window sills and behind a picture hanging on the wall of the stairs, making sure she wasn't in view of any cameras. She spotted one on the wall looking at the front door so would have been seen coming into the hall, but not placing the hidden microphones. One was also embedded in the envelope addressed to Detroski.

Still no sign of the man who opened the door. Angel turned to go back out when, momentarily, she noticed the shadow of a hand rising above her head. Then a sharp pain in her neck and darkness. She slumped to the ground. The attacker picked up her body and placed it on a chair. He searched her pockets, found the pistol, her ID and wired communicator; the earpiece had fallen to the ground.

Spear had seen her going into the house and through the open door saw her attacker striking her head. Then the door closed and cut off his view.

'Is she the police or MI5?' shouted the woman.

'If she's the police then we can expect more visitors, but MI5 or MI6 would just send an agent. She didn't have time to make a call or send a message, but we shall know soon.' The man examined her identity card. 'This is faked,' he said.

'Then she must be an agent, but how did they know we were here?' asked the woman who looked worried.

'Maybe they didn't, but were just checking up on Detroski,' he said.

Katrina Vasalov made a call to Seperkov and told him what had happened. His optimism was shattered. He went into a rage. His plan was now threatened. He was still about twenty minutes' drive away from Riverside.

'We need to bring forward the next step of the plan. Take the prisoners to the boat moored at Pangbourne. Hunter is waiting there. Make sure the explosives are in place,' he said.

'We will need to drug them since I only have four men and there are now three people to deal with. Also the police or a SWAT team could arrive at any time,' she said anxiously.

'Do what you think necessary, but leave Detroski for me and make sure they arrive at the boat. Don't worry about the police, that won't happen. MI6 and CTU want to keep this to themselves. So far they haven't involved the police. Our diversions seem to have worked.'

Vasalov's training made her sceptical about Seperkov's assurances. She never underestimated the British Intelligence agencies, but she was unaware of the greater political implications and the personal vendetta that was driving Seperkov.

'What are you going to do about Sean O'Brien?' she asked.

'Leave him to me,' he snapped.

Alicia locked her office door and reviewed the situation. She had ordered that a satellite surveillance of the area in the UK where Curly was travelling be sent to CTU. One was about to come into position over England. The cell phone signal was weakening and before talking to Curly she wanted to see the terrain. She wasn't familiar with the geography of that part of England, except she knew the Thames Valley had many large country houses owned by rich celebrities. She had another concern. Had the Russians found a way to decode the phone calls since those from Cane had stopped and unauthorised signals had been detected coming from CTU? Did she have a spy in the camp, even amongst her hand-picked agents?

After the moles had been found at Langley working for The New Order, she learned to trust no one. She rang Stefan Lewis, the CTU Head of Administration and Human Resources. He was in charge of all staff files and had assisted her in recruiting people. He knocked on the door. She unlocked it and let him in.

'Stefan, I want to see the personnel files on Pat King and Brad Walker.'

He looked at her and, detecting anxiety in her face, asked, 'What is the problem?'

She didn't answer his question, but asked another.

'Who knows or has access to my cell phone encryption codes other than the analysts King and Bradley?'

'Nobody else, that was your order,' he replied.

'Can you send me a list of all calls or messages sent from CTU using those codes in the last week?'

'Yes, but you can access that yourself by using your own password followed by the following entry code. No other staff member except me can access those files.'

He wrote down a series of letters and numbers. The computer

would recognise them and select the list she wanted from the mainframe computer. It would give the time, date and identity of the sender.

'Thanks. I may call you later,' she said.

Alicia locked the door behind Lewis. She hoped the files would only reveal the calls made to Curly, Cane, Angel and the White House. It was a relatively short list. Then she spotted something that shocked her. Pat King had sent two coded messages to a cell phone in London two days previously at about the time when Paul Cane was abducted. It had only lasted for a few seconds. Was she the mole in CTU?

Alicia had to find out. She called Lewis and instructed him to immediately remove King's security clearance so she couldn't access CTU's files. Five minutes later he brought Alicia her file. After carefully perusing it, she ordered that King be arrested and placed and locked in CTU's secure room until she could be interviewed. Assuming the worst case scenario, Alicia called Curly who was swiftly driving to Riverside.

'Don't use your cell phone and discard it immediately. I think the Russians have our encryption codes and may be intercepting our calls. If so, they could also be tracking you. Are you being followed?' she asked.

'I don't think so,' he replied.

Risking being overheard, she told Curly to buy a new cell phone in a local shop or make calls from a phone box since there was more he should know.

Curly looked in his mirror, but couldn't see any cars that were obviously following him. He pulled over and stopped the car near a small row of shops and waited before getting out. A number of cars and vans passed by on the busy road. After a few minutes he noticed a large SUV with darkened windows pass by. They were the types of vehicles used by politicians and celebrities who wanted to conceal their identities. Using his small Sony camera, he took photos of their number plate.

Curly was a professional. He deleted all the files on the Sim card in his cell phone, but leaving it still active. He switched it back on and waited for an open lorry travelling in the opposite direction and threw the phone into it. The signal could still be picked up by whoever was monitoring the phone, but it would lead them on a false trail.

He found a Curry's store, bought a cell phone and paid for a connection. Unfortunately, it would take a few hours before he could use it, so he had to find a public telephone to call Alicia. Such phones were becoming rare outside the large cities, but he eventually found one in a side street.

Curly asked the operator for a reverse charge call to the US. It took some time before Alicia was able to respond. She was clearly pleased to receive his call and to know he had carried out her instructions.

'Sean, two Russians who worked for Seperkov were arrested in Pakistan. Certain measures familiar to them were used to extract information. It looks like Seperkov was behind the London bomb and is in England. He must have travelled on a forged passport and a different identity, maybe even disguised. He could have used the Russian diplomatic channel. If so, it would suggest he had help from one of the Russian government agencies. He may have also had help from someone senior in the British government or the security service.

'It looks like his prime target could be Oleg Detroski, but you may also be on his list if he has been monitoring our calls, since he will know you are going to Riverside. I was also told by the Head of MI6 that his agent, Angel, has been caught and taken into the house. Beware, MI6 have a sniper, who was sent to protect Angel; he doesn't yet know about you and is hiding in the woods near the house. I will try and get a message to him through Angel's boss at the MI6 Headquarters, but that might prove difficult since our lines have been compromised.'

The phone was suddenly cut off. People were queuing outside and getting anxious, so Curly went to go back to his car. He now had to rethink his strategy.

The driver of the car spoke into the microphone to Seperkov, who was in the back seat.

'Something strange has happened. The signal from the agent's phone is getting weaker and according to the GPS map he seems to be travelling in the opposite direction. Perhaps he's going back to London.'

'Pull over,' ordered Seperkov. He examined the picture and saw the vehicle stop at a truck depot.

'He's abandoned his phone to distract us, which means he knows he's being followed. He could only know that if someone has informed him, probably CTU or MI6. Driver, proceed fast to Riverside – that's where he'll be heading, nothing changes except he will be expecting us. We will not disappoint him.'

Cane heard the commotion coming from the hall. Shortly after, the door suddenly burst open and to his amazement an unconscious woman was brought into the room by two men, who flung her onto the bed. It was Clare Angel whom he had seen drive up to the house earlier. Seeing the open door, he was about to run out, but his motion came to an abrupt end by a burly Russian woman holding a pistol to his head.

'I warned you not to try and escape, Mr Cane. I've brought you a companion whom you may recognise. When she wakes up she will feel a little dizzy from a bump on the head.'

The three then left the room and locked the door. Cane took a wet towel from the bathroom and placed it on Angel's head. After a few minutes she opened her eyes and colour returned to her white face.

'Where am I? Who are you?' she asked, holding her head. As full consciousness and colour returned to her face, she smiled at Cane and apologised for not recognising him.

Cane smiled back and held her hand. Her eyes looked through him. For a very brief moment in time, he felt intimately connected to her. It was the same feeling he'd experienced when they first met. It actually spooked him.

'I saw you at the front door then lost sight of you. It seems as though someone didn't want you to see too much of the house.' Aware of the active camera on the wall, he helped Angel off the bed and took her in the bathroom. Once inside and beyond the view of the camera, he whispered, 'We're being watched so don't say anything you don't want them to hear.' She pulled him close to her mouth.

'I have planted some miniature microphones in the hall and in an envelope addressed to Detroski. It's unlikely he will be given it, but we will be able to monitor speech in part of the house. There is a highly trained SAS sniper hidden in the woods overlooking the house who can also pick up sounds from them. He will have seen what has happened and will report back to SIS. They will know what to do.'

What she really meant was the information would only go to BS not to anyone else.

'Have you seen Detroski? He owns this house and is supposed to be here.' She suddenly realised Cane wasn't supposed to know that she was from MI6. But by now he had probably guessed.

'No, I was drugged, brought here and kept locked in this room. Can you tell me exactly what's going on?' he asked.

Angel told him what she knew and that CTU's satellite had picked up his phone message so they were able to track him to the house.

'We believe Seperkov is on his way here, probably to kill Detroski, unless he's already dead. Our own lives could be in danger so we have to get out fast.'

Cane's thoughts went back to the plane and the loss he had suffered. The man who was probably responsible was actually coming to the house. It was his chance to take retribution. Before leaving the bathroom, he asked Angel why the British Police and John Nicholas hadn't been informed about her mission.

'I can't give you an answer at present, so we're on our own.'

Cane, being now more politically aware after the millennium bomb incident, thought once again he was in the middle of a political conspiracy or someone's personal vendetta.

'How do you propose we get out of here?' he asked.

Angel took off her boots and unscrewed the heels. Concealed in them were four sealed metal capsules. She took out two. The others contained a highly toxic compressed gas. They were her reserve armament. She walked out into the room and surreptitiously placed two small plastic discs from one of them onto the wall near the barred windows. She then took a sheet of paper that was lying on the table and, out of sight of the camera, scribbled a long message. She folded it up and gave it to Cane. He took it to the bathroom to read it.

Have placed miniature radio microphones around the walls. They will transmit speech to Spear positioned in the woods. He can re-transmit them back to SIS. Spear has enough fire power to blow a hole in the wall of the room and take out all the people, but he won't act until I give the order. We need to wait for Seperkov before taking any action. If these people were going to kill us they would have already done it. They must have a plan and we need to know it.

Cane realised Angel was a serious woman with a mission. That mission was also his mission, but she knew how to carry it out. The Russians had been planning this for some time and were no fools. He had great misgivings about what might happen. Like a suicide bomber, he no longer cared about himself, but only on seeking justice for the death of his wife and the passengers and crew of BA66. He hadn't forgotten Christine Hunter, who had led him to the house and was probably working with Seperkov. The day of reckoning had finally arrived.

Spear put on the earphones Angel had left him so could hear the conversations in the house. His first task was to transmit them straight to BS using the equipment in Angel's box. Within minutes his cell phone rang and the SIS director was acknowledging the messages.

'What is your assessment of the situation?' he asked.

'Angel is locked in a room with Cane, but seems to have things under control. They are expecting the arrival of Seperkov. No sign of Detroski. I can blow a hole in their room at any time, but for now am keeping undercover. Your woman is a resourceful gal. Where did you find her?'

'That's my little secret. Just make sure you bring her back to us alive.'

'I'll do my best,' said Spear.

'There is one more thing you need to know. An Irishman who works for Alicia Garcia, the Head of CTU, is on his way to Riverside. He's an undercover contractor, not a CTU agent. He's the Americans' contribution to finding the plane bomber and is the only person who knows what Seperkov looks like. The problem is, Seperkov also knows him as the killer of his half-brother so a personal vendetta is also involved in all this. Make sure you don't shoot the Irishman if he tries to make contact. The man has many aliases. I had to tell Garcia about your role so hopefully she'll have passed it on to him. Unfortunately, she thinks that Seperkov may have the cipher key to the encrypted text messages the agent had been sending to her, so he was forced to discard the phone. I don't know what he plans to do when he arrives, so be on your guard as things may get complicated. Seperkov and his men are travelling in a black SUV. They had been following the Irishman to Riverside until they lost him and so he could arrive first. He is driving a blue BMW. You should know this man is a trained ex-SAS and MI5 officer, but now, like you, is a freelance. Garcia won't release his true identity, but I understand he has a bad reputation.'

Spear searched his memory for such a man, but there were many who could fit the description. Using his earpiece he was now able to pick up talk coming from the house. Angel's voice was clear because she knew where the microphones were placed. It was now a waiting game. The next move would have to be made by Seperkov.

CHAPTER 17

The Final Reckoning

Curly followed the route given by his satellite navigator and arrived at a road close to the house at Riverside. He parked on a lay-by in a wooded area and noticed two other vehicles also parked further along the road on a path in the woods. The house was visible from a clearing. He estimated it to be about five hundred metres away on the bank of the River Thames. His first priority was to contact the SAS man to avoid being shot. But he would be covering his back.

Spear's adrenaline was rising. It made him alert. He removed his eyepiece just a few seconds to make an adjustment and heard the crack of a broken twig. Someone or something was approaching. It could be a rabbit, a squirrel or some other woodland animal, but they would make further noises. This was someone trying to avoid being heard. Danger lurked nearby. He turned around to be confronted by a man with a pistol pointed at his head.

'Don't move or I'll shoot,' said the intruder.

Spear sensed the man meant what he said. He froze. But his rifle was pointed at the intruder's chest; they were both locked in a kill situation.

'I don't know who you are, but since you probably know me, you will appreciate that unless we point our weapons away from each other, we could both be dead men. I guess we're here for the same reason.'

Spear gave his SAS identity number used by field operators. Curly immediately recognised it and lowered his pistol. Spear did the same. They shook hands. In the exchanges that followed they identified mutual acquaintances from their army days. Although the two had never met, they had gone through similar training.

Spear showed him the rocket-propelled grenades that could breach the house windows and even the walls of the house if necessary, but he had orders to wait for Angel's command and only use them if the need arose. She had placed microphones in the rooms so he could hear what was being said, but there was no way of sending a message back since their cell phones and communicators had been taken by their captors.

After they had updated each other on the situation, they worked out a strategy. Curly would go to the house and try and find a way inside while Spear covered him. The first priority was to remove the abductors and rescue Cane and Angel before Seperkov arrived. Curly had the advantage; he knew from a photo he had once seen what Seperkov looked like.

Spear gave Curly a bullet-proof over-jacket. He was amazed at the range of weaponry in Spear's case. Curly made his way towards the gardens of the house, avoiding the paths, assuming hidden cameras would be observing people using them. Fortunately, a gardener's shed was located in a shaded corner of the lawn giving a good view of the front of the house and drive. He made his way to it and was surprised the door wasn't locked. It was an ideal lookout.

Curly settled down and tried his cell phone. It had been over an hour since it was activated and was now on-line. But he wondered if it could be monitored by the people in Seperkov's car. He decided, at least for the time being, not to take the risk of using it. Curly reviewed the layout of the house. He was close enough to see that some of the windows were blacked out and probably alarmed. There was a rear door, but that would almost certainly be protected.

Curly heard a door open and someone muttering.

'Where are you taking us? I need to speak to Oleg Detroski,' Angel said.

Then a woman replied, 'You both have a choice. Come quietly or you will be drugged. You are going on a river boat to see an old friend.'

Cane shouted, 'First, we must know if Detroski is in the house.'

'Why are you so concerned about that traitor?'

The woman spoke a Russian vulgarity, which demonstrated her hatred of the man whose house she had taken over.

'He's a British citizen and you have no right to kidnap him or us,' said Cane, realising that his remarks would go unheeded.

The last words Spear heard from Angel were, 'Why are you binding our hands and blindfolding us?' She then said the word 'SWANS'. It was a password she had agreed with him, meaning don't attack but follow. The Russian woman heard what she said and looked at her in a strange way. Angel pointed to the window – swans were swimming on the river.

Curly saw Cane, Angel, the Russian woman and two men get into a SUV parked outside. The vehicle drove off down the gravel path to the road. Now was the time to use his phone. He called Alicia and told her what had happened. She replied in an untypically anxious voice.

'We have a satellite positioned over the area tracking the vehicles. Spear is leaving his position in the woods and following it. Seperkov and his followers are close and will arrive at the house at any time. You must make your own decisions, but don't take on the men since there are at least four of them, including Seperkov. They are likely to be well armed. We are watching you now, but will lose the satellite pictures in the next thirty minutes.'

'Why is there no back-up?' Curly asked.

'I can't tell you that now. You're on your own, but then that's how you like it.'

He ended the call for fear of it being traced on his insecure line.

Spear found the vehicle on his tracker and discreetly followed it. BS had called him and repeated the need to protect Angel and Cane, but not to involve the police or anyone else. He was told that Seperkov was on his way to Riverside where it was likely Detroski and his bodyguard, Voss, were being held. Spear thought to himself, *I hope my old SAS colleague knows what he's up against.* But then he didn't really know how ruthless Curly was and of the personal issues between him and Seperkov.

The SUV sped up the drive and parked in front of the house. Four men emerged and went inside. A few minutes later, Curly heard two shots that appeared to come from an upstairs room. Two of the men came out into the garden. Curly didn't recognise them, but became concerned when one, with a pistol in his hand, started to walk towards the shed. He fitted the silencer and released the safety lock on the Sig. He positioned himself directly in front of the door, which, if opened, would give him a direct frontal shot. It was the split second element of surprise that gave him the advantage since any searcher wouldn't expect to be faced with his quarry. The other man went around the house and was out of sight when the door opened.

The Russian opened the door and looked straight down the barrel of the Sig, but, before his brain had time to register what he was facing, a bullet had removed part of it, together with the front of his face. It was spattered over the wooden wall of the shed. The muffled sound from the silencer couldn't be heard from outside. Curly searched the pockets of the dead man and took a wallet and what looked like an ID pass to the Russian Embassy. It was time to leave the shed.

Curly ran to the front door of the house that had been left open. He cautiously went inside. Russian talk was coming from upstairs and he heard a door close. Curly went into a large lounge and crouched down behind a settee. A mirror was mounted on the wall to the right that gave him a view of the hallway and the door of the room. Two men came into the room. He recognised one as being Seperkov. His hair and beard were greyer and he was much thinner than the image in the photo. Here, at last, was the architect of the worst terrorist crime in British aircraft history. That thought filled Curly with an immediate desire to kill the man. But there were others involved and Seperkov was the key to their identity. Yes, he would kill him, but not now. He had to be taken alive. First, there were two bodyguards to be removed. Also, he had to find out who was upstairs. Curly had been in many such situations like this one when instant thinking and reacting had saved his life. Again his main weapon was the element of surprise. He would use it.

With his faithful Sig gripped in his hands, Curly stood up, confronted the two men and pointed it straight at them. The bodyguard reacted instantly and went for his shoulder holster, but never reached it; the bullet put a neat hole into the front of his cranium. It was meant to enter through the mouth, but Curly's hands were cocked a little high. The effect, however, was the same and the man went down like a stone, spilling blood onto the cream carpet.

He repositioned the Sig to Seperkov's face. Instead of an expression of horror, expected after just witnessing the violent death of his associate, Seperkov's lips widened slightly, showing the glimmer of a smile, as he said, 'Well, at last we meet, Mr O'Brien. I was expecting you. Although, I didn't think you would be here when we arrived. Pity our meeting has had to start like this,' pointing to the poor man lying on the carpet. Still in a calm, unruffled voice, he continued. 'Yes, I know we want to kill each other and with good reasons, but you and I aren't so very different. I have been following your career over the years and am very impressed. You are physically different to what I expected, but in previous photos you were probably in one of your ridiculous disguises.'

Curly knew he was playing for time, hoping the three men would come to his rescue. It was an old trick, but Seperkov didn't know there were only two left and that Curly was aware of them. The one upstairs would by now have heard what was going on and be preparing to act.

Showing anger at Seperkov's demeanour, Curly said, 'I'm not here to listen to your rambling. I want to know what you've done with Oleg Detroski.'

'Oh, that traitor. He's been punished for his misdeeds. Why have MI6 and the CIA been so concerned about him? Like the other traitors who stole money from our country, he has been served justice.'

'Stop pretending you're a patriot. You're just a terrorist and a criminal. You haven't answered my question,' said Curly.

'The answer's upstairs,' he retorted.

Curly noticed a shadow in the hallway getting larger. A hand gripping a gun then appeared just after a shot grazed Curly's left shoulder, taking with it a piece of his bullet-proof jacket. He was glad Spear had given it to him, otherwise he would have sustained a shoulder wound. Curly lowered the Sig and fired. The explosive bullet took off the hand still clutching the gun; blood spurted out from the wound as the man yelled out and staggered into the doorway. The second bullet produced a large bloody hole in his chest and put the poor wretch out of his misery. The sound of the shot brought the man from the garden, who unwittingly rushed into the room, only to be halted by a third round from the Sig. Curly's swift reaction now left him alone with Seperkov whose expression had now changed to one of horror. Taking advantage of Curly's distraction, he rushed towards him wielding a knife he had concealed in his pocket. The two men wrestled on the carpet. Seperkov was strong and, although at least ten years older, was physically fitter. Curly didn't like hand-to-hand fighting, but he knew that, for the man gripping him around the throat with one hand and knife hovering above his face in the other, it was a life or death struggle. As he tried to lower the knife onto Curly's face, Seperkov muttered, 'This is for my brother.'

With his adrenaline flowing at maximum, Curly summoned all his strength and kneed Seperkov in the groin and then, with his free right hand still holding the Sig, he crashed it onto the back of his assailant's skull. Seperkov loosened his grip and dropped the knife, narrowly missing Curly's head, and slumped forward semi-conscious.

Curly stood up and dragged Seperkov onto a chair. He noticed fresh scars on his neck and forehead. He took out some plastic binders from his pocket and pulled them tight around the man's hands and legs. They were part of the kit he always carried with him and superior to conventional handcuffs that required keys. When Seperkov came round he wouldn't be able to move. Placing the Sig back in its holster, the next task was to go upstairs. He entered the bathroom, after looking in all the bedrooms, and was shocked at the scene that confronted him. The man, whom he assumed was the Russian oligarch, Detroski, was lying in a pool of blood in a bath with a bullet wound in the back of his head. The front of his face was blasted away leaving a gruesome bloody sight. His hands had been tied and a gag placed in his mouth. He had been executed with the traditional shot to the back of his head. This was yet another murder Seperkov would have to pay for, but did he do it for himself or for someone else or for the Russian government? When he talked about 'our country', it implied the latter. He was known to have close associations with the Kremlin. How otherwise was he able to enter Britain? But the killing of Detroski was a small crime compared with the murder of 349 people on the BA plane.

Curly called Alicia and updated her on events and told her that Detroski was dead, knowing she would inform others who were in the communications loop. She told him the car carrying Cane and Angel was tracked going to a boat moored at a village called Pangbourne, on the River Thames. Spear was following and standing by since he didn't know who was on the boat or the intentions of their captors. She added that having Seperkov in custody would certainly change plans and would pass that information to Spear.

The big question for Curly was how to deal with Seperkov? Alicia just told him to find a satisfactory outcome and clearly didn't want to give him any orders. After seeing what he had done to Detroski, Curly was even more outraged. There was no fitting punishment for such evil acts. He had to find out who else was supporting Seperkov. If he could, he would gladly hand him to al-Qaeda. That fate would be more painful than he could expect from his enemies here. The answer could be on the boat at Pangbourne.

The boat, a large river cruiser, was moored upstream of Pangbourne village on a quiet part of the river. Vasalov removed Cane and Angel's blindfolds and with their wrists still bound, led them onto the boat.

During the journey, Angel and Paul Cane had been sitting close to each other on the back seat of the car. He had felt the warmth of her body. Their hands were bound, but they were able to touch. Cane's emotions were raised. His pulse rate increased. He had experienced it the last time the two of them were close. There was something going on he couldn't explain. From her responses he sensed she also felt it. They were in a dangerous situation not knowing their fate or where they were being taken, but being together produced a feeling of calmness.

Angel had placed one of the metal capsules she had concealed in the heel of her boot, in her bra. It contained a liquid that, when exposed to the air, would rapidly evaporate into a gaseous vapour and temporarily incapacitate anybody who inhaled it. AL had given her the device for use in a dire emergency. She would only use it if their lives were threatened.

Vasalov led them onto the boat. It was then Cane saw her. The dark-eyed, evil woman who had tried to kill him and Valerie. He assumed it was Christine Hunter. That was confirmed when Vasalov said, 'Christine, here are the people you were expecting. Gregori should be joining us soon. He wanted to know if all the arrangements are in place.'

'Yes, they are. When will he be here?' she asked.

'He's had some personal business to deal with at Riverside,' replied Vasalov.

Looking harassed, Hunter shouted, 'He was supposed to call me and hasn't, so I left a message on his phone.'

Turning to Cane with an angry scowl on her face, she said, 'So you've found another woman already.'

The remark was meant to rile him. It succeeded. He had to be restrained by the two men who had brought them from Riverside when he tried to punch her in the face.

Without showing any emotion or saying anything, Angel gave Hunter a penetrating look. It was one that killers know. She would realise that a dangerous adversary had now arrived.

'Take them down below,' ordered Hunter.

The two men grabbed Cane and Angel and pushed them down some steps into a small rear cabin. They thought it was below the waterline. Angel feared their captors might be planning to sink the boat with them locked in the cabin. She began to wonder if Spear had successfully followed them.

There was no sign of a camera in the tiny cabin so she took off her bullet-proof vest, unbuttoned her blouse and removed the capsule from her bra. Cane looked on in amazement. It was impossible for him not to be aroused at the sight of her shapely figure and well-rounded breasts.

Seeing Cane looking, she quickly covered herself, saying, 'Sorry, don't get any ideas. It was the best hiding place for this little device. When it comes into contact with air it will produce a powerful gas that will temporarily blind and choke anyone within two metres'

'If we're kept in here, how are we going to use it?' Cane asked.

'Let's wait for the opportunity. I'm sure Spear will provide it,' she replied.

BS called Spear and told him about what had happened at Riverside. He was able to give him Curly's new cell phone number that Alicia had obtained so they could communicate. She had her experts at CTU encrypt the number so nobody else on the network could monitor calls. Spear was not surprised to learn that Curly had killed Seperkov's men and had him alive. Like himself, legally Curly didn't exist and had no official authority so he could do what he wanted.

BS was worried about the situation. He had lost control now that Angel was in the hands of the terrorists. How could she have been stupid enough to let herself be taken prisoner and allow Alicia's loose cannon to run amok? It was going to be difficult to contain the secrecy of the operation now that dead bodies were laying around in the house. He called Davenport and told him about Detroski's murder and the events that had taken place. The two men agreed his death had to be kept a secret and the mess at Riverside cleaned up before the local police or media found out. Seperkov and the rest had to be eliminated as a matter of urgency. But no bodies had to be found. Davenport told BS it was a job for

Alpha group. BS agreed. They would be dispatched as soon as night descended on the area. A mock accident would allow them to close the road near the house and men in police uniforms would patrol the area to keep out any curious on-lookers. Alicia was told about the clean-up operation. She ordered Curly to do what was necessary to Seperkov and leave the house.

If what happened at Riverside was discovered, there would be a mammoth political fall-out for the government and everybody concerned. Many heads would fall. BS would be the first casualty. But in the chain reaction, others would follow. On the positive side, the man responsible for the London plane bomb had been found and would be eliminated. It would complete the mission. Once that was achieved then it could be classified and except for a few selected individuals, no one would know that it ever happened. No one would know that Seperkov had ever been in Britain. If the Russian government did know, they would never admit their involvement. BS wondered what had happened to Voss, Detroski's so-called bodyguard. Was he one of Seperkov's men? It was Voss who had initially suggested his boss went to Riverside.

Curly returned to the lounge where Seperkov was still lying unconscious on a chair when he received a surprise call from Spear.

'I know what has happened, but you need to drive here as soon as you can and bring Seperkov if he is still alive. Cane and Angel's lives are in danger and Seperkov could be our bargaining chip to save them. I am on a small boat near a bridge at Pangbourne. Call me when you get close. I am sending you the GPS coordinates.'

Curly had to leave Seperkov to get his car on the other side of the wood. His hands and feet were tightly bound, but an extra tie was placed around the leg of the settee.

Twenty minutes later Curly arrived at the front door of the house in the BMW. Feeling some apprehension, Curly ran into the house only to find no Seperkov. He must have regained consciousness and broken the binding cords. Seeing a blood-stained knife on the floor that Seperkov had tried to kill him with, he was supplied with the answer as to how he had removed the binds. Where was he? Drops of blood led to one of the bodies in the hallway, then outside. He must have picked up the gun from the dead man who came in from the garden. Curly had forgotten to remove it. So there was now a very angry terrorist with a bump on his head, armed with a gun, somewhere in the grounds. Fortunately, Curly had Seperkov's cell phone, but no doubt others were stashed away in the SUV. It was then he noticed that the SUV was missing. Seperkov had escaped just after Curly left the house.

Curly called Spear.

'Seperkov has escaped and is likely to be heading for Pangbourne to join the others. I have the GPS of your position so am on my way.'

Looking through his binoculars, Spear saw the SUV drive up to the boat and Seperkov get out. He was greeted by Vasalov and Hunter. He looked dishevelled, was bleeding and angry. Examining the cabin cruiser more closely, Spear noticed boxes stacked around the deck connected by cables that went into the cabin. He had seen something similar before.

'Good God. It's rigged with explosives,' he said to himself.

He now realised that he had to act quickly and get Cane and Angel off the boat, but he would need help. Curly was only minutes away. He estimated there were three men and two women onboard and Cane and Angel, who he assumed were locked away in the cabin below the deck. The Russians were all armed, but that didn't present him with a problem. Spear had taken on a whole platoon in Iraq single-handed, killed everybody except two, whom he took as prisoners. No doubt the man who would soon be with him could boast a similar record.

They would have all the bad people in one place so the plan could work. There was only one problem. It was a summer's evening and still light. There were a number of pleasure boats on the river and the village of Pangbourne was only half a mile away, so any shooting would be heard and attract attention, then the local police would arrive and their mission would fail.

The villagers and tourists enjoying a summer evening on one

of the quietest and most rural parts of the English countryside were unaware of the existence of two of the most sought after terrorists in the world in their safe environment.

Spear called up his boss, BS.

'Seperkov escaped from Riverside and has now joined his comrades on the Thames boat, including the woman I believe you call Hunter, so we have all the rats in the cage. First, we have to get Angel and Cane out because it looks like they had planned to blow up the boat with them in it. The Irishman is on his way, so I have enough back-up to continue with the mission. Do I have your permission to proceed?'

'Yes, but get Angel and Cane out first. I know I can depend on you, Bill. After, call and say 'SUNSHINE', if all goes well. If not, say 'STORM'. I think someone is trying to tap into my phone so no more conversational calls.'

Spear liked a challenge and wanted to repay his old friend BS for saving him from a possible court marshal from the SAS after breaking the rules while on a second mission in Iraq.

The door to the cabin on the boat opened. A hard-faced, angry Russian stood in front of them.

'So you're Paul Cane,' he said.

Angel looked at him and said calmly, 'And who are you?'

Taken aback by her calm manner, he replied, 'The reason why you're here.'

'So you're Seperkov. I am disappointed; having heard so much about you, I was expecting a smarter-looking man.'

Cane noticed Angel gripping the capsule in her hand. She was cleverly engaging Seperkov and playing with him like a cat plays with a mouse before it strikes. Hunter was close behind and the others out on deck. Spear hadn't done anything so this was their only chance to escape. The door was wide open with the key in the lock.

She saw that Paul Cane was directly behind her in the confined space of the cabin and he was looking down at her hand. She unscrewed the miniature capsule using her long fingers. It was difficult, but worked. Suddenly the air was filled with a suffocating gas. Seperkov, taken by surprise, started coughing and moved back, placing his hands over his eyes. Cane saw Hunter's dark eyes staring at him. She too was coughing. Angel pushed Seperkov and Hunter aside and went through the narrow door space. She had ripped off her blouse to cover her face and Cane followed with his coat over his head. The compressed form of CS gas was effective at temporarily immobilising their captors. It would only last for seconds, but it was enough. Angel turned around and pushed Seperkov and Hunter into the cabin and locked the door. Fortunately, they had left the key in the lock.

The two Russians on the deck rushed towards them. Cane punched one in the face, but his eyes were smarting and he was no match for the burly Russian. Angel was doing well using her judo moves on the other man who was almost twice her size. She slammed his face against the cabin wall with a crack that sounded like a fractured skull.

Ten minutes earlier, about two hundred metres away, there was a tap on Spear's shoulder. Curly had arrived. They shook hands.

'Glad you could join the party. I nearly expected to have to go it alone and I'm not well dressed. I've spoken to the boss and we have a go situation. First, we must get our friends off the boat and then kill the bastards. Basic problem is, we have to do it quietly so the people in the other boats moored along the river don't hear anything.

'It looks like they packed the boat with explosive and were going to blow it up, so first, we need to deactivate the firing mechanism.'

Curly smiled. 'No, we don't. They provided us with the perfect tool. We blow them up with the boat. Seperkov likes blowing up people in airplanes so we'll give him a dose of his own medicine.'

Spear smiled. 'Why didn't I think of that?'

'All we have to do is take them by surprise, rescue Angel and Cane and lock them in the cabin, light the fuse and bang – it's all over and with no body parts that could be recognised; then we wait to read all about it in the newspapers tomorrow.'

Curly put a new cartridge loaded with non-explosive bullets into his Sig. They were more appropriate for the task ahead. He fitted the silencer while Spear checked his own Hecker Koch pistol, also loaded with short-range bullets. He put some stun grenades in his pocket. They tried to look like two tourists out for a walk along the river, looking for a place to fish. But their guns and bullet-proof vests concealed under their anoraks did make them look a little overdressed for a warm summer's evening, but there were no people about, so hopefully they wouldn't be seen.

They were just fifty metres from the cabin cruiser when they heard a muffled cry and saw what looked like smoke coming out of the boat's cabin. A woman was seen running towards one of the SUVs parked on the roadside near the moorings. Spear saw it was the Russian, so took aim and fired. She staggered and dropped a box she was carrying, but managed to get into the vehicle and drive away. Spear ran after her, fired a round at the car but missed. He was too late. He picked up the box and found it contained what looked like a timing mechanism with a control switch attached.

Curly ran towards the boat with his pistols ready to fire. Spear ran back to join him. They saw Cane and Angel fighting with two men on the deck. Spear was the first to arrive and took on one of the men, a tall Russian he had seen leaving Riverside. The Russian pulled out a knife, but before he could use it, a red spot appeared on his head and the man dropped like a stone on the deck. Curly lowered his pistol and at point blank range aimed a second shot at the other man, who had a gun pointed at Angel's head. He fell back onto the deck clutching his chest wound. Cane and Angel, having now disengaged from the dead Russians, leaped off the boat onto the bank.

Angel turned to Spear and cooly said, 'What kept you so long?'

But he was in no mood for jokes. She then shouted, 'We've locked Seperkov and Hunter in the cabin, but the other woman, Vasalov, ran off after we released the gas.'

'What gas?' asked Spear.

'It was contained in one of these,' she said, placing a small, empty metal capsule in his hand. It held a special compressed type of CS gas mixture that when released in the atmosphere formed a dense mist. An unpleasant concoction of toxic gases designed to disarm and temporarily blind anybody within a few metres.

She continued. 'Our man at SIS engineered a miniature capsule that was concealed in the heel of my shoe.' She pointed down to her rather oversized boots. 'They certainly feel lighter now I've got rid of it.'

Curly couldn't believe what he had just seen and heard. 'Did you say that Seperkov and Hunter are down there locked in a cabin?'

'Yes, and they will be feeling very sick, having inhaled some gas, but it won't kill them, so we still have work to do.'

'Can't we not just open the door and shoot them both?' asked Spear.

'Yes, we could, but we don't want their bodies found and anyway that death's too quick for them.'

Pointing to the boxes, Curly said, 'Have you seen the drums of explosives on the deck? They were going to blow the boat up with you both in it. I think it was Seperkov's plan to include me, but that went wrong at Riverside.'

'OK, but let's not disrupt their plan,' she said.

Spear and Curly had expertise in explosives and soon found primed detonators attached to the drums. Spear produced the box he had picked up from the escaping Vasalov. It contained a remotely radio-controlled firing circuit. He switched it on and a red light appeared. He then promptly switched it off. All that was required was to send a signal to detonate the explosives. The timer on the box could be overridden by a manual switch. They reckoned there was enough explosive, which looked like Semtex, to completely destroy the boat and all its contents.

Curly said, 'The people who put this together were professionals. I don't understand why they went to so much trouble just to kill us when a few bullets would have been easier. There's more to this than we're seeing. But we can sort that out later. Let's finish the job they started and get the hell out of here.'

Angel had been collecting stuff from the boat, including the log book, clothes and articles stowed away in the lockers. It was all evidence for later. She made one last visit to the cabin and heard some whimpering sounds coming from within, but no hammering on the door or signs of them trying to get out. Perhaps in the confined space of the cabin, the gas had made them unconscious. It slightly lessened what they were about to do. These people did deserve to die, but killing people in cold blood didn't come easy, even to Angel.

The four went to the small boat under the bridge where Spear had his equipment. It was time to take retribution. But who was going to be the executioner? They all looked at Paul Cane.

'Paul, you've suffered the greatest loss from the people locked up in that boat. Now is your chance to serve justice.'

He took the control unit from Curly. His hand hovered over the firing button. Tears flowed from his eyes as he thought about Valerie and all those people on the plane. And the others who had been killed and injured in the past by the acts of evil perpetrated by the two people on the boat. But did he have the sole right to take retribution and kill them for their crimes? They had intended to do it to him and many others. Did the hangman think about what he was about to do before he opened the trap door?

Angel, sensing Paul's hesitation, looked at the others. The message was clear. They all placed their hands on the fire button and together pushed it down. After a few seconds' delay, a massive explosion erupted into a fireball that spread debris over a wide area. Nothing was left of the boat and mooring. Whoever had planted the explosive didn't want any evidence left behind.

They had to get out of the area quickly. The explosion would soon bring people to the scene. Cane agreed to go with Curly since he didn't have a car. Angel agreed to go with Spear, who was charged with protecting her. He thought the lady didn't need protecting; she was a winner, a survivor. BS knew what he was doing when he gave her the mission. Before leaving, the four shook hands. Angel came to Cane and gave him a close hug. Her look left him in no doubt that she wanted to see him again. Her eyes, her expression, her manner were identical to those he once saw in Valerie. It was the third time he had noticed it.

Spear remembered the call he had to make. When he heard the click of the receiver being lifted, he said, 'SUNSHINE'. Then it went dead. Angel decided not to ask any questions, but guessed it was a coded message to BS. They needed to get back to London post-haste. But first, Angel had to get back to her own car parked in the woods so she could drive a different route from that taken by Spear since they must not be seen together.

Seperkov's SUV was badly damaged, but they had to remove the number plate. It was burnt out so nothing was left inside that could identify the driver. Vasalov had obviously escaped in the other vehicle, which gave them a problem. Who was she? Why did she leave everybody and not attempt to protect them? Why did she have the firing control unit? They were questions that had to be answered.

It was late in the evening but still light when Spear drove back to the wooded area near Riverside where Angel had parked her car. She wanted to go back into the house and asked Spear to come with her. He advised against it, but the lady insisted and she was the boss.

The front door was partially open so they went inside. The bodies of the two Russians were spread out on the floor. On the table in the corner of the room she saw her bag. It still contained among other items her treasured Walther P99. She wanted to go upstairs to see Detroski's body, but Spear told her they should leave as the police would be at the scene of the explosion and would soon be putting up road blocks. They left and returned to their cars. Angel thanked Spear, gave him a hug and kissed his cheek. He smiled and said with his usual humour, 'Glad to be of help. We should do it again some time.'

They drove away separately in the direction of London.

Curly and Cane drove at speed back towards Reading and the M4. At first, the two men didn't speak. Curly was not a talkative person, it was his nature, but eventually he said, 'Well, Paul, how do you feel having rid the world of a mass murderer?'

Cane paused before replying. The shock of what had happened during the last few days was just beginning to take effect. When the adrenaline subsided the body took time to re-adjust itself to normal. A horrendous experience could leave its mark from which recovery could take a very long time. For some, there was no recovery and lives could be irreversibly changed.

'I should feel pleased that justice has been done. We took retribution on those who were behind the terrorist act. But are there others higher up the chain who may never be brought to justice? Seeing Seperkov and Hunter face-to-face brought everything back to me. But their deaths haven't brought me closure. My wife's death and all the loss of life on the plane were so unnecessary. What did it gain the terrorists? They had no cause, no reason, nothing but their own self-interest. What we did was right, but will it change anything? We thought that after the millennium bombs. The main culprits were eliminated, but others took their place. There is just an endless chain of retributions.'

Curly listened sympathetically.

'Paul, it may not be a consolation to you, but I've been through what you're feeling many times. In fact, I only came over a few days ago from the US to stop a man who wanted to kill me and was threatening the lives of my sisters. After I retired from the army at the end of the IRA troubles in Northern Ireland, the man's brother murdered my parents after being released early from prison. I knew if he had been caught by the police, who at that time were told not to do anything that threatened the peace process, he wouldn't be charged or prosecuted. I, therefore, delivered my own justice and shot him. You are right about the retributions. The brother, who was released from prison a month ago, came after me. After holding one of my sisters at gunpoint, threatening to kill her, my other sister killed him with her stiletto shoe seconds after I shot his hand, so, although I didn't actually kill him, it was my intention to do so.'

'I know you've worked for Alicia for many years and by now must be hardened to killing,' said Cane.

'No, I'm not. When possible, I arrange others to do it. But it became my job in the same way that a soldier kills the enemy of his country without worrying about the morality of his actions. We are just soldiers doing a job. More freelance agents are being used by the security services because they are not restricted by the rules, which these days favour the bad guys instead of the victims.'

Cane began to like his new companion. He was quite different to what he had imagined.

'So you weren't sent here on a mission to find Seperkov?'

'No, not initially. Alicia asked me to talk to you since I was in London, but that was before she received the phone call about your abduction by the terrorists. That changed everything because she had an agreement with Angel to help identify the plane bombers. CTU had suspected it was Seperkov, so passed that onto MI6.

'I had arranged for Seperkov's half-brother to be assassinated in Moscow since he was the aid to the Russian member of The New Order's Cabal, whom we now know ordered the placement of a live atomic bomb on the Thames barge. He therefore had a personal vendetta against me. You were the bait that brought me to Riverside. Unknown to us all, a CTU staff member on Alicia's inner team had given Seperkov the cell phones' encryption codes so he was able to monitor our exchanges.'

Cane looked puzzled. 'There are many things I don't understand. Why didn't Angel inform John Nicholas about what was happening? He had all the official resources to capture Seperkov and save Oleg Detroski and us?'

'I don't really know except people higher up the political chain didn't want it made public and involve the security services when they discovered the Russians, and not al-Qaeda, were behind the plane bomb. My guess is the government didn't want to jeopardise its relationship with the new Russian president by making public that one of his known friends was responsible for an appalling terrorist act. Seperkov was videoed going into the Kremlin a few weeks back before he disappeared. You could visualise the political consequences. That is the reason why Spear and I were brought in to help since we have no official status. If we had been killed, it would have been unmarked graves in some field or, more likely, a cremation and ashes used to fertilise a prison garden. I assume you realise that you were never at Riverside. Nobody must connect you with the events of the last two days.'

'But who made the decisions and controlled the mission?' Cane asked.

'It had to be Angel's boss, the Head of MI6.'

They were approaching the end of the M4 motorway. Curly switched on the car radio to hear the special news bulletin about a massive explosion on a boat at Pangbourne. Police and fire engines were at the scene.

Curly dropped Cane off at his apartment in Knightsbridge. Before leaving, he said, 'I don't know if we shall ever meet again. Since I know your name, you should know mine. My real name is Sean O'Brien. They shook hands. Then he got back in the BMW and drove to the city.

Cane had thought that he would never see his apartment again. Henry, the security guard, greeted him in the entrance with a surprised look.

'Glad you're back, Mr Cane. Everybody's been looking for you. I've had the police here four times. Are you alright?'

'Yes, Henry. I'm OK. Just very tired. Can you make sure no one disturbs me? I'll call the police later.'

Henry never asked questions. Discretion was why he was paid so much.

Cane woke up in the night. That was nothing unusual. He had done so since leaving the hospital. He had stopped taking sleeping pills since the physical pain had lessened and he wanted his body to return to normality. But the mental anguish persisted. The events of the last twenty hours had drained him; but now, alone again, he thought about his wife. Killing Seperkov and Hunter hadn't reduced the hurt they had inflicted. But this time it was a high-pitched sound and cold blast of air that had woken him. The windows were shut and no doors were open. The central heating was off so there was no source of cold air, but he certainly sensed it. The sound was like a distant cry for help. Faint but real.

In the darkness of the bedroom, near the window, he saw a flickering light. It was like a candle blowing in the wind. He pulled back the curtain, but apart from the distant light of the city there was nothing nearby. He closed the curtains and went back and sat on the bed. Then he saw the light again. It was in the form of an apparition, which moved slowly across the room. Cane had never believed in ghosts. But this was real. It stopped moving and what he saw made him freeze. His heart missed some beats.

Just a few metres in front of him was a ghostly image of what looked like Valerie's face looking at him. It lingered for about ten seconds then moved. She looked happy, even smiling. She turned, seemed to wave, before fading into the wall of the room; then it was all over. Cane tried to say something, but no sound came out of his mouth. Was it a final goodbye? Her killers had been served justice. Was she finally at peace? He tried to raise himself off the bed, but he couldn't move. Some force was holding him back. Was he dreaming? He fought it, but became very tired; then sleep took over. In the morning he remembered the dream or was it a dream? He felt more relaxed. The tension was gone. It was like a weight had been lifted from his mind.

The blue BMW was parked outside the Connaught Hotel.

'Nice to see you back, Mr Ryan,' said the doorman.

'Thanks, please look after the car. Here are the keys. It has to be returned to the hire company. I won't be requiring it again since I'm going back to America tomorrow.'

'Hope your business trip was successful, sir,' said the doorman.

'Yes, very successful,' said Curly.

Angel drove straight to her apartment in Kensington. On the way back she called BS on his special number, but there was no reply. The message she left simply said, 'Mission completed.'

She looked out of her bedroom window. The city lights were

coming on. The sun had set, leaving a red-purple sky. It was a clear, still night. It had been a long day – a very long day. She was exhausted. She stripped off all her clothes and boots. She kissed the boots. She owed a lot to Alan Leeke for the capsules; they had saved her and Paul Cane's lives. She went into the shower and as the warm water trickled over her body, she felt relaxed and thought about Paul, alone in his flat. She would definitely see him again. She dried herself and fell naked onto the bed and was soon consumed by sleep. Tomorrow would be another day.

CHAPTER 18

The Clean Up

Davenport's cell phone pinged. He knew who was sending the text message by the code on the screen.

'*Mission accomplished, but there are complications. We need to meet now. Absolute security essential.*'

BS rarely invoked urgency in his messages unless it was absolutely necessary.

Davenport typed back, '*Churchill Room at the club in twenty minutes.*'

Davenport excused himself from his dinner guests and walked to Albemarle Street, only ten minutes' walk away from the restaurant in Piccadilly where he was entertaining guests. He knew the location of all the street cameras so was able to avoid being seen by them. He was just one among many strolling in the streets of the West End on a warm summer's evening, so he wouldn't be noticed. BS would use his usual disguise. It never changed, which made it less effective for those who had seen it before.

Davenport's first task was to open a bottle of wine. The Churchill Room always had bottles in the refrigerator. It was his private room. Only he, or anyone with his permission, could use it. If the walls had recordings of some of the conversations that had taken place in the room over the years, then many government files would have to be altered.

BS looked grim as he took out the papers from his small, black briefcase. He explained to Davenport what had taken place at Riverside and Pangbourne relating to the death of the Russians, including their friend Oleg Detroski.

He said, 'Angel and Spear had done a great job, but

unfortunately couldn't prevent the murder of Detroski. It was Alicia's guy and Spear who saved the day after Cane and Angel had been taken by the Russians. But at the last moment, Angel used her wits and discharged one of AL's gas capsules to escape with Cane from the cabin on the boat where they were being held. Afterwards, she locked Seperkov and Hunter in the same cabin.

'The clean-up team went to Riverside and recovered all the bodies and documents. They were able to do this under the noses of the police, who were at the time fully engaged with the boat explosion at Pangbourne, which fortuitously gave them the diversion they needed. Anyone reporting it would assume that the two events were associated. But it was what was found at Riverside that is worrying. One of the dead men was Voss. It looks like he had been working for Seperkov. It was him who had suggested Detroski went to Riverside to hide from people who had threatened to kill him. The killing of Detroski was obviously Seperkov's main mission. The Russians took Cane as a hostage because Christine Hunter wanted him dead. They also thought he knew too much about the plane bomb. Seperkov had been able to monitor telephone conversations with Cane because a mole at CTU had given him the cell phone encryption codes.

'We don't have Seperkov's body, but do have his fingerprints and DNA. He wasn't very careful at Riverside. Although there is no doubt about Seperkov's responsibility for the bomb that blew up the BA plane, he must have had some high-level backing to be able to enter Britain and acquire all the resources he needed. We believe the Kremlin's hands are dirty, but, when that suspicion was raised with the PM, he categorically stated that all knowledge of Seperkov or what he was doing must be kept top secret. Only he and the Home Secretary would know the facts. That was the reason why we didn't alert Nicholas's people to what we had discovered. You can see the political consequences for us all if this gets out into the media.

'The problem is, one of the Russians, a Katrina Vasalov, escaped the carnage at Pangbourne and disappeared. She was an embassy official and the person who abducted Cane outside the

Russian Embassy in Kensington Palace Gardens. Spear thinks he wounded her before she jumped in the SUV at Pangbourne. That SUV was found burnt out in a field just outside Reading. But she knows everything. We know she hasn't tried to get back into the embassy since all entrances are under surveillance. I placed a watch on all airports and ports, but had to be careful no questions were asked by the police. The boat at Pangbourne was registered by a London company, but the owner was thought to be Russian. It's likely the police will track down the owner, but it was probably rented out. Vasalov would have used an alias to escape. There was clearly a strong relationship between her and Seperkov. At present the police aren't connecting this, or the incident in Kensington, to the Russians. But it won't be long before the local police report it to Special Branch, who will then involve the Counter Terrorist people.'

Davenport poured himself another drink.

'So, Alpha did a good clean-up job at Riverside?'

'Yes, they recovered everything, but we have to decide what to do with Detroski's body. We can make his death known to his wife or say he and Voss just disappeared. She is in France so won't want a lot of publicity. We can arrange for her to go into hiding. She will think that one of her husband's many enemies has taken him and could also be seeking her and their daughter. Our greatest problem will be the police and MI5. We must stop Detroski's PA or his wife from revealing that he had gone to Riverside.'

'I'll take care of that,' said Davenport. 'How are you going to deal with MI5? You know you've stolen their clothes on this one. Mrs Fancy Pants over at Thames House will be incandescent if she finds out what you've done.'

'Don't worry, that won't happen. That contingency is well covered.'

'Well, Henry, how did your girl perform?'

'Just as I expected. I haven't had a chance to talk to her yet, but Spear tells me she took control and used her capture to advantage. It enabled her to get close enough to Seperkov and his people, including Hunter, to orchestrate their demise.'

BS looked worried and embarrassed. Davenport knew his friend well enough to know something was bothering him.

BS poured out another glass of wine and said, 'You are my oldest and trusted friend. There is something I want to tell you since you mentioned Jayne. Early yesterday morning I received a call on my private phone, the number of which is known only to you and a few others. It was from Jayne's mother, Laura. I don't know how she obtained the number and code. She told me that I had to arrange for her husband, Norman Goodfellows, who is Jayne's stepfather, to be released from police custody or she would make it known that Jayne was my daughter. It was a bombshell I wasn't expecting. It came at a time when Jayne was a prisoner at Riverside and I was uncertain of her fate. There is no way her mother could have known about her situation. When Spear called, I told him to get her out of Riverside, but it was too late for him to act. I was trapped in a situation of my own making.'

'Did you believe her?' asked Davenport.

'I thought long and hard and, after considering everything, believed it was plausible. It was a long time ago. Yes, we did make love before I went away overseas, but after, she never replied to my letters, I assumed our affair was over. I did start seeing other women and knew she had met a Polish man, so naturally believed Jayne was his daughter.

'As you know, members of the same family cannot be employed by MI6, but, unless suspicions are raised, checks are not made on new recruits. There is one way I can establish the truth, but I haven't yet done it. All my staff's fingerprints, retina and DNA have been recorded for recognition purposes. The DNA results would prove it.

'My problem is, do I submit to her mother's demands to keep the secret or risk releasing a man who could be part of Seperkov's team? We don't know how much he knows or even if he is connected. The police are questioning him and his partner after Jayne raised suspicions following her visit to Kensington House that we now know the Russians were using as a safe house. They haven't been charged yet, but Nicholas has no other leads at present, since he doesn't know about what happened at Riverside.'

With a smile on his face, Davenport said, 'Get the man released and let her have him back. He would be small fry and anyway, if he's connected, it would be for money and we can deal with him later. Tell Nicholas that you need to have him free and kept under surveillance as he might lead to other terrorists. He should buy that.'

BS still looked worried. He clasped his hand over his face.

'I almost got my little girl killed.'

'Did you never have your suspicions, Henry, when you looked at her? She seems to have inherited your rash behaviour. You should be a proud father. But she mustn't find out the truth. It would destroy your relationship with her and she would lose her job and you yours. Just add it to our pack of secrets. I hope Goodfellows doesn't know Laura's secret, otherwise we do have a problem.'

BS reacted quickly to Davenport's concerns.

'I doubt Laura would share it with anyone,' he said.

'But she must have been desperate to contact you. Do you think she and her husband could be part of the conspiracy? How did she know that Jayne worked for you at SIS? And how did she know your private number? You have to find that out, otherwise we are all in danger.'

Davenport drank the remnants of the wine.

'Henry, I need to get back to my dinner party and will talk to you tomorrow. I assume you've changed your codes and now have a secure line?'

They shook hands and left the club at intervals so as not to be seen together.

For the first time in his life, Henry Barrington-Smith was uncertain what to do. Before, decision-making was easy because it didn't involve his family. Now everything was different. He had a daughter, a brilliant daughter, a woman who, single-handedly, had taken on ruthless terrorists and eliminated them, as demanded by the mission with which she was entrusted. She wouldn't get any recognition for her deeds. Was that fair? But it's the nature of the job. And she loved her job. He would see her tomorrow and get a full report. But when he looked into her eyes, he would see a different person.

He decided he would arrange to meet her mother, Laura. He had never stopped loving Laura. He wondered after thirty-four years what she was like now. The thought actually excited him. Back in those days they had shared many happy times together. They had loved and, for a short time, belonged to each other. But he left and it all went wrong. He had been a fool. Laura Clayton was a beautiful woman that any man would have been proud to have had as his wife.

Now, they shared a deep secret. He wanted to know why she hadn't told him about Jayne. He wanted to know about her life. But he must find out how she had tracked him and Jayne down; that scared him. It was late and he needed sleep. He broke the law driving back to his apartment after consuming half a bottle of wine. But his troubled mind was on overdrive so sleep wouldn't come easy.

CHAPTER 19

Chequers

After a good night's sleep, BS had gone early to his office. Angel was waiting to see him with her report.

'Come in,' he said, responding to her soft knock on the door.

A beautiful young woman, his own flesh and blood, sat before him in the comfortable black chair. It was the same one she had sat in when he first briefed her on the mission. It seemed like a long time ago, not just a few weeks. He smiled and looked at her. Yes, he saw himself, not in the dark eyes and impish face, that was her mother, but in the determined expression, the desire to succeed, the cunning of a wild animal setting up a trap for its prey. She had her mother's looks, but his character. He wondered what she would do if she knew he was her father. How would she feel? How would she react? He decided that for now the risk would be too great. He would take Davenport's advice and get Laura her husband back.

'Congratulations – you did it. Spear did call me yesterday and told me what had happened.'

She looked surprised at his positive approach.

'We still have serious problems,' she said. 'The Russian woman, Vasalov, escaped and knows our identities. It seemed that she intended to blow up the boat with everybody onboard, including Seperkov and Hunter, so someone else was giving the orders. If Spear hadn't shot her hand and made her drop the firing box, she might have succeeded in killing us all since there was a time when we were all on the boat.'

BS said, 'I believe there was someone in the Kremlin protecting Seperkov and pulling the strings. He was the puppet not the puppeteer. But, whoever it is, he will know we are closing in on him. My immediate task is to brief our political masters so they can deal with the other security agencies and take us out of the firing line.'

BS knew that wasn't completely true. Politicians could not be trusted and would readily sacrifice him and anyone else to save their own skins. But he and Davenport had been in the game much longer than the current politicians and always had their backs covered. The latter had long-established, high-level contacts that even the most senior politicians wouldn't dare to cross.

'What about Alicia and her man called Curly?' she asked.

'Don't worry about the CTU people. I'll take care of them. Alicia is in a similar position with the CIA and FBI, who are also searching for the terrorists not knowing that she is working with us. But they have their own problems with al-Qaeda. Remember, CTU reports directly to the White House. We don't have that degree of protection.'

Angel listened, but her mind was elsewhere. She was actually thinking about Paul Cane and wondering what he might be doing. They had shared an unforgettable experience and faced near death at the hands of their captors. She didn't understand her feelings. It was as though some attractive force was drawing her to him. Hearing her name mentioned brought her mind back to what BS was saying.

'Jayne, I'm giving you a short holiday. You deserve it. Why don't you go away?' he said, thinking it would give him time to talk to Laura.

'Thanks, but I would rather keep working and find Vasalov.'

He was expecting that reply, but it was worth a try.

'Well, at least take a few days off,' he said, hoping that would work.

'I may do that since I want to see my mother. She might believe the arrest of my stepfather was my doing if his assistant recognised me at Kensington House.'

It was the last thing BS wanted to hear. He now decided he would have to keep her busy.

'OK. Let me brief you on what we've discovered so far. Using a satellite connection we tracked Vasalov's movements after she abandoned the burnt out SUV in Reading. She boarded a train to Portsmouth on the south coast. There she took a ferry to Cherbourg. Then we lost her because we didn't have access to videocams and didn't want to involve the French authorities. It's likely she's now back in Russia. She was travelling alone, but there was a report from French immigration at Cherbourg that a Russian woman named Berinski, who seemed to be in a hurry, passed through them on her way to Paris. It may not be Vasalov, but it's unlikely that two Russian women would be on the same ferry from Portsmouth. Passport control at Portsmouth confirmed someone named Berinski boarded the ferry. We checked all flights and trains leaving Paris for Moscow, but didn't get anyone with that name on any passenger list. She virtually disappeared, probably using another alias and travelling by road. These people are well trained and know how to avoid being traced. The Home Office Minister challenged the Russian Ambassador about Katrina Vasalov and was told that she had returned to Russia some months earlier. That would have prompted messages being sent back to the Kremlin and alert whoever is involved. They would certainly be helping her to get back.'

Angel suggested that she spoke to Alicia since CTU and CIA had agents and contacts in Moscow who could help find Vasalov. BS agreed, but warned her to only discuss it with Alicia because the situation was politically sensitive.

Angel left the office. The first task facing BS was to call John Nicholas and get Goodfellows and his assistant released and any proposed charges dropped.

They had a long and difficult conversation. Nicholas had tried to contact Paul Cane and, having failed, was worried that Hunter might have abducted or even murdered him. BS said he was safe and had gone away for a few days after the threats. He didn't know how much Nicholas knew about the Russians and Detroski so he had to be careful what to say. Nicholas was no fool and would have been making his own investigations. He accepted the argument BS put forward about keeping the two men under surveillance to find out who their contacts might be. Nicholas asked him if Jayne wanted her to work with his people. BS thanked him, but said that she was following up other leads with the Americans. Nicholas tactfully reminded him that any information gained had to be shared; it was an embarrassing moment.

BS searched the files and found Laura Goodfellows' telephone number. He made the call.

Laura's voice hadn't changed. He mentioned the possibility of agreeing to her request if she was prepared to meet him. At first, she was hesitant, but when Jayne's safety was raised, she agreed to meet him that night at 7 pm at the eighteenth-century Crown Pub and Hotel, located in the village of Cookham on the River Thames, near Maidenhead. Kenneth Graham, the author of *The Wind in the Willows*, once lived at the village where he had the inspiration to write the famous book. BS thought it strange that she chose that particular place. Then it came to him. It was the last place at which they had partied before he went overseas. Could it have been where Jayne was conceived?

BS rang the hotel and booked a room for the night using an alias. He was still in deep thought about how to handle Laura when his red phone rang. That meant only one thing.

'The PM wants you at Chequers at 12 noon for an important meeting,' said the voice. (*Chequers is the official country residence of the Prime Minister located near the village of Ellesborough in the Wycombe district of Buckinghamshire.*)

No reply was required. His presence was expected. The PM's office would know he had received the call and it was an emergency.

BS speedily read through Angel's report and the notes made from the telephone conversation with Spear. He reviewed all the intelligence papers and reports on the plane bombing and the Russian Embassy business. He suspected it was the latter that had triggered the PM's concern. It was going to be an interesting day.

After security and identity checks, BS was led into an office in the house. The PM was seated with two other men, one whom he

216

recognised. They rose to greet BS. The PM introduced him to the others as Henry Barrington-Smith, the Head of MI6. Each man shook his hand.

'This is Jack Linderman, the President's Chief Political Advisor and you know the Home Secretary.'

The four sat down. Coffee and sandwiches were on the table.

'Henry, this is an unofficial meeting. No minutes, no recordings. What is said in this room stays in this room. I assume you have no problem with that?' The PM looked straight at him, expecting an answer.

BS simply said, 'No problem.' He was aware the men in the room were three very powerful politicians and he was about to be drawn into a web of conspiracy.

The PM continued.

'Gentlemen, this morning I received a personal call from the Russian president, warning about the consequences of the British security services harassing Russian Embassy staff and making false accusations of Russian terrorist groups being involved in the London plane bomb. He denied any knowledge of such groups and wanted proof to back up such statements. As the new president, he wished to build better relations with the British government and help to fight the al-Qaeda terrorist threat that Russia also faced. He offered the assistance of his security services to track down the al-Qaeda terrorists responsible for the London atrocity. He hoped that the recent incidents would not set back such intentions.'

'When was the call made?' asked BS.

'I received it at nine o'clock UK time this morning.'

BS spent the next twenty minutes giving them a detailed report on what had taken place during the last three days, starting with the discovery of the tunnel from the Russian Embassy to the house that had been occupied by suspected terrorists, the events at Riverside leading to the death of Gregori Seperkov and Christine Hunter on the boat on the Thames. He told them Seperkov's main mission to murder Detroski was successful. He reminded them that Seperkov was the cousin of Alexander Larinko, the Head of the Kremlin's Security and a friend of the president.

BS noticed the surprised look on the face of the American, but the Home Secretary and PM's expressions didn't change. Perhaps they already had knowledge of the events that took place at Riverside. Had Davenport done his work?

Linderman looked worried. 'Henry, how sure are you that this guy Seperkov was behind the London plane bomb?'

The Home Secretary interrupted and abruptly answered the question. 'Very sure. It was your people at CTU who gave us the information about an al-Qaeda man called Malik, who we are certain detonated the bomb on the plane. Two CTU agents on the plane had him under surveillance. CTU supplied proof that he had been duped by one of his own people working in Afghanistan for the Russians.'

'What about the woman who escaped?' he asked.

BS answered. 'That's a problem. She knows who we are.'

The three men now looked concerned so BS decided to give his view of the situation.

'Gentlemen, I suspect that the Russian president's call is a warning that the whole matter needs to be kept secret and swept under the carpet unless we want to face an international political crisis. He must know what occurred at Riverside. I suspect Vasalov, who is obviously an SVR agent, has already reported to him or his advisors and this is their reaction. I doubt if she is yet back in Moscow, but no doubt would have sent a message to her bosses soon after the Pangbourne event. She must have had an escape planned and help in executing it. They know we cannot afford to expose them and are offering us a way out. The reference to al-Qaeda tells us they want us to pursue that terrorist group for the plane bomb. Remember, it was one of the reasons why we believed Seperkov organised the atrocity. There is another more sinister element – the murder of Detroski. The Russian president considered him a threat. We are currently investigating Detroski's past and his connections. I believe he may have been funding an underground movement in Russia to depose the president. If that is true then it would provide a motive for his killing. My agent uncovered a treasure trove of evidence at Riverside that is currently being checked out. It might reveal answers to some questions.'

The Home Secretary interceded.

'Legally, since Detroski was a British citizen, those responsible should be brought to justice, but in this case it's unlikely to happen, particularly as the murderer is dead. One might say justice has been served. With the current terrorist threat and the highly volatile situation in the Middle East, we need Russia on our side, so this cannot be made public and involve a police investigation; it has to be covered up.'

The PM was looking worried, knowing that he was personally in a grave situation. If a hint of a cover-up got into the media, it would finish him and his government. The Russians had him cornered.

Linderman, who, so far, had been quiet, suddenly said, 'I need to tell you we now have firm intelligence of an al-Qaeda plot to bomb US facilities. We don't have details yet, but CTU are following up leads from the person who gave them knowledge about the Russians' involvement in the London bomb. We think that event may have delayed or even changed their plans. Due to the links with the Russians it's essential we keep everything top secret. Al-Qaeda has cells in London and in many US cities and we don't want to alert them until we know more about the targets. Remember, Malik was al-Qaeda's money courier who was going to London to furnish funds for British terrorist groups.'

The colour returned to the PM's face. This was just what he needed to justify the cover-up of the Riverside affair. Strict security clamp-down because of the new al-Qaeda threat to Britain and the US.

'I assume we can include the threat extends to British cities since al-Qaeda sees us as your close ally.'

'Absolutely,' said Linderman.

The PM turned to the Home Secretary.

'You must make sure Scotland Yard and MI5 divert the attention to al-Qaeda for the plane bomb and get the Russians off their radar. I'm due to chair a COBRA meeting tomorrow so in the national interest I will ask all the chiefs to do likewise. I shall have to tell them about the Russian president's call to reinforce the need to concentrate all efforts on al-Qaeda.'

BS seized his opportunity.

'Prime Minister, you or the Home Secretary may need to have a word with Rupert Arnold and John Nicholas who are pursuing the Russians for the London plane bomb since they don't know about Riverside. Nicholas did arrest two British estate agents whom he suspected knew about the safe house in Kensington Palace Gardens. It was one of my agents who raised the suspicion. I have since asked him to release them so we can place them under surveillance. We can do that, but the case needs to be boxed.'

The PM asked the Home Secretary to see to it. BS was relieved since he could now agree to Laura's terms. A more relaxed atmosphere permeated the room and coffee was poured.

BS took Linderman aside and asked him to thank CTU and in particular Alicia Garcia for her invaluable intelligence and practical help in tracking down the Russians. Linderman told him the President had put a lot of faith in CTU since both the CIA and FBI had failed in the past to deliver reliable intelligence. CTU was small but operationally more efficient and had already proved its value, even if it had to remove a mole who was being blackmailed by Seperkov into passing him telephone encryption codes. But Alicia had quickly resolved that problem. He told BS that she had really good operators in the field and wanted to continue working with the British team.

The meeting broke up and BS drove back to SIS. On arrival, Bob Bradley, Jayne's assistant, gave him a message from her. It read, '*I am doing some checks on the material that I retrieved from Riverside since there are some things that still bother me. But afterwards, I will take up your offer and take some days' leave.*'

BS hoped she didn't intend to see her mother before he had a chance to meet her that evening.

CHAPTER 20

The Reunion

BS arrived early at the Crown and booked into his room. He had time to reflect on the last time he and Laura were at the hotel. It was June 1969. He remembered making a fool of himself at a birthday party for one of his army friends. Rooms had been reserved at the hotel for those too drunk to go home. Girlfriends were invited. He recalled the night of passion with Laura. It raised his blood pressure. Now he was about to meet her again. Like a schoolboy on his first date, his feeling of excitement was tempered by a little apprehension.

Major Henry Barrington-Smith had known Laura only a few months and been out with her on about five occasions. Her father was from army stock and took an instant liking to the young army officer. When a girl's father likes her boyfriend then courting becomes an easy next step. Laura saw Henry as a possible future husband. It was a tradition that upper-class girls married at an early age if their parents approved of the man. Laura was a beautiful girl and had everything going for her, but for Henry, marriage wasn't on his mind. He loved the army and the freedom it gave him. The Cold War was at its peak and he had been selected for special ops in Germany. It was the wrong time to have a wife.

The party went on until the early hours and Laura and he had become very drunk. Laura was a party girl and, once drunk, was game for anything. Some of Henry's friends started to make affectionate moves towards her, so, in a fit of jealousy, he decided to take her to one of the bedrooms for himself. It wasn't long before they were making love and afterwards fell asleep.

The next morning Henry had to return to his unit so their

goodbyes were short. He promised Laura that he would write as soon as he could, but, since his mission was secret, couldn't say when it would be. Unfortunately, tight security around the operation meant he couldn't do that for a month. His scribbled letter was full of apologies, but he promised to see her on his return to England. It would be many months before that took place. Unknown to him, his letter never arrived. Laura was upset and assumed that she had been abandoned. It was after that she met a Polish builder, named Janusz Bronowski, who had been commissioned to do work on an extension to the family mansion. It wasn't long before he filled the vacant place in her heart left by Henry.

After a short courtship they became engaged and married. She thought she was pregnant before the relationship started, but didn't tell him. He believed the baby was his so they married before anyone noticed the pregnancy. She regretted the deception and still loved Henry. She heard from one of his friends that Henry had a girlfriend in Germany. Since she hadn't received any letters or calls, she decided to try and banish him from her mind and keep the secret to herself. She knew that one day she would meet Henry again and then tell him about his daughter and the hurt he had caused her.

On his return to England after the secret op was completed, Henry went to Laura's house to find out what had gone wrong with communications, only to discover she had left home and was now married. Laura's parents explained that she now had a child and it would be best if he didn't contact her. He realised what a fool he had been, but accepted her parents' advice. He was heartbroken and volunteered for more overseas service.

It was 7 pm. He was sitting in the bar, sipping a glass of whisky in anticipation of the arrival of Laura, a woman he had left with his child that, until a few days before, he didn't know about. He wasn't sure what to expect. Would she be pleased to see him? Would she be angry? He didn't know what he would say and almost forgot he needed to find out how she knew he and Jayne worked for the

SIS. This was passing through his mind when he felt a light tap on his shoulder.

He looked around and there standing before him was a slightly older version of Jayne. Physically she hadn't changed much. Her figure was more rounded, but it still retained the correct proportions. Her black hair showed strands of grey, but her dark complexion, high cheek bones and brown eyes reminded him of the girl he had once made love to in a room just a few metres away from where they were standing.

'Hello, Henry,' she said in a low, soft voice.

For a moment Henry said nothing, but just stared. He was spell-bound by her beauty. Old feelings came flooding back.

'Well, aren't you going to offer me a drink?' she asked.

Henry gathered his wits.

'Yes, of course. It's great to see you after so many years. What would you like?'

'Vodka and orange, please.'

He ordered the drink from the barman and asked for another whisky for himself. They sat down in an unoccupied room at the back of the pub. Henry spoke first.

'I've ordered dinner for 7.30.'

An awkward silence ensued. They just looked at each other not knowing what to say. Then they spontaneously laughed at each other's embarrassment. That broke the ice.

'Do you remember the last time we were in this bar?' said Henry.

'I remember we were both very drunk, but everything that night is still a little hazy,' she said, smiling. 'Henry, let's get to the point of our meeting since we both know why we're here.'

'OK, but before we talk about Jayne, I need to ask you how you discovered that she worked for me at MI6? I had no idea that she was our daughter until you called me. If that had been known, it would have been impossible for her to have been employed by the SIS.'

Laura looked away.

'I owe you an apology for keeping it from you for so many

years. It was wrong and painful for me and I don't want to go through all the reasons why I did it now. My marriage to Goodfellows was a mistake and we have been living separate lives for some time, but after he was arrested he told me it was Jayne who had raised suspicions about him and his partner after her visit to Kensington House. His company looks after the estate and manages properties for foreign owners. As far as I know, he does nothing illegal, but does protect the confidentiality of his clients and gets paid well for it. He does have contacts and it was through one of those that he found out that MI6 and the police had the house under surveillance. Jayne's disguise wasn't very convincing and when he showed me the photos I immediately recognised her. It didn't take much effort to find you. After that I knew our daughter worked at that funny-looking building at Vauxhall Cross. Goodfellows doesn't know Jayne is your daughter, but if the police charged him then things might have become difficult for all of us.'

'Thanks for being so honest. Don't worry about Goodfellows and his partner, they have been released today and if they keep quiet no further action will be taken. Our problem is Jayne. She has been on a very special assignment in the last few days that carries a top secret classification and has done an excellent job. She loves her work. Now is the wrong time to tell her the truth. I cannot say more because national security is involved, but let's wait until the time is right. She's a tough and intelligent woman and I know if you are honest about the reasons for not telling her before, she will understand.'

Laura smiled and placed her hand on his hand. He felt an upsurge of emotion. It was like the clock turning back. She looked as beautiful as she did all those years ago. Henry's life had been his job and although he had many friends and led a full life, deep down he was a lonely man. Many women, mainly widows, had tempted him, but none had touched his emotions like the one sitting opposite. He had thrown away his chance before and wasn't going to make the same mistake again.

The waiter arrived with the menu. Henry ordered a bottle of champagne and two sirloin steaks with all the trimmings.

They agreed to draw a line under the past and not talk about it. Henry told Laura that he had booked himself a room for the night. She suggested that they could perhaps relive the night they both couldn't remember. It was an invitation even in his wildest dreams he didn't expect to hear. He was determined this time to make up for all those lost years.

Moscow
Two days later

Katrina Vasalov hid her bandaged hand under the table. It had given her much pain since Spear's bullet had shattered the wrist bone. It meant she wouldn't have a strong left grip, but fortunately she was right-handed. She put that to good use when making love to her partner, Josef Krinsky, who was sipping wine from a glass and already feeling the urge. It was the first time they were able to relax in a secluded restaurant on the outskirts of Moscow since she had left to work in London for her boss, Alexander Larinko.

They mused over their successful assignment and her escape from MI6 and the British police. But Katrina Vasalov was worried since she had failed to blow up the boat with everybody onboard. If the two Englishmen hadn't killed the guards, forcing her to flee, then her mission would have been successful. Now she would be hunted as they knew her name and Russian Embassy connection. Being back in Moscow under Kremlin protection would give her some security, but once Detroski's death was made known, his friends and supporters in Russia and elsewhere would want retribution. Al-Qaeda was also seeking retribution for what the Russians did in duping Malik to blow up the London plane.

Seperkov had achieved the mission he had been set and successfully convinced MI6 that he was the man behind the London plane bomb. But although he was dead, they would be seeking his and other connections to the murdered oligarch, Detroski.

They had just finished the dessert and bottle of wine when Vasalov's phone rang. A car was being sent to take her to the

Kremlin for an urgent meeting. That meant the political repercussions had started. She was expecting good news from her boss and a huge reward for serving her country so well. Within minutes a black Lada estate car with dark-tinted windows pulled up outside the restaurant. Two men got out and opened the door. Katrina Vasalov kissed her friend and told him to wait at her flat for a call. She was ushered to sit in the back seat. The car drove at speed out of the city in the opposite direction to the Kremlin.

The bullet entered her forehead. She died quickly; that was her reward. Her body was deposited in a deep hole on a building site just before the concrete was poured into it as part of the foundations of a new apartment block. Many such blocks were being built on the outskirts of Moscow in a modern style to replace the old drab Stalinist ones that still littered the landscape. She was now part of the new Russia.

Alexander Larinko had already received a full report of what had happened at Riverside and Pangbourne from his British contact. He made a phone call.

'The mission is completed.'

A final retribution had been made. But that wasn't the Kremlin's reason for killing Vasalov.

PART TWO

CHAPTER 21

CTU Langley
July 2001

Alicia's cell phone signalled a call coming through. Curly had arrived back and was at their rendezvous hotel. She didn't need to speak. Owing to the need to change security encryption codes, they now used coded messages to pass information. This time the meeting was personal, a homecoming. For the first time in her life, she was glad to know that her agent and lover was safe. She knew this new vulnerability wasn't good and wondered if their working relationship could endure. It placed them both in danger.

Much had happened during Curly's absence. In addition to the traumatic events in Britain, CTU had given top priority to tracking down al-Qaeda operatives in the US and following up intelligence leads. They were dealing with a new breed of dangerous terrorists who were deliberately setting false trails to conceal their real objectives. The FBI was taking the lead, since the search was concentrated on US soil. All intelligence acquired by CIA operatives in Middle Eastern countries was being fed to them and CTU. The Vice President wanted all the agencies to share information, but Alicia had decided to pursue her own leads in the US. She knew the same issues between the agencies still existed and, although inter-communication had improved, the same management structures dictated how agents operated. She was sure not everything was being disseminated and distributed. The career prospects of agents still depended on identifying and catching terrorist suspects.

Alicia still hadn't had any contact with her old friend Mark Brooks at the CIA and wondered whether her messages had been passed to him. She didn't trust the people at Langley and knew they didn't like CTU.

Curly wanted to go to Moscow to find out more about Vasalov and the people she worked for, since he believed that Seperkov had been acting under orders. But Alicia wanted him to stay in the US and find the terrorists behind the latest threats.

The mass of new information meant Alicia had to take on two extra staff since she had lost Pat King after her arrest. This had greatly upset Alicia, who had personally recruited her. All new members of staff had to go through more rigorous background checks and would, in future, have all their communications monitored.

Two known al-Qaeda suspects, who had entered the US earlier in the year, were being kept under surveillance. Others who were believed to have passed through immigration with false documents were being sought. Three men were arrested placing explosives under the Golden Gate Bridge in San Francisco. Under interrogation they admitted to being members of an al-Qaeda cell in California, but stated they knew nothing about any wider plot. Another group was caught trying to blow up a nuclear power station in Michigan. Both operations were clumsy, leading the FBI to believe the terrorists wanted to be caught. It strengthened their belief that these events were some of the many subterfuges being carried out.

It was not a coincidence that Khalid al-Mihdhar and Nawaf al-Hazmi, who had US visas, were living openly in San Diego, California. But no actual connection to the men arrested could be made to them. They were on the FBI's watch list. In fact, al-Mihdhar had been travelling to the Middle East freely during the last year, finally returning to his home on 4 July 2001. The FBI failed to inform US immigration about their suspicions, so they were allowed into the country.

CTU investigated a report that two Arabs had approached a farmer in Idaho seeking employment as pilots for planes carrying out crop spraying. Their strange request made him suspicious so he refused and reported them to the local police, who informed the FBI, but the two men disappeared before they arrived. Their descriptions were placed on file.

Another report, related to two men of Middle Eastern origin paying for lessons at a flying school in Florida on a Boeing 727 simulator, was filed. They only seemed to be interested in knowing how to manoeuvre the planes and not in taking off and landing procedures. The instructors thought that was strange. The two men, according to their certificates, were already qualified pilots for light aircraft. The obstreperous attitude of the men caused the head of the school to call up the flying school, also in Florida, to check on their credentials.

One of the instructors, a woman, told the investigators that one of the trainees, being a Muslim, objected to being taught by a woman. He did eventually qualify, but his attitude and demeanour left a bad impression at the school. His name was Mohamed Atta, an Egyptian national. Good descriptions were obtained of the two men and placed on file. This interest in flying training raised concerns with Alicia after the reports about the use of aircraft for terrorist activities, the London bomb being uppermost in her mind.

CTU and the FBI knew there were four al-Qaeda suspects, all interested in flying planes in the US. They were Mohamed Atta, Marwan al-Shehhi, Nawaf al-Hazmi and Khalid al-Mihdhar. The men had obtained their visas in Saudi Arabia. Applicants at the embassy didn't have to go through the vigorous background checks because the consul general in Riyadh believed that the Saudis were not security risks. It was a poor assumption and displayed a lack of political will to aggravate the allies of the Gulf War and suppliers of most of US oil. Later, the consequences of this lax policy would be far-reaching.

Alicia was reviewing intelligence information when her phone rang. She was expecting a call from Burger, but to her great surprise it was Mark Brooks.

'I can't speak on the phone. Can I come over and see you now?' he asked.

'Yes,' she replied, sensing he was under pressure and couldn't speak freely.

An hour later, Mark arrived in her office. He had lost weight since she had last seen him and looked worried.

Embracing him, she said, 'I'm glad to see you again. I have been very worried that something bad had happened and the CIA weren't telling me. Am I allowed to ask where you've been and did you get my messages?'

'Yes, I did and I'm sorry that I couldn't call you before now, but I didn't get them until yesterday when I returned to my office in Langley. I have been undercover in Iraq. I was sent there after the London bomb on a secret mission. The CIA wanted to know if the Iraqis were involved, particularly if Saddam Hussein could be implicated in the attack.'

'Why did they think that?' she asked.

'The intel came from a Saudi agent in New York, who claimed he had obtained a document from an Iraqi secret service defector, stating that an Arab called Malik had been duped by Iraqi agents into believing he had received an order from bin Laden. Apparently the Iraqis had planned and funded the whole operation.

'I found no justification to the Saudi claim, but my DG insisted that I sought out one of our undercover agents in Baghdad who befriended one of Saddam Hussein's aides. He knew nothing about such a plan and thought it was one of the Saudis' many dirty tricks. I made a report back to Langley, but was told that, since I was in the country, to also look for evidence of Saddam's biological weapons and other potential weapons of mass destruction. The UN weapons inspectors had left Iraq and although they were forced out before every site had been searched, they didn't find anything that would fit into the category and were convinced that Saddam either didn't have any such weapons or had destroyed them.

'It was known he had been planning to make chemical and probably biochemical weapons, but although some preliminary work had been done they never went into production and only a few crude prototypes were found. Some bombs may have been taken to Iran together with military aircraft, but no convincing proof was uncovered. The inspectors' report was sent to the

Secretary General of the UN. The British member had sent a separate secret report to his own government at their request. It clearly stated that no significant evidence existed that Saddam Hussein's regime had weapons of mass destruction. It was not a finding that the US President and the UK Prime Minister were expecting or wanted.

'I spent some difficult days in Baghdad and nearly got arrested. Eventually I managed to get out through Kuwait. Langley told me it was important to come back with positive evidence that would implicate Saddam. Apparently the orders had come from the White House, which worried me. When I returned yesterday and read the report from Eli that you requested, I was convinced that once again we were being dragged into another political conspiracy. The White House clearly was looking for reasons to construct a new UN resolution against Iraq.

'It's obvious that al-Qaeda is planning something big in the US. What is most worrying is there are people in our own government who are trying to divert our attention in other directions.'

Alicia told Mark what had been happening in England and about the intelligence her agents had gathered on al-Qaeda's activities in the US. He was amazed how much more she knew than the CIA about the British success. She told him the FBI was taking the lead on the tracking down of al-Qaeda cells in the US, but most of the information was coming from the Middle East, sometimes from dubious sources. However, it was clear an increasing number of al-Qaeda cells were being set up and funded. There was uncertainty about how much the Saudi community in the US supported al-Qaeda. CTU was investigating the source of funds being channelled to cells in the US since it could lead to finding those involved. In the interest of national security, CTU was able to access bank accounts of foreigners without seeking a warrant from a judge. It was legally a grey area so any action had to be done with stealth.

Mark warned Alicia that some CIA senior staff didn't want to cooperate with CTU as they resented its direct connection to the White House. He told her that he wanted to help, but had to be careful since he was being watched by people who knew about his past relationship with her. They both decided to secretly exchange information. Alicia was trying to find out how many of the estimated three million Muslims living in the US belonged to militant bodies. It was a huge task because of the wide diversity of the population and the lack of true census statistics. This was compared with about six million Jews. For political reasons the various communities deliberately exaggerated their numbers.

Bin Laden had appointed Mohamed Atta to be the leader of the al-Qaeda hijacker team in the US. He was given the responsibility for choosing the targets to destroy. His nineteen team members had all completed their training, which, for four, had been rigorous since they would pilot the planes to be hijacked. There should have been twenty members of his team, but one member was refused entry at immigration in Florida due to inconsistencies in his visa documentation. In addition to himself, the pilots were to be Hani Hanjour, Ziad Jarrah and Marwan al-Shehhi. The team was broken up into four sections, each led by one of the pilots. Fifteen of the nineteen were Saudi citizens. All the men were chosen for their readiness to die as martyrs – and the ability to obtain a US visa; they masqueraded as businessmen or tourists to get their visas. Much of their training had taken place outside of the US.

After the London plane bomb disaster and the loss of Malik, KSM was being hunted by the FBI so bin Laden replaced him with one of his supporters, a wealthy Saudi codenamed Ali Baba (AB) to manage the cells in the US and UK. Hijacking a plane in London would be difficult because of the heightened security now in that city's airports. A new plan was therefore conceived. A new target had been selected in the UK. The action would be synchronised with the US ones for maximum impact.

AB had acquired one of the new laptop computers with encryption software. He had successfully used it to communicate with his US team members. They limited themselves to three-minute online sessions to minimise being traced. The internet was becoming more convenient than cell phones, since anyone with a little knowledge could set up a server and operate a network. After some extensive interrogation of suitable candidates, a cell leader for the UK attack was found at the University of Southampton. He was provided with appropriate software and key codes to use.

CHAPTER 22

Southampton
31 August

Kasim Hadjab was a first-year student at Southampton University in England studying marine engineering, but he already had a degree from Cairo University in industrial chemistry. He was born in Gaza of Palestinian parents. Both were killed when an Israeli plane fired on their house in reprisals for an earlier Hamas rocket attack on Jewish homes. After, it was his uncle Mahmoud Sasha who smuggled him to Egypt to stay with wealthy friends. It gave him a chance for further education and win a place at university. While at the university he became associated with militants and jihadists. Seeing that he had a deep hatred for Jews and their protectors, they encouraged him to become one of them. One day in Cairo he met Mohammed Fakri, at a local mosque. He asked Kasim to go to England and become a student at an English university since it was an easy way of entering the country and obtaining a visa. He was given the task of identifying two other students of similar minds and to form a secret al-Qaeda cell. He was told that money would be sent to a British bank via a Swiss bank by a man, codenamed AB, in the US who was responsible for funding cells. The funds were for an important mission. His cell would be part of al-Qaeda's global network, whose objective was to remove all non-believers from Arab lands, including Palestine. The latter was enough to persuade him. After his parents and other members of his family were killed, he had vowed to seek retribution on those who supported Israel.

There was no shortage of young men in Britain who were willing to die for the cause. They all wanted to be martyrs for Islam. The first Gulf War had been a good recruiting ground and although many of the Arabs didn't like Saddam Hussein, they saw the attack on Iraq as an attack on Islam. But the West's support of Israel was the biggest incentive.

Kasim and his team would receive instructions through coded messages on an internet website. Only he would possess the key to decode the information. Secrecy was to be absolute.

Southampton, the major commercial port on the south coast of England, was the home of Cunard and the P&O fleet of cruise ships. Kasim, being a student studying marine engineering, had a detailed knowledge of ship design. He took a special interest in the new P&O cruise ship, *Prince Charles*.

He had already received AB's plan and the approximate date for its implementation. At first, it surprised him that such a daring plan could be conceived, but, after thinking about it for some days, he realised not only was it feasible but it would attract worldwide publicity. A similar attack had worked successfully in the Yemen so could work in England. His name would go down in the history of Islamic martyrs. He felt honoured to have been selected for such a task. But it worried him that time was short to make the preparations.

The two other members of the cell would be told on the day before about the attack to avoid breaches of security. Both were dedicated jihadists and wanted to be martyrs. Ali Hussein Shumari and Ali Kusak were from Iraq and also engineering students at Southampton. Kasim avoided being seen with them at the university because they thought, being Muslims, it was likely they were being watched. Since the London plane bomb, the movements of all Middle Eastern students and visitors were being logged. The University of Southampton, however, was not high on the police watch list. What Kasim didn't know was al-Qaeda's other attack was planned to be carried out at the same time in the US.

The material to be used for the explosives had already been purchased and stored in a warehouse by members of another cell, who had no knowledge of its intended use. It had been purchased by three companies from a variety of traditional suppliers to farmers and building contractors.

8 September

John Nicholas received an email from GCHQ highlighted as 'Significant'. This separated it from the normal daily reports he received. It related to unusual large purchases of fertiliser chemicals made by three different companies, who were new to the list of buyers, at a time of the year when such materials were not normally used. Conscious such materials could be used to make terrorist bombs, Nicholas ordered his agents to make enquiries and find out who had bought the material and for what purpose. It didn't take them long to discover that all three companies were bogus with fictitious addresses in the area of Southampton. That was enough for the police to start a full-scale search of the area, including warehouse and storage units.

A day later, a vigilant local police patrol car noticed a new shiny lock on a double lock-up garage located on the edge of a council estate. It was an area they frequently patrolled owing to reports of break-ins in the area. Lock-up garages were often used by thieves to store stolen property. Being aware of the search being carried out in the area for possible explosives, Nicholas's team was immediately notified by the local police.

A call was made to the army bomb disposal unit and explosives experts placed on standby. Nicholas decided that before breaking into the garage he would put a surveillance team in place. It was important to find out who had purchased the material.

Infrared camera and other sophisticated detection devices confirmed that the garage contained a large quantity of ammonium nitrate, a common component of explosives. Nicholas informed Arnold that they had uncovered a cache of explosives that could be used to make a bomb. He told the Home Secretary, who alerted the Prime Minister. Surveillance of the whole area would be carried out without raising suspicions amongst the local community. It was important to catch all those involved before a terrorist act could be committed.

A decision was taken to pick the garage lock, remove the explosive material and replace it with a similar–looking, non-explosive compound. It would be a hazardous operation and would only succeed if the terrorists didn't have an explosives expert who would notice the material had been switched. The police would follow the terrorists to their intended target and arrest them in the act without endangering the public. The army experts knew exactly what to do, so Nicholas had every confidence the deception would work. He wanted to arrest the whole team and find out who was behind the plot. They waited and observed.

Arnold and Nicholas looked at likely targets in the area. They listed the Fawley Oil Refinery, the local airport and the Southampton Docks where cruise ships were always moored. It then occurred to them that the new cruise ship, *Prince Charles*, was about to dock and take on passengers for its maiden voyage to New York on 11 September. Arnold called the Managing Director of the P&O company to alert her about the potential terrorist threat since the new ship was on the list of vulnerable targets.

Late in the evening, a van parked outside the garage and two hooded men emerged. They unlocked the garage, loaded three boxes of the material into the van and drove away. A black SUV with four armed agents followed discreetly behind. The van went to a deserted warehouse near the River Itchen where the two men unloaded the boxes and then drove away. A car pursued the van and the surveillance team found a secluded area opposite the warehouse and waited. The two men parked the van in a side street and went to separate houses. Their addresses were noted and put under police observation. Enquiries were started to find out the names of the occupants. The surveillance team took up their positions.

Kasim went to an internet café to access messages from AB. They were encoded in adverts on certain websites. He was expecting to be given the time and date for the attack on the cruise ship, but instead he received a warning that the police had found the cache of explosives and had placed a surveillance team on the lock-up garage where they were stored. AB had received urgent information from a source in London about the police discovery. Kasim was therefore instructed to execute Plan B.

Plan B was for him alone to drive a motor launch packed with explosive into the weakest part of the hull of the ship. It wouldn't sink the ship, but could damage it enough to cause an evacuation and stop its maiden voyage. Al-Qaeda had used the same technique to damage the USS Cole in the Yemen. Other al-Qaeda operatives would provide the boat and make the new arrangements. He actually liked the new plan. It would enable him to take retribution on those infidels who had killed his parents. He would be able to join them and all the other martyrs in the promised heavenly paradise.

Some operational issues associated with working alone would have to be overcome. The other two cell members would stick to the original plan so providing a diversion to the police who would believe they had stopped the attack. It was likely they would be arrested, but martyrdom might be preferable. He would use the internet to tell them about the change of plan.

AB was in New York to oversee the arrangements for the hijackers. Finding planes that were scheduled to take off within short flying times of New York and Washington was a challenge.

The date planned for the hijacking of the planes had to coincide with the departure of the cruise ship from Southampton. This was to maximise the impact on the world's media. Since television cameras would be covering the UK's largest cruise ship on her maiden voyage to New York, it was an opportunity not to be missed. He knew that bin Laden and his many followers would be watching events in their hideaway in Afghanistan.

9 September

The cruise ship, *Prince Charles*, was being prepared at Southampton for her voyage to New York. She was the pride of the P&O fleet, being not only the largest ship in the fleet, but also in the world of passenger ships. Her gross tonnage was one hundred and fifty thousand tonnes. She had all the latest technology that included a new propulsion system. The crew of one thousand serviced three thousand passengers. But on her maiden voyage only one thousand selected passengers would be onboard; these would include government officials, showbiz celebrities and business leaders. Some minor members of the royal family would also be included.

Captain Chris Rogers and his officers started to make preparations for the ship's maiden voyage to New York. He had been informed that the Managing Director of P&O and a number of senior company executives would be joining the ship together with the celebrity actress Lorna Green, who had accepted the honour of being the ship's godmother. It was a tradition for all ships to have an adopted godmother. It was a big event for P&O so certain members of the media were also invited. Rogers was worried about the huge number of smaller vessels that would be accompanying the ship though the Solent. At normal times, with the variety of ferries traversing that waterway, it was always very busy. He remembered what had happened to the Titanic at the commencement of her ill-fated maiden voyage.

The Captain had just sat down to lunch when he received an urgent telephone call from the company's MD. She informed him about a possible terrorist threat. He immediately ordered restricted access to the ship and a thorough search of cabins and all public areas. Contingency plans to deal with such a situation had been rehearsed on other ships, but new crew members had been assigned to the ship so now each one had to undergo extra screening. This could delay the sailing date scheduled for 11 September. A berth had been reserved in New York for a specific time and date, which couldn't be changed. Extra staff and police would have to be drafted in to help, but without raising alarms in the media. The company's PR person had handed out a brief to the press and TV producers, explaining the security concerns after the London plane bomb, hoping it would explain the increased police presence. Nobody would see the four police marksmen with sports bags, dressed in clothes similar to those worn by the crew stationed at vantage points around the ship.

CHAPTER 23

Manhattan, New York
11 September 2001

It was a glorious sunny morning with a clear blue sky when Robert Carville drove into the underground car park of the North Tower of the World Trade Centre in lower Manhattan. He took the elevator to the 83rd floor. As it quietly ascended he checked the time on his wristwatch; it was 8.25. He liked to be punctual for his clients, particularly when a banker like Julian Richards was involved. Chuck Thompson was one of Hollywood's leading producers who had partnered with a group of investors to make a film about a young pop star growing up in Manhattan. They needed a bank to underwrite their investments. Robert had facilitated a number of successful deals with Richards' bank in the past so offered his brokerage services to Thompson and his partners.

Chuck had just arrived when Robert entered Julian's office that overlooked the Hudson River and New Jersey. The air was so clear that visibility extended for many miles. The three men shook hands, knowing that their meeting was only scheduled to last for thirty minutes. Julian Richards was a busy man and believed that any deal worth doing had to be concluded within that time. They helped themselves to coffee from a small machine neatly placed in a corner outside the office. Robert, who was seated opposite Julian with Chuck next to him, had a panoramic view through the window of the sky extending down to the distant horizon. They made some small talk while putting papers on the table. The time was 8.40. Robert was looking out of the window and noticed a small moving dot in the sky, which seemed to be getting larger as he watched. It was unusual to see a moving object in that part of the sky. Chuck had sorted out his papers and was about to say something so Robert momentarily glanced in his direction and wasn't looking when the dot in the sky had become a large plane heading straight for them. The time was 8.46 am.

The whole building shook; breaking glass could be heard amongst loud explosions above. Through the office window, still unbroken, they saw debris falling and liquid running down the windowpanes. The noise was horrific; screeching, grinding mixed with a cacophony of other sounds. The desk and other furniture in the office moved back and forth and the walls shuddered as they would during an earthquake. Then everything stopped moving, but the sounds continued above; but this time people were running along the corridors screaming down cell phones. Julian, who had been thrown to the floor, picked himself up and all three stood in silence trying to comprehend what had happened. Chuck was the first to speak.

'I saw it coming to the building – a massive plane. It must have hit us some floors above.'

At that moment they saw black smoke streaming out from the building. An acrid smell of burning aviation fuel filled their nostrils. It was the liquid they had seen on the window.

A steelworker had just climbed to his high perch on a building a few blocks away from the North Tower to start his shift when he heard the deafening roar of jet engines above, followed by the vision of a large low-flying aircraft. It just scraped over the Empire State Building and sliced straight into the North Tower between the 93rd and 99th floors. He was horrified to witness an orange fireball as the building exploded, showering debris over a wide area. Seconds later he saw thick, black smoke emanating from a jagged opening as thousands of gallons of fuel burnt and consumed everything in its path.

Fire alarms and the screams of men and women descending the stairs could be heard. Panic had set in as the smoke became thicker and what was a bright, sunny morning had become a dark night. Robert and his companions decided to use their cell phones to find out what had happened and what they should do next.

Julian called his bank manager who was located on floor 101. People on this floor could see the extent of the damage. They were horrified to discover that all the floors directly below them had been blown out so no escape was possible. The stairs on the floors above led to the roof, but all the doors to it were locked and since the electric cables had been severed the elevators and electronic locks couldn't function, it was impossible to open them; so access to the roof was blocked. Police helicopters hovered above, but were useless because of the dense smoke and in any case nobody could be seen on the roof.

The only escape from floor 83 was down the stairs, but no one knew how safe they would be and thousands of people would be using them. They decided to stay in the office until help arrived, unaware of the further danger that was about to make their position perilous.

At 9.03 a second plane struck the South Tower between the 77th and 85th floors. The loud explosion and devastation shook the North Tower and the office where Robert and his colleagues were sitting. They were on the opposite side of the North Tower where the first plane had struck so at first they didn't know it was a terrorist act. It was only when Julian heard from a newsman on his cell phone that a second plane had crashed into the South Tower did they realise an attack on America had started. It was the incentive to finding a way out as quickly as possible. Anxious, panic-stricken people blocked the narrow stairwells. Many fell over and were badly hurt.

The three men decided to wait until the stairs were less congested, unaware of the massive structural damage that had occurred above them. Julian wanted to try and reach his colleagues in the bank, but there was no way of reaching them. The density of smoke outside the window of their office was increasing and the temperature was rising. Robert looked up and, to his horror, saw a man jumping from an upper floor. He was followed by others, some holding hands, preferring an instant death in the fresh air than being roasted alive in the inferno above.

It was that sight that made the three men make calls to their families and friends. Robert didn't have a family so called Paul Cane. Since there was no reply, he left a message saying that he was OK, but in the North Tower of the World Trade Centre with business colleagues. He knew TV pictures would be beamed around the world and people with family members and friends would be trying to make contact so many lines were overloaded and out of action. Robert thought Paul might be calling since he knew about his frequent visits to see clients whose offices were in the North Tower. He recalled Valerie's sense of fear when she was close to the building during their short stay in New York in 1999.

Against all pleas from Robert and Chuck, Julian left the office to explore ways to the upper floors where his colleagues were trapped. The others pleaded with him not to go. He ignored their pleas so Chuck and Robert headed for the stairs going down. Julian was never seen again. Debris was falling from the South Tower, which was burning more fiercely and looking to be in an unstable condition.

CTU Langley

Alicia and her staff watched the awesome sight of the burning towers on their TV screens. Calls were coming in from everywhere. The President was on Air Force One flying back from Florida and the Vice President and his staff had been taken to the secure room under the White House. She was told that two other planes were unaccounted for and could have been hijacked. It wasn't long before she received the news that a Boeing 757 had crashed into the Pentagon. This was too close to home so Alicia ordered everyone to the bunker under the building. It had duplicates of all the communication equipment.

Alicia was angry, very angry that CTU, the FBI, the CIA and the NSA had not exchanged all their intelligence that might have prevented what had happened. She knew that al-Qaeda were responsible. They almost had some of the hijackers within their clutches. If they had been arrested by the FBI then they wouldn't be looking at the horrific sight before them. She wanted to call the Vice President, but knew he would be pre-occupied with the crisis.

Curly, who was in New Jersey, called Alicia to say he could see the burning towers. He was following up some leads on a man known as AB who was al-Qaeda's operations chief and likely to be responsible for the final stages of the hijacking, having replaced KSM. Alicia told him that was now a priority. She feared that the US would soon be at war, but with whom? This attack had raised the level of the hunt for those behind this latest atrocity.

The Solent, Southampton
1.00 pm

The Head of Administration of the ship reported to Captain Rogers that security checks and formalities for sailing had been completed and all passengers were aboard. He was pleased to be on schedule and thanked the crew for their efforts. The weather report for the local area and the Eastern Atlantic was excellent, so the ship would have a pleasant voyage through the English Channel.

Using the side thrusters, the giant ship was able to manoeuvre away from the dock with ease and into Southampton water. A pilot boat and four police launches accompanied her to ensure a safe passage through the numerous small craft that turned out to see this latest wonder of marine engineering. Thousands of cameras recorded the event. The VIPs onboard were on the top deck for a good view.

Thousands of people were waving and cheering as the *Prince Charles* left the dock and glided silently onto the calm waters of the Solent. Rogers and his senior officers were stationed on the bridge watching the many displays that provided all the information on the ship's operating systems and progress. Gone were the large steering wheel, the compass and range of navigational instruments that had helped past mariners to safely traverse the narrow channels out to the English Channel and the seas beyond. Now, small sensitive joysticks connected to a bank of computers and GPS systems did all the work with only minimal human intervention. Rogers' mind, however, was still troubled by the terrorist threat. Extra police had been placed onboard and in boats alongside his ship. He hoped, like on other occasions, it was a hoax perpetrated by warped people who derived pleasure in propagating fear and disruption. After the London bomb, everybody expected further acts. *Prince Charles* gained speed and continued through the Solent.

1.40 pm

Matthew Jones, the First Officer on the bridge, who was actually in charge of the sailing, noticed on the radar scan a small boat travelling fast towards the ship. It was only about five hundred metres astern. He took out a pair of binoculars and saw a motor launch with the word 'Ambulance' boldly painted on its side. It looked like some emergency had taken place, perhaps on one of the many other boats sailing out. But there had been no notification on any radio about such an event so his suspicions were raised. The police had issued warnings to all boats to stay well clear of the cruise ship since they had their own escort boats around it.

The ambulance boat seemed to have only one man aboard who looked to be of Middle Eastern appearance. This raised alarm bells on the bridge. Jones informed the captain, who called the police to report his observations. They were immediately relayed to the escort boats. The intruder had found a gap between the escorts on the port side near the stern of the ship and was heading at high speed straight for it. Two police launches did a three-sixty degree turn towards the boat, but, before they were close, it exploded within about five metres of the stern. A huge plume of fire, smoke and water erupted into the air. It quickly diminished as the escorts approached. The *Prince Charles* carried on cruising almost unaffected by what had happened behind her.

A hooded man standing on an isolated spot at the stern of the ship quickly packed away a rifle into his sports bag and went below to the crew's quarters. He took off his top clothes, placed them in the bag and stowed it in a locker. He made a call on his cell phone and merged with the crowds on the deck.

Other escorts were busy picking up small amounts of debris from the ambulance boat. A few TV cameras had filmed what had happened, but it was missed by the main ones who were showing scenes from the bridge. It was doubtful many people would have seen the explosion outside of the immediate area, but those on the shore and on the many small boats would have witnessed it.

Rogers was concerned that the ship's propellers and port side thruster might have been damaged by the explosion since they were not responding well to controls and warning signals were being flashed on the screens. Many passengers on the deck heard the explosion, but didn't actually see it. The chatter about it was overridden by music coming over the ship's speakers. What was about to happen in New York would soon take over the conversation. The cruise ship had slowed down to about five knots owing to the damaged propeller.

John Nicholas switched off his cell phone and smiled to himself. Unknown to anybody except his marksman, a major terrorist incident had been averted. The two al-Qaeda terrorists, who were part of Kasim's cell, had been arrested loading what they thought was explosive material onto two small motor boats. Previous to their arrest, GCHQ had found the website Kasim had used to inform them of the change of plan. It didn't take long for the experts to decode the message. They then knew about the subterfuge plan.

Nicholas and his men had carried out a search of all boats on the river, but didn't find Kasim on any boat. He then decided to put his best marksmen on the ship to stop any boat that tried to get close. It was calculated that any boat approaching would come up river from the stern. The calculations proved to be correct. A tank-busting grenade fired from a rifle directly into the fuel tank of the approaching boat was sufficient to take it out and cause the explosives onboard to detonate. AB's Plan B, his prelude to what was about to happen in New York, passed without having any significant impact. It had failed owing to the efficiency of GCHQ's watchers.

Many crew members and passengers were busy on the ship and missed the TV pictures coming directly from New York that showed the first plane hitting the North Tower and the resulting explosion. Captain Rogers and the officers on the bridge did have a TV on, which, up to the point when the BBC interrupted programmes, was showing the progress of their ship sailing through the Solent. Everyone looked aghast at the images on the screen. Having just been spared what Rogers believed was a terrorist attack on his ship, he was aghast at what he was now seeing. Was there a connection to what had just happened? The timing couldn't be coincidental. Fifteen minutes later they saw the second plane hit the South Tower. It confirmed they were witnessing a terrorist attack on the US.

It wasn't long before the MD, who had been outside with guests, asked Rogers and Jones to her cabin. She had just received a call from the Home Secretary informing her that New York was closed down so the ship would have to return to Southampton. Rogers told her the ship had sustained some damage to its propellers and would have had to return anyway. The public and media didn't need to know because after the New York announcement a return would be expected. Rogers was ordered to make an announcement to the passengers and crew. The Home Secretary wanted it played down until he had received a full report from the police.

Knightsbridge

Since the Riverside incident Paul Cane had taken some rest. Recovery from his leg and other injuries had been set back by the recent events. But during the last few days, regular exercise and walking had helped to stimulate his muscles and he was slowly returning to normal. After taking a walk in Hyde Park he went to one of his local restaurants for lunch in Knightsbridge when he saw the *Prince Charles* sailing out into the Solent on a wall-mounted TV.

In the picture he saw the cruise ship shudder slightly and heard what he thought was a muffled sound of explosives. The commentator said a minor incident with a boat had taken place behind the ship. A brief picture from another camera showed some smoke hovering over debris in the water some distance behind the ship. He hadn't been in contact with his friend John Nicholas or anyone else since Riverside, so was unaware of the real drama that was taking place at Southampton.

Cane was just about to drink a cup of coffee when the BBC newsreader interrupted the scenes from Southampton for an urgent news flash.

'In New York at 8.46 this morning a plane crashed into the North Tower of the World Trade Centre. Many thousands of people were at work in the building, but the number of casualties is not yet known. It is not known at this time why the plane was flying so low in a restricted area. Further bulletins will be issued when more information is available.'

The announcement was followed by terrifying pictures of fire and smoke bellowing out from the tower.

Then it came to him. It was Valerie's behaviour when she sensed that something bad was going to happen there. He felt sick remembering her reaction to Robert's suggestion to go up the North Tower. Seventeen minutes later while he was still thinking about that, the commentator screamed out that a second plane had crashed into the South Tower. This time a picture was shown of the plane entering the building and being swallowed up until a huge explosion of fire and black smoke shot out. There were gasps from people in the restaurant whose eyes were transfixed on the screen. The time was just after two o'clock, but it would be just after nine o'clock in Manhattan when most people would be arriving for the day's work in one of the busiest parts of the city. The world then knew that America was under a terrorist attack. Cane felt sick at the sight as did many of the others in the restaurant. This time the terrorists had gone too far. War would be declared on those who supported and nurtured them.

Cane paid the bill and hurried back to his apartment. He switched on the TV only to see even more horrific pictures. A third plane had been hijacked and crashed into the Pentagon. It was believed more planes could have been taken over by terrorists.

Being distracted by the TV pictures, he hadn't noticed the light flashing on his phone until he went to make a call to Alicia. Someone had left a message. He was shocked to hear it was from Robert Carville, who was trapped in the North Tower. He cursed for not being home to answer it. He immediately called the number, but there was no connection. He then dialled Alicia, but her cell phone was engaged so he left a message asking her to find out more about Robert's situation. But he knew she would be overwhelmed with calls. New York and Washington were in lockdown – a state of emergency existed. Cane went back to watch the television to see more scenes of horror of people emerging from the burning towers. He scanned in vain for Robert, but most people were covered in dust and unrecognisable.

At 9.59 am New York time, the South Tower collapsed, followed at 10.28 am by the North Tower. *Did Robert get out in time?* he wondered. He believed the worst since no further calls had been received. Perhaps phones weren't working and maybe he was injured and in hospital. Robert only had an aunt who lived somewhere in Hampshire and no other relatives, but did have many clients and friends whom he could call. Unfortunately, Cane didn't possess any telephone numbers.

Cane had lost his wife and now he may have lost his best friend to terrorists. He was filled with anger. He knew the war on terror had now taken a huge leap. The US had been attacked on its own soil. He recalled last time that happened at Pearl Harbour, when war was declared on Japan. But this time the likely culprit was al-Qaeda. It was a nebulous network with bases in many countries, but was extensively supported by the Taliban in Afghanistan. He had read reports that some politicians believed Saddam Hussein in Iraq also supported al-Qaeda, but evidence for it had yet to be found.

The Global Economist had been in contact with Cane and wanted him to write an article on the current situation in the Middle East concerning the controversial issue of the weapons of mass destruction that many thought Iraq was developing. It was a follow-up on the work he did for the journal in 1998. It was prepared to offer him a commission to travel to Israel and Jordan to interview people, but he told them he needed more time to recuperate after his recent experiences. Now the Middle East might become a more dangerous place. He was feeling despondent when his cell phone bleeped. It was Alicia calling him back.

'Paul, I have some news about Robert. It's not good. He and a client called Chuck did manage to escape from the North Tower before it collapsed. They are badly injured and in intensive care in a New York hospital with severe body injuries. I used my authority to get that information since you will appreciate many thousands of people are missing and an information lockdown exists in New York while searches are made amongst the rubble. The President has told the FBI and CIA to make finding those who supported the hijackers a top priority. We are now working with them and already have many leads to follow. We saw what happened in Southampton and believe it was al-Qaeda trying to deflect attention away from what was happening in New York, but it failed. I have spoken to John Nicholas, who did a great job in tracking the people responsible and stopping a boat packed with explosives from hitting the cruise ship. They managed to keep it away from the media so al-Qaeda didn't get the publicity that they wanted. We believe the man behind it and the hijackings is somewhere in New York. He will be found. This is an encrypted call that will automatically be deleted when I finish. I will text you the name of the hospital where Robert was taken. Take care.'

Before Cane could say anything, she rang off. He was both relieved and anxious. He would go to New York when it was possible to see Robert. Thinking back to earlier in the year, it was Robert who probably went through the same anxiety after the London plane bomb when he was in hospital. Fate has a strange way of dealing. Once again, just when he thought his life could return to normal, fate had plotted out another course for him.

Later in the day, Henry, the security man, called on the intercom to say that a woman was at the desk wanting to see him – her name was Clare. At first, the name didn't register and then to his surprise he realised it was Angel or Jayne Clayton-Browne.

'Ask her to come up,' he said.

Cane felt excited, but slightly nervous. It had been a day of mixed emotions. Before she knocked, he opened the door to see standing before him a different-looking woman to the one he was with a few weeks back. She was dressed in jeans with a sloppy jumper and her dark hair pulled back in a ponytail style. Her warm smile and relaxed expression displayed a friendliness that made Cane want to kiss her, but he resisted the temptation.

'Hello, Jayne. This is a pleasant surprise,' he said as she walked into the apartment.

'I hope you don't mind me calling on you without letting you know I was coming, but I was out walking in the park and did wonder how you were after hearing the news from New York.'

Cane was wondering what she meant when she continued.

'Alicia called and told me about your friend Robert Carville.'

'Yes, it was a shock. Unfortunately, I cannot get to New York to see him owing to the flight ban and am waiting to know the name of the hospital where he was taken. Sadly, he left a message on my apartment phone before he started to leave the North Tower, but I was out and didn't see it until just before the building collapsed. Thankfully, he's still alive.'

She noticed tears in his eyes and quickly changed the subject.

'I'm taking a leave for a few weeks on orders from my boss, but it looks like I shall be sent on a mission to the Middle East very soon.

But this action in New York could change things. The Riverside business is still not finished. But we may never know what happened to Vasalov and any others involved. They would have gone underground by now. The Kremlin would have made sure all the tracks are covered. I think the PM wants to draw a line under it. Everyone will be now focused on tracking al-Qaeda and bin Laden. I can see the US attacking the Taliban in Afghanistan, if they don't arrest him, which is unlikely. The Iraq situation is also worsening so we could be on the brink of new wars. Anyway, enough about terrorists. Have you recovered from the Riverside experience?'

She looked at him with her large, brown eyes, waiting for an answer.

'I'm not sure. After returning that night I had a strange experience. I saw a ghostly figure of Valerie here in this apartment. I don't know whether it was real or a dream. But after I woke up, everything changed. She seemed to be at rest, saying goodbye. I felt better. My sadness remains, but my mind is less troubled. Does that make sense?'

Jayne gave Cane a warming smile. 'Yes, it does,' she said.

'Do you believe in ghosts or restless spirits?' he asked.

'Yes, I do,' she replied, coming close and taking his hand.

Cane felt a flow of warmth running through his body. One again his emotions were being raised.

'I think I saw my father's ghost after he died. Something I will never forget. But last week I found out that he wasn't my father. It was shattering news because I really loved the man who brought me up and whose name I took. I'm trying to forgive my mother for what she did in keeping the name of my real father from me all these years. Fortunately, my stepfather never knew, but now my actual one does.'

'Do you know the identity of your real father and have you met him yet?'

'No, my mother refuses to tell me and I'm not sure I want to know. My mother begged me not to try and find out because she thinks it will affect my life and career. I have my suspicions and one day when the time is right I will find out.'

'Perhaps your mother had good reasons for not telling you,' Cane said.

Jayne changed the subject and clearly didn't want to talk about it. Before she left, they talked about their lives for some hours. This time they parted with a friendly kiss. No fixed arrangement was made to see each other again, owing to the uncertainties of what might lie before them, but her visit helped to off-set the bad news Cane had received earlier. He still awaited further information from Alicia about Robert's hospital location. He had to find a way of going to New York. He owed that to his dear friend.

Cane watched the TV coverage of the events in New York and Washington and realised that the world had changed. The war on terror had now become a reality. He now had a personal involvement and he was determined to play his part in that war.

The news from New York and Washington put the total dead at the time of the attacks as 2,996, of which 1,466 were in the North Tower and 624 in the South Tower; the others were on the ground near the towers, at the Pentagon, and in other places. This death toll was greater than the loss of life at Pearl Harbour. The US would soon be seeking retribution for these acts of terror.

EPILOGUE

The events that had taken place in the US on 11 September 2001 occupied most of the world's media for many weeks. In some Arab countries there was celebration on the streets, while in others a realisation that war was about to start. Mullah Omar, the Taliban leader in Afghanistan, had refused a US request to arrest bin Laden. The bonds between the two men were too deep, even though both knew the consequences. The large CIA team on the ground in Afghanistan had already provided money and arms to the anti-Taliban warlords and after an intensive US bombing of Taliban positions they defeated the Taliban soldiers. With US backing, the Northern Alliance took over the government of the country. Bin Laden and his followers went into hiding in the Tora Bora Mountains close to Pakistan's Tribal Areas. It would be many years before he would be found and killed. But before then a guerrilla war would engulf the country. It would be the start of a long bloody conflict in which thousands of Afghans, US and European soldiers would die and be injured.

Curly had found AB in New Jersey at a location close enough for him to have witnessed the planes crashing into the Twin Towers. Angel passed the information to the FBI whose agents stormed the building and arrested him. At the time of his arrest they hadn't enough real evidence to charge him for the attacks, but only with being a suspected member of a terrorist organisation. He was taken to a country outside of the US for questioning where the law permitted unconventional ways of extracting information. He died later in captivity before giving any useful information.

The real architect and mastermind of the hijackings, Khalid Sheikh Mohammed (KSM), had already left the country and was back in Pakistan. It wouldn't be until March 2003 when he would be arrested in Rawalpindi, Pakistan, after an informant had given information to the CIA. He ended up in Guantanamo Bay military detention camp for alleged acts of terrorism and mass murder and faces the death penalty. But since he admitted to those acts while under torture the evidence has so far been deemed inadmissible.

Angel and the CTU continued to seek out those who had supported the hijackers in the US. She knew it would be a difficult job since many had either left the country before the event or buried themselves within the community. After it was announced that fifteen of the hijackers were Saudis, she was alarmed to discover that a private charter plane had been given presidential permission to leave the country carrying certain members of the Saudi Royal Family and their friends back to Saudi before US airspace was re-opened. Some of them were thought to be connected to bin Laden. The FBI told Alicia not to officially investigate these people since they had been given clearance by the State Department. Curly found out through his contacts that within twenty-four hours of the attacks, nine million barrels of oil were despatched from Saudi Arabia to the US. After that order was given many wealthy Saudis left the country. Someone had found out about Curly's contact. He was later found with his throat cut in an alley in Washington. Angel was worried that the informer might have been tortured and identified Curly.

John Nicholas and the Scotland Yard Counter Terrorist team had obtained a lot of information from the members of Kasim's al-Qaeda cell, whom they arrested before the attack on the cruise ship, *Prince Charles*. Many other arrests followed, but the mole in their own ranks still couldn't be identified. New intelligence protocols were put in place so it was only a matter of time before he or she would be caught. The *Prince Charles* was repaired and did finally make her maiden voyage to New York.

Barrington-Smith did have his night to remember with Laura. They decided to continue to have a secret relationship and made the venue at Cookham a monthly meeting place. For the Head of MI6 it proved to be a very bad mistake. The first rule of intelligence is never to use the same public place for meetings. Someone will always notice you and it will be the wrong person. It would be the start of his journey into fast retirement.

Cane did eventually get Alicia to arrange clearance for him to fly to New York to see Robert. He was badly injured and, although his injuries were not life-threatening, he was not expected to leave hospital for many months. The disturbing sights in his perilous journey out of the North Tower had traumatised Robert. It would take months and maybe years for him to recover. Having had a similar experience, Cane knew exactly what his friend was enduring. Unfortunately, Robert's client Chuck, who was with him when the plane struck the building, had died from his injuries. After scrambling over debris and dead bodies, they had found a way out after almost giving up when the staircase below them was blocked. Carrying Robert down the last five levels, Chuck had saved his life. In doing so the exhaustion had taken its toll on Chuck's body. Later his heart failed.

While in New York, Cane went to the site of the demolished towers that became known as Ground Zero. It was a disturbing experience that left an indelible mark, heightened by the premonition that Valerie had experienced on their last visit to the site. Afterwards, Cane flew to Washington to see Alicia. He didn't want to fly back from Kennedy since it would invoke too many bad memories. It wasn't easy for him to fly to New York, but he decided he had to overcome his fear of flying across the Atlantic. The urgent need to see Robert was the incentive, particularly as Alicia had spoken to John Nicholas about granting him security and medical clearance.

Cane met Alicia at a downtown restaurant. It brought back memories of his meeting with Valerie back in 1999. He found it uncannily therapeutic to be near to the place where they had met. She was now at rest. Her brief appearance in his bedroom had given him some peace. He had sought and now taken retribution on those who had taken her from him.

Alicia had changed in appearance since they last met. She was less formally dressed and seemed more relaxed, more feminine and looked happy, like a woman in love. She responded warmly to his kiss on her cheek. He thought her demeanour a little surprising since she must be under extreme pressure after the terrorist attacks. He thanked her for all the efforts in getting him to New York and for finding Robert. She was saddened by what had happened and told him that she would make sure Robert was well looked after. He had kept the apartment in Washington she had given him during Project Whirlwind.

He learned that the President was sending troops to support the CIA in Afghanistan, but also secretly going after Saddam Hussein in Iraq. Washington was in a state of frenzy, almost panic after the failure of the intelligence services to stop the hijackers. Now the blunt instrument of bombs and missiles was to be used against the terrorists.

Cane related his personal experiences at Riverside and his meeting with Curly to Alicia. At the mention of Curly her eyes lit up and even her dark skin couldn't hide her arousal. Cane now knew her hitman was much more. The woman in front of him was in love. She quickly changed the subject and asked him what he was going to do.

'I have been offered another writing assignment by *The Global Economist*, but it means going back to the Middle East. I'm not sure it's the best time to go, but then that's why the journal needs a reporter in the region. I guess it's going to be a busy time for everyone soon. The Iraq situation is getting dangerous. This time the UN is unlikely to support another invasion,' he said.

Alicia wanted to tell him more about Iraq, but resisted owing to him being a friend and not a colleague. She knew that the White House and the military had plans to launch an attack on Iraq if they couldn't achieve a new UN resolution. But first, bin Laden and the Taliban in Afghanistan had to be their immediate focus.

'There might be something you could do for CTU if you go to the Middle East,' she said with a wry smile.

She knew that he really wanted to be an unofficial agent, like

Curly. She was offering him a way in. Probing her, he asked, 'What would that be?'

'I can't say at present, but if you're interested, I will keep you in mind, that is assuming you accept the journal's offer.'

She observed a glint in Cane's eye and knew she had hooked a potential agent. Perhaps it would take the pressure off Curly, who she could keep in the US. She had, of course, a personal motive. After further exchanges they said their goodbyes and he flew back to London.

Cane arrived at his apartment in Knightsbridge early in the morning after an uneventful flight. Henry greeted him at the entrance and handed him a sealed envelope he had been given by a woman on 2 November for personal delivery. He went to his apartment and anxiously opened it to find a handwritten note. To his surprise and delight it was from Jayne.

> *Dear Paul,*
>
> *I hope you have recovered from the Riverside experience. I assume that you have been to New York to see Robert and hope he is recovering. You may remember that I told you I may be going to the Middle East on an undercover assignment. Well, although it's classified and I shouldn't be telling you, I am leaving tomorrow, sooner than expected because of the new situation. I didn't know when you would be returning so it's unlikely I shall see you before I leave. Therefore hoping everything goes well and that one day we may meet again. I hope you will look after yourself and take some much earned rest.*
>
> *Jayne x*
>
> *2nd November*

Cane noted it was dated and delivered after the day of his meeting with Alicia in Washington. He then realised Alicia and Jayne were close colleagues and although they had never physically met, they had a secure telephone connection. The offers made by *The Global Economist* and Alicia now became much more interesting.

Lightning Source UK Ltd.
Milton Keynes UK
UKOW05f1513151113

221156UK00001B/42/P